MW01049921

# A
# HOUSE FOR
# MISS PAULINE

## Also by Diana McCaulay

Daylight Come
Dog-Heart
Gone to Drift
Huracan
White Liver Gal
Writing Jamaica: People, Places, Struggles

# A
# HOUSE FOR
# MISS PAULINE

## DIANA McCAULAY

ALGONQUIN BOOKS OF CHAPEL HILL   2025

Published by
Algonquin Books of Chapel Hill
an imprint of Little, Brown and Company
a division of Hachette Book Group, Inc.
1290 Avenue of the Americas
New York, NY 10104

The Algonquin Books of Chapel Hill name and logo are registered
trademarks of Hachette Book Group, Inc.

© 2025 by Diana McCaulay. All rights reserved.
Originally published in Great Britain in 2025 by Dialogue Books.

Hachette Book Group supports the right to free expression and the
value of copyright. The purpose of copyright is to encourage writers
and artists to produce the creative works that enrich our culture.
The scanning, uploading, and distribution of this book without
permission is a theft of the author's intellectual property. If you
would like permission to use material from the book (other than for
review purposes), please contact permissions@hbgusa.com.
Thank you for your support of the author's rights.

Printed in the United States of America.
Design by Steve Godwin.

This is a work of fiction. While, as in all fiction, the literary perceptions and
insights are based on experience, all names, characters, places, and incidents
either are products of the author's imagination or are used fictitiously.

The publisher is not responsible for websites (or their content) that are not
owned by the publisher.

Library of Congress Cataloging-in-Publication Data is available.
ISBN 978-1-64375-722-3 (hardcover)
ISBN 978-1-64375-724-7 (ebook)

Printing 1, 2024
First U.S. Edition

To my women friends
my two blood sisters, Marilyn and Suzie
my (almost) lifelong sistren, Celia and Rosemary
And to Nancy McLean, in tribute, sorrow and
remembrance

Colonization is always about the land.

Viet Thanh Nguyen,
*A Man of Two Faces*

*Nkakat itaha ekpeme, eto akpa ayak*
*oduñg, sia odung edi ûkú eto*

(The termite can never devour a bottle,
a dead tree will always leave a root to
become the fountain for rebirth...)

Efik proverb

# A
# HOUSE FOR
# MISS PAULINE

# Chapter 1

When Miss Pauline finally comes to understand that the stone walls of her house have begun to move, she knows she will die before her hundredth birthday, just over a month away. She sleeps in her mother's iron bed, under a light sheet, the mosquito net pulled close, and for the past seven nights she's been woken by unfamiliar noises. The first time it happened, she considered getting up to investigate but the noise stopped. Country night fulla sound, she whispered aloud to reassure herself.

She's not someone who has struggled to sleep at any point in her life, not after bereavements, not with newborns, not when her baby father went to build roads for months, or when her boy child came home with torn clothes and swollen eyes, not when her girl child became a mother and took up with a man she disliked, never with indecision or worry, sickness or remorse. Not when her monthlies stopped coming. Not after the wounds of loss or disaster. Not even when her dreams became the recurring nightmare of an underground cavern below an unreachable hole in the rock, arousing guilt that clung like mortar. Not when she began calling herself old at eighty. But night after night, she's been roused, first by her body, and then by the noises. Her stomach cramps. Her fingers ache. She's thirsty. One night, a rustling, easily dismissed as small nocturnal animals outside, going about their business. The next, a swishing, like a storm through trees, but when she goes to the half-open sash window, the night is windless. On the third night, she hears the scrape of a heavy stone being pulled through pebbly mud, wet and grasping; the fourth brings the rumble of river stones being sieved. The fifth and sixth nights are split by a cracking, like men breaking stone with hammers and pickaxes. Men hauling stone, men quarrying.

She shudders and fear feathers her skin. She pulls the sheet up, but it presses down on her body. She thinks of a shroud. Her mouth fills with saliva and she swallows. She reaches for the cup beside her bed, River's cool water, and drinks. The noises are not only strange and too close, but they are directed at her. For her. Chuh man, Pauline, wha do you? she demands out loud. How much tings mek noise a nighttime? Rat. Cat. Croaking lizard. Dawg. Bat. Owl. Mongoose inna the chicken coop. 'Tap you rass foolishnis. You inna safe place. But she well knows that dangers hide in safe places. If a man—a tief— is in her house, he'll be sorry. On the seventh night, she gets up and reaches for the 'lass stored under her bed, her knees crackling. She holds one of the bedposts and pulls herself up, thinks of her baby father, Clive, who gave her the cutlass and the leather scabbard, made with his own hand.

Her son, Alvin, insisted on installing electricity. She's never liked or trusted the wires that run along the walls of her house. Alvin had a banking job in Kingston, and he used to pay her bill. She's often imagined complaints from his unpleasant town wife about the money he spent on her and what her son might have said in response: If she has light now, I don't feel so guilty for not visiting her in Mason Hall.

Alvin, her firstborn.

The handle of the 'lass is smooth against her palm, but heavier than it used to be.

Is not heavier, girl, you is weaker. Out loud she says, Weaker is not fuckin *weak*.

In the central room of her home she stands, holding her breath. She fumbles for the switch, annoyed at her sudden reliance on its power. The warm, flickering glow of a kerosene lamp, which can be adjusted depending on her mood—bright for cooking, dim for thinking—is much better. But perhaps the harsh electric light will solve the mystery of the sounds. Wild hog, mebbe? Yellow snake? Foolishnis. No snake has been seen in Mason Hall in living memory and feral hogs are rare.

She throws the switch and squints until her eyesight adjusts. Goes from room to room, cutlass raised, staring up at the underside of the zinc roof, looking behind furniture, curtains, under beds and rugs. Not a lizard, mouse, cockroach or stray cat. Nothing fallen off a table. Certainly no mongoose, snake or hog. No tiefin man, lying in wait. Just anodda fuckin dream. She turns the light off.

Back in her bedroom, she lays one palm on the walls of carved limestone blocks. The stones feel dry, papery, as if they might crumble to dust through her fingers. Her left arm cradles her stomach, trying to soothe it. She fights to swallow. She knows every fault and blemish the stones hold, their fissures and holes and the faint shapes of insects captured by the rock as they died. Then, against her palm, she feels a vibration, like an electric shock. Snatches her hand away. Is it the damn wires? She's cold, too cold. She reaches out again, this time with her fingertips. The stones tremble, sending a jolt from her fingers to her chest. She sets her jaw, leaves her fingers where they are and closes her eyes, thinking of the men who helped to build this house arguing about whether cement was the right kind of mortar. The wall itself shivers like a living thing.

Hairs rise on the back of her neck, but she wipes her palms on her nightdress and kisses her teeth, impatient with herself. She stands tall and speaks directly to the walls of her house. Stone is not dawg or man. Stone cyah move.

Her mouth tastes of metal. The cup on her bedside table is empty. She sits in the armchair in the corner of her bedroom, the cutlass in her lap. She'll clean and sharpen it after she's had her tea in the cool of the early hour. Then she'll slide it under her pillow where it will be easy to reach. In case she needs it. She thinks of other mornings, the steady, rolling days of the life she has built for herself—weeding the kitchen garden at the side, raking up leaves for mulch. Tidying her house. Fetching water from River for storage in her stone jar. Preparing meals, using her own vegetables and seasonings. Reading time in the afternoon, when it's too hot for exertion. Crackers and cocoa tea made from her own plants, enjoyed on the veranda after the sun goes down, a welcome retreat to her bed. She's empty with a cavernous loss, hollowed out by a force she doesn't understand. She waits for dawn, startling when a pair of croaking lizards begin their call and response.

The sky lightens and just as her spirits lift, a damp spiral of wind whispers against her face. Raas, she hisses. Over at the window there is no draft coming from outside. Are the stones themselves breathing out? She smells stagnant water. Something wet and rotten. Something dead.

'Tap you bloodclaat foolishnis, she says, glad there's no one to hear her, but the wind still swirls and her voice shakes.

Then she speaks her own name. Pauline Evadne Sinclair. If you going talk to stone an youself, talk the truth. You need some help.

When the sun is fully up, she uses the flush toilet—waste of clean water—and goes into the living room. Her stone house is a simple rectangle with two bedrooms on one side, the larger one facing the road to Mason Hall and the smaller one at the back. One sparsely furnished large room runs through the center of the house, from the front veranda to the back door, containing a small side table, a bigger kitchen table with four chairs, and a threadbare couch that's hardly used. The large kitchen and small inside bathroom are on the other side. The living room tends to be dark—the exterior doors are narrow with a single window beside each, one at the front, the other at the back. She likes the dim coolness of the main room, although she spends most of her time on the veranda, where there is her glider and an uncomfortable wicker chair.

Sitting at the narrow side table in the living room, she rummages for paper and pen in the single drawer. She will write to her granddaughter, Justine, living in foreign. Carol's daughter. Carol, whose birth nearly killed her. Fraidy-fraidy Carol who migrated in the five flights time in the 1970s, sponsored by Evon Marshall, her *stush* American spouse. Justine, the only one of her grands she has spent time with, sent to Jamaica for a month every summer until she was sixteen. Justine, playing skipping games in the square with the children of Mason Hall. Justine, refusing to use the outhouse after Miss Pauline gave her a chimmy and insisted she deal with the contents herself. Her disgusted face as she took the chimmy outside. Plaiting her granddaughter's hair. Justine loved ribbons when she was young.

Who, in all of her life, has Miss Pauline ever asked for help? Clive, her baby father. Her lifelong friend, Zepha, and Zepha's man, Jiwan, the ganja grower. Never her children. She smooths the sheet of paper torn from an old accounting ledger and begins to write. The words come slowly with many crossings out and she's not sure of her spelling anymore. Should she write down what she's heard? Felt? Remembered? Dreaded? She knows, though, that if she tells anyone that her house itself is moving and making noises, that the past is coming for her, they will seek out her four grandchildren, three she's never met, and two words will chart her final days. *Mad ooman.*

Some tings not good to talk.

# Chapter 2

Miss Pauline dresses in an ironed white blouse, the neckline slightly frayed, a long skirt with a faded pattern. She settles her tie-head and decides she doesn't need the 'lass for a visit to the post office.

She walks through her living room, trips on Zepha's hand-made rag rug. Tek time. Nobaddy to find you if you drop. Searches in the same drawer for an envelope, leans over to pen the address, hopes the one she remembers is accurate. She won't reread what she's written. She drops the envelope and a pen in one of the deep pockets of her skirt in case there are forms to be filled out at the post office. She can't remember the last time she had posted a letter to anyone and she hasn't seen her granddaughter in twenty years.

On her veranda, she stops to take in the morning light, drinking her tea. Although the sun is well up, dew still glints on the patchy ground cover in front of her house—shame-old-lady, buttercups, waving grass—and she remembers the month she spent over sixty years ago now, tramping the land around Mason Hall, until she found this site, the place she planned to spend her life. She drew the footprint of this house from her mind's eye into the dirt, using a piece of quick stick. Small rocks in each corner; larger, flat rocks in the middle of each room. Sitting in the tall grass, she listened to the hum and scratchings of insects, and imagined the walls rising around her. She used a hoe to look for pockets of soil on her chosen land. It sloped, but not too much, which meant good drainage, and it faced the trade winds that brought cooling year round. In the shade of a gnarled breadfruit tree, she planned a kitchen garden and the trees she would plant—orange and lime, Otaheite apple, ackee, Julie mango. There would be banana and cocoa walks. And at least one panganat bush, her favorite fruit. But the land also faced the full force of storms. She waited a second month to see it in all phases of the moon. She knew she should assess the impact of both wet and dry seasons over an entire year before choosing, but her desire by then was too urgent.

The events of the last several nights seem impossible in the bright morning, but she wants to be out of this house. She puts the half-full mug on the floor and slams the front door behind her.

She shakes out her puss boots to make sure no insect has taken up residence overnight, slides her feet into them, and leans down to tie the laces. Her head swims. She reaches behind her for the arm of the glider and collapses onto it. Can she even make it to the post office? Is it finally time for a walking stick? Is she sick and that is all? Or worse—is she losing her mind? Stone is *not* dawg. Nor man.

She takes deep breaths and her dizziness ebbs. You nuh eat anyting since mawnin, she admonishes. Jus tek you time.

But she wants her letter to go on today's pick-up, so she can't dawdle. She laces her boots and stands, steadying herself on the arm of the glider. She's okay. She takes the front steps one at a time, thinks: shoulda put in a handrail, ma Clive.

It's a short, downhill walk on an unpaved marl road to the village center. Other similar roads bring people from their homes in the hills, winding between grassy banks, crumbling in places. Just wide enough for a taxi, with only a few places carved out of the banks where cars can pass each other. All the roads converge on Mason Hall's triangular central area, called the square by all. She greets all those she encounters and they respond.

Mawnin, Miss Pauline.

Bless.

Give t'anks.

You out early, Miss P. Mawnin, mawnin.

Respec'.

The exterior of the post office has been painted red by a cell phone company, a color she considers has only certain appropriate uses and this is not one. But it's not the first coat of paint to be applied to the buildings of Mason Hall, and after that time the heritage people came in the sixties she was glad the old stones were hidden. She can still see their shapes through the paint, the small gaps in the mortar, the uneven surfaces, but now it's easy to think the post office walls were just poorly rendered.

It's not much past nine o'clock and she wonders if she'll have to wait for opening time, but the door is ajar. Inside, Miss Marcelle, the postmistress, is leaning on the counter, listening to a talk show, staring at one of the new phones, a mug beside her. The zinc roof has holes in it and buckets half filled with scummy rainwater are placed under the worst leaks. The single louver window is missing three blades, but Miss Pauline sees the stones stand strong. Still. Unpainted inside, giving off their familiar cool glow. She suppresses an impulse to nod to them in acknowledgment or inquiry. A single lightbulb hangs from a cord and throws her shadow against the stone walls. Her back is hunched. That is not her, cannot be her. She pulls her shoulders back and the shadow does the same.

Miss Marcelle turns the phone face down and looks up. You reach you century yet, Miss Pauline? How you so strong? You go live forever, nuh true?

Miss Pauline hears this often from the people in the village of Mason Hall, parish of St. Mary, island of Jamaica.

Don't chat fuckery inna ma ears, she says to Miss Marcelle. Nobaddy live forever. Nobaddy *want* live forever.

Youngsters laugh at an elder swearing, the church sisters shake their heads. Miss Glad, her mother, said badwuds were forty-shilling words, because that was the fine for using them back in the day.

You too bad, says Miss Marcelle, playful. Miss Pauline knows the postmistress wanted her to swear, because she finds this entertaining, coming from an elder. The much younger woman drinks from the mug. The lemony smell of fever grass drifts across the counter. Pastor Edmond Slowly's drink. Pauline's stomach roils.

She puts the envelope on the counter, says, Turn that ting down, nuh? You soon deaf. How much for the stamp-them? She searches for the cloth purse in her pocket.

For the U.S.? Same as ever. You hear 'bout the eart'quake? You feel it?

Miss Pauline looks up. Nuh-uh. What eart'quake?

It come on the news, Miss Marcelle says. Two o'clock a mawnin time. Three point four them sey. Right here in Mason Hall. Three in a week. Tremor from two week before that. Them sey we must look out for aftershock.

*Aftershock.*

Were the sounds she heard and felt nothing more than the earth gathering itself for a quake? She remembers the one after the devastation of Hurricane Gilbert, the primal terror she felt, exploding from the shaking ground itself. But no, there was that clammy, interior wind inside her bedroom, that smell. Tremor cyah mek breeze. She grits her teeth. Girl, nuttn wrong wit' you mind.

Me never feel it, she says. She seals the envelope using the small round sponge on the counter, hands over the money and the letter to Miss Marcelle.

Outside, she doesn't know what to do with herself. How long will a letter take to get to New York? What will Justine make of what she wrote? She should have read it over before sending it. She's not hungry, has no inclination for the usual household chores, wants to be away from her house. She should have brought her water bottle with her, then she could have filled it at River's banks. A simple, daily task. Her mind feels cottony, her legs uncertain.

Her footsteps lead her toward River. She'll be able to make it down, because now there are concrete steps and a rope to hold on to at the steepest places. She stops at the top of the slope, and suddenly she's seven, looking at the dangerous, divided path to the river, holding a clean glass bottle that once held white rum. The first time her mother sent her to collect water. Then, there were occasional tree trunks to hold on to—rose apple and anchovy pear—and a few rough steps cut into the hillside. The height made her dizzy. Women and girls were already at the riverbank, and she could just hear their voices above the chatter of the water.

Steep, eeh, Puss? her father had said from behind.

She nodded. She wanted to ask him to hold her hand and come with her to River, but she knew he wouldn't. He pointed with the cutlass that would later kill him. Go the long way. Not the shortcut. Next time, tie the bokkle to you waist. Leave you hand-them free.

She fell that first time. The rum bottle went flying but didn't break. It rolled down, finding its way, clinking against rocks. She liked the don't-care attitude of the glass bottle. She cut her right elbow and bruised both knees.

First time? a girl said, peering at the cut on her arm. This way. We get drinkin water upstream where it more clean. You can wash off too. Pauline, right? Me will call you Paulie. You soon come school, right? How old you is? Me is eight. Me is Zepha.

River became her favorite place, and she claimed the best rock for drying clothes as her own. She named it Sollah, after the wise man in the bible Pastor Edmond Slowly talked about in school.

She traces the old scar on her elbow; then reaches for the new rope. Steps down, once, twice. The concrete blocks are too far apart. A female voice behind her calls, Miss Pauline?

She turns to see who it is and misses her footing, twists her ankle, almost falls. Whoy, what you doin, Miss Pauline? Cyah still be climbin down to River when you have pipe water inna you house! Dat nuh mek any sense. It's Lora, Zepha's youngest child, now an elder herself, buxom and cheerful, wearing the green, black and gold of the Jamaican flag, carrying an empty basket. Come back up, she says. She holds out her hand and Miss Pauline takes it.

What you doin? Lora says. You need sumpn?

Miss Pauline blurts, How long a letter tek to get to New York?

What? Lora wrinkles her brow. Letter? What letter? Why you lookin for a letter at River? Wha' going on, Miss Pauline?

Nuh matter which letter. Nuttn going on. Jus did tink you might know.

Nobaddy write letter anymore. Only person can tell you dat is Miss Marcelle.

Just comin from there.

Well, go back. Ask her. Who you writing to, anyway?

Ma grand, Justine. She tries to remember if Lora ever met Justine but can't.

Why you don't just call her? Or go to the library and Skype? You know Miss Amoy's grandson, him always over there, him can show you. Lamont him name. You want me come wit' you?

No, chile. You go about you business. Me is good.

Lora looks unconvinced but turns away to begin her own climb down to River, her steps confident, swinging the basket as she goes. She doesn't hold on to the rope.

*

Miss Pauline sets her face in a frown to discourage any unwelcome observations from Miss Marcelle and goes inside. Stupid to be returning so quickly, she should have asked about the time the letter would take to be delivered on her first visit. The post office is empty.

Of course a letter is not the best way to get in touch with her granddaughter. Before Alvin died, he often badgered her about getting a smart phone (which she had ridiculed at the time) or showing her how to use the computer terminal at the refurbished branch library. Lawks, Mumma, you could talk to me anytime you want, Alvin said, his irritation obvious. She misses him, although she knows he found her a trial.

She had not wanted to outlive her children.

She never hears from Alvin's wife, Leesha, which is fine with her. She migrated with their two babies and she and Alvin never lived together again. One of their children, the older girl, became an airline pilot in Canada, and this gives Miss Pauline a sense of unreality—that in her own lifetime, it has become possible for women to fly airplanes, taking hundreds of people from place to place, across oceans and mountain ranges. She's never been on a plane, never will now. The younger girl—Alvin never complained about not having sons, at least not to her—left Canada for Australia. Miss Pauline knows nothing of her life—what she does for a living, whether she married, if she has children. She has photographs of her other grands, Carol's children, Jacob and Justine, at various stages of their lives, which she keeps in the cedar chest in her bedroom. If she were deemed to have lost her mind, she supposes her fate would rest with Carol, Jacob or Justine.

She's leans on the counter. Her mouth is so dry. She should have gone down to River. Of course she can still make it down that hill.

She calls out again and bangs on the counter. Sounds come from the back, but no one answers her. Wutless ooman. Maybe she should just go to the library, seek out Miss Amoy's grandson. It's no longer the dilapidated, intimidating room of her childhood and Miss Adina, the woman who swung the door of literacy wide open for her, has been dead for five decades. She's been there over the years, and she's seen the computer terminals, fed by something called WiFi (which she translates as Why Vi, as if it's a question to an unknown woman), and the shelves of new books with bright jackets. She doesn't remember when last she visited, and she hates it that her time there as a girl is sharper in her memory. She stopped going once she started to reread the books she owned as the old friends they were.

Impatience becoming anger, she shouts for Miss Marcelle. In daylight, noisy, shaking stones are bare foolishnis. The post office is like her, a creature of another time, long past its relevance. She's fading, her brain cells flaking like paint, her spine crumbling, joints fusing, the past seeking its reckoning. Well, high time. She never thought she'd live to see the date change from the 1900s to 2000, marking a whole new century, and now that is almost twenty years ago.

Soon come! Miss Marcelle finally calls from the room at the back. There's a catch in her voice. A man speaks in an undertone. Probably Miss Marcelle's man. Those days of lust, so long ago. Sometimes she dreams about the sweat and slide of desire, not of particular men, or of sex itself, but of that heady, life-affirming, reckless drive, and she loves those rare dreams. In her waking hours, she doesn't miss lust or sex, but she wonders if her cells still hold that hungry longing, and if not, where it went.

Maybe, like a body, stones can hold on to yearning.

Mawnin again, says Miss Marcelle, emerging from the back. She clears her throat. Her T-shirt is ripped and one eye is half closed. You, ahhm, you forget sumpn, Miss Pauline?

Miss Pauline frowns. Wha' happen to you?

A man she doesn't know walks up and grasps Miss Marcelle's neck from behind. She flinches. Nuttn happen to her, he says. He holds a steaming mug, brings it to his lips. More fever grass tea. Pastor Edmond Slowly.

The man slurps, smacks his lips. What you want, old ooman? Don't you same one was jus here? You tun eedyat or what? He's short and rail thin. Not young. Shaved head. Two gold chains. Expensive clothes and polished shoes. Not from country. Maybe a politician.

Miss Pauline glares, takes a step closer to him, the counter between them. You is *renk* an outta order. Me is here to discuss post office business wit' the *postmistris*, Miss Marcelle. You is who?

The man cocks his head on one side and sips. A condescending smile flickers behind a wispy mustache. Miss Marcelle looks at the ground, straightens her T-shirt. Miss Pauline makes an irritated "now what?" gesture with her hands, and the man nods. Awright, Granny, you do you business. To Marcelle he says, Mek me know when you dun.

Me is not you fuckin Granny, Miss Pauline snaps.

The fever grass smell wraps around her, like the damp wind invading in her bedroom, and she thinks of bloody underwear and the churchman.

# Chapter 3

Her mother laid a handful of diapers, cut into long strips, on the rickety table where she was doing schoolwork. She looked a question at Miss Glad. Soon you start bleed, her mother said. Every month. Use these to soak up the blood. Inside you draws. Only you to wash them, unnerstan'? Only you to touch them.

Bleed?

Ee-hee. Big woman business. You monthlies. The curse. An nuh mek no man nor bwoy fool aroun wit' you, you hear me? When you start bleed, you will breed.

What you mean, bleed every month? Forever?

Until you is old.

She sought out Zepha, who was a year older, to find out if she knew about this bleeding business. She found her friend sitting on a stool under an ackee tree at the side of her house, mending her brother's baby clothes.

Don't Saul too big for them now? she asked, walking up.

Mumma sey she go try sell them.

Pauline sat on the ground in the dusty shade, watching Zepha's fingers fly. The hole in Saul's shorts disappeared. She was embarrassed to ask about the bleeding but didn't know why. After all, she had washed her brother's diapers, sopped up her sister's vomit, taken her mother's chimmy to the outhouse. Miss Glad had shown her how to kill a chicken, chase it around the yard, put a bucket over its head, then administer a clean swipe to its neck, blood spurting. She had seen goats butchered and gutted fish herself. Mess and blood were part of life, but this type of blood seemed different.

She took a deep breath. You start bleed yet, Zeph?

Zepha didn't look up. She made her last stitch and bent down to bite the thread. Ee-hee. Mebbe eight month now.

How it feel?

Feel? Messy. Like runnin belly. She shrugged. Dunno what else to sey about it. Jus' mean you tun big ooman. But her eyes were sad.

You awright, Zeph? Pauline touched her shoulder and Zepha nodded.

Me is good, Paulie. But hear me now. When you start bleed, man will come after you. All kinda man. Old man, bwoy. Watch out for Pastor Slowly.

Him? Who teach we? Him nuh look like him can mash ants! Hear what me sey.

For a few weeks afterward, she watched the Pastor from the desk she shared with her classmate *bufutu* Martha in the windowless room he had built at the side of the Anglican church, but he was the same, writing his lessons on the blackboard, making his students chant the answers, while he stared over their heads. Twelve times twelve? One hundred and forty-four, her classmates called out. Had Martha started to bleed yet? The other girls?

By the time she woke, months later, to belly cramps

pulling downward, she had forgotten the conversation with Zepha. Wetness between her legs. Had she wet the bed, as her older brother Troy used to do, earning a beating from Miss Glad? She hurried to the outhouse in the gray dawn, frogs jumping away, her feet bare. She held her breath before going inside, sat on the seatless chair her father had installed. Easier than squatting. Touched herself, brought her fingers to her nose. The iron smell of blood. After, she washed her hands in a basin of River's water outside and went to get the strips of cloth her mother had given her. She had just turned thirteen.

Pastor Edmond Slowly, the only teacher in Mason Hall, knew. Somehow, he knew. After school was let out early that same afternoon so the classroom could be painted, he concocted a detention for disrespectful behavior. She was to return the next day, a Saturday, and write out lines he had written in a new exercise book. He made her read them out. I must be hum-ble and obe-ee-dee-ent, she said out loud. His eyes shone.

She didn't tell Miss Glad about the detention, waiting until her mother was occupied with getting ready for Saturday market. She put on her school uniform. The Pastor was waiting for her, wearing his church collar. The smell of fresh paint made her sneeze. He watched her fill in the first ten lines, and left. Not everyone in the Pastor's class could read or write and she was proud of her letters, but now she wanted to be outside, skipping with her friends. She wrote faster and her handwriting became careless.

When I run out, you run in, the girls outside sang in the sunshine. Saturday market was starting. Handcarts bringing produce from the fields creaked and people greeted each other. She was too old for skipping games now.

The strips of cloth in her underwear were already wet. She would soon need the outhouse. Her body was betraying her.

She was at line forty-two when the Pastor returned, shutting the door behind him. Line forty-two, Pastor, she said. Soon done.

Eyes on your book, he snapped, standing behind her. Too close. Heat rolled off him. She smelled the starch used on his white shirt by Miss Blessing, who washed his clothes, and the fever grass tea on his breath. She tried to stand, but he put both hands on her shoulders, holding her in her seat, and began to pray, loud enough for anyone passing to hear. He prayed for her immortal soul, that she would be rescued and protected by Jesus, that she would accept his guidance in the Lord's name, that no rod would be spared to keep her feet on the path of righteousness. And then he ran his hands over her shoulders and down to her painful breasts and he squeezed them. Hard. His nails bit into her nipples and he pulled them up and out, as if he wanted to tear them off her chest.

She grabbed his hands, jumped to her feet and faced him. He was sweating and his eyes had smalled-down. What you touchin me for?

You are a vessel of god and I am his messenger, he said. She felt the weight of respect for authority, the burden of it, handed to her by her grandmother, mother, father and every elder in Mason Hall. It was at war with her wish to bite the pastor. Hit him. Hurt him. She took a step back, but he moved quickly. He got her wrists together with one large hand, held them above her head and she registered his unexpected strength. She had never seen him engaged in a manual task. Hold still, he said, his face close. He shoved her against the wall and pushed one knee between her legs. Silent, she struggled, but his body was too heavy. Then, with his free hand he reached under her skirt and into her underwear. His fingers wriggled like worms, trying to find their way inside her, and she cried out, shame and rage rising in equal measure. Shut you mouth, he whispered, his breath hot and aromatic. Alla you force-ripe gal the same. Hm-hmm. You wet and slippery like mawnin grass. He pushed two fingers inside her. Nice and tight, he said.

She spat in his face, and he recoiled, letting go of her wrists. He saw the blood on his fingers and a flash of revulsion crossed his face. Today not the day then, he said. But you is more than ready.

You tink me fuckin 'fraid of you? she demanded, and he laughed.

Miss Glad should wash out you mouth with soap and bird pepper, *facety* gal pickney. Maybe I tell her what you sey to me.

Fuckin tell her.

I like your spirit still, he said. Me and you, our time will come. Soon. He pinched her cheek, and she smelled fever grass again. Gwaan now, he said, staring at the menstrual blood on the fingers of his other hand, rubbing them together whether in enjoyment or disgust she could not tell. Dutty gal, he said as she dashed for the closed door.

# Chapter 4

Miss Marcelle didn't know how long her letter would take to get to New York. Coulda be a week, coulda be a month, she said. It was time to take Lora's advice and find her granddaughter in a different way. Modern time now.

Miss Pauline trudges up the hill to the library. Earlier, when she took the 'lass from under her bed, she thought it had become heavier so she left it there. Now the road seems steeper than it used to be. The sun hammers her neckback. She's left this journey until too late in the day and she should have worn a hat or carried an umbrella. She tries to remember what Lamont looks like—she's seen him around the village, a gangly teenager in washed-out clothes, his face expressionless, eyes sliding away. Something suppressed about him. Not going like showin one old ooman how to Skype, she mumbles as she walks. Mebbe him not even at the library.

The library is painted a bright yellow with white trim and had been renovated in the old colonial style by some foreigners about ten years before. The contractors had tried to get the earlier white paint off the stones, describing it as a desecration, but the porous stones held on to the paint which hid their origins. She remembers where the stones came from, who moved them, and how numbering them with a stick of coal helped with fitting them together afterward. She sees the faces of the men who helped her, the elder Ras Kyah, Clive and his friend Lizard, and she remembers again the argument about the right kind of mortar—the Ras insisted on white lime, oxblood and animal hair, but no one knew where to find an ox. Were all the stones of Mason Hall now moving too, making a haunted night chorus? There would be no one at the library at night to hear them, but what about the other buildings? Were other villagers lying awake too? Are they afraid to speak about what they heard? Which would she prefer—that what she heard was real, or the product of a failing mind?

The coal marks she made with her own hand are long gone. A painted wooden sign hanging from the eave announces it is the library, in swooping, pretentious letters. Pastor Slowly called that type of writing cursive. Too damn hard to read, in her opinion. Also unnecessary. Everybody knows it is the library. She grasps the handrail and starts up.

At the top, she slows her breathing, peers through a tinted glass door, but can't see inside. She turns the handle, but it doesn't open. She pulls and pushes at the door, tries the handle again. A buzzing noise, like a swarm of carpenter bees, causes her to look around but she sees nothing. Used to be easy to open the fuckin door. She pounds on it with her fist.

A boy she doesn't know pulls it open. He's wearing pants below his underwear and gleaming white athletic shoes. You no hear the buzzer, Mummi? he demands, using the term for a female elder. When she was younger, she insisted on being called Miss Pauline. She was not missus anybody. But she has come to like the affectionate, respectful familiarity of Mummi.

Me hear it, yes, but me dunno what it for, she snaps, walking past him before she can see disrespect in the youth's eyes. Where Lamont is?

Office. Over dere, the boy says, pointing with his mouth. He looks about fifteen. She's sure he'll leave Mason Hall for an uncertain future in one of the bigger towns as soon as he finishes secondary school, maybe with one or two subjects to his name. Miss Glad used to say, The girls breed, an the boys leave.

The office door has a sign done in the same irritating letters, LIBRARIAN, but only the boy called Lamont sits inside. He barely looks up from the screen when she enters, gives no greeting, does not stand. She's amused by her annoyance, given her selective rejection of such rules, depending on who was insisting upon them.

You the librarian now, yout'? she says. You is Miss Amoy grandson, don't it? Lamont?

Lamont looks confused and she points at the open door with the sign. Nuh-uh, he says, understanding Miss Pauline's error. Librarian soon come. Mi is Lamont, ee-hee.

Is you me looking for still.

Mi?

You. You can show me how to Skype? Want speak to ma grandpickney in New York.

The boy lifts his hands as if he wants to sink his face into them but stops. He rolls his eyes. Miss Pauline waits, biting back a retort. She needs this youth's help. His face is watchful, suspicious. She wonders if he's working out a fee in his mind, or if he'll flatly refuse to help her. Then a flicker of a smile touches his eyes, and he says, You come to di right person, Mummi. You have her Skype name?

Me have her real name.

Siddown, Mummi. We look for her. Maybe she on Facebook too.

He puts two gray blobs in his ears and moves in his chair, she assumes to music she can't hear. Miss Pauline is tone deaf and doesn't understand music. When her mother took her to church in childhood, the singing made her put her hands over her ears until her mother slapped them away. She sits back in the chair, stretching her aching back, and thinks about Zepha, and their first encounter with this library, the same, but not the same, after she left school. Five books cyah give you a education, Zepha said, referring to the books she had taken from Pastor Slowly's schoolroom after his assault. It was Zepha who ridiculed her wariness about Miss Adina; Zepha, who ran up the steep hill with her, past the younger children playing hopscotch and jumping rope, past the skylarking boys, past *bufutu* Martha who was said to be sick with sugar, which they didn't understand, past Maas Delroy, drunk every day before eleven, stopping to give a penny to Maas Ezekiah, called Bicycle, due to his severely bowed legs. Breathless, they stopped in front of a small, rust-colored building, made of what Miss Glad's landlord, Peanut, called Spanish wall, some of the ochre clay fallen away from the rough white stones and lying on the ground. The door was open, and it was dark inside. The old library looked like it had grown from the soil.

You go first, Pauline said to Zepha.

No, you, she responded and pushed her.

They skylarked together, laughing, until an old woman dressed entirely in black appeared in the door and shouted, Hi! What is this devilish commotion?

Zepha looked down and mumbled, Good mawnin, Miss Adina. We come to look for books.

You can read, Zepha Daley? And you, Pauline Sinclair, I hear you are no longer in school. What do the likes of *you* want with books?

Miss Adina spoke as if her mouth was full of boiling porridge and Pauline barely understood her words. She received the sentiment behind them, though—no place for you here. The new ember of rage in her chest kindled by the Pastor glowed hot.

Nuh you business if we can read, she spat, hands on her hips. Library suppose to have book, you suppose to care them, an we suppose to look at them. Don't it?

Out of order pickney, said Miss Adina, but she took a step back and the scowl on her face eased. She muttered about the children of today and people getting above their place and the dying trial she faced every day in trying to keep the library from sinking into disorder and chaos.

And Miss Pauline remembers how, on that first day, she suggested Zepha borrow a book as well and her friend said: You read yours to me.

Zepha could write her name but never learned how to read, although she remained in school until her first pregnancy at sixteen.

The computer makes a whirring noise. Connectin now, Lamont says. His fingers fly over the keyboard, pictures flash on the screen and are gone before she can see what they are. She's not sure she's up to date on her granddaughter's last job in New York—maybe she won't be able to take time off. Christmas is a good time to visit family, but it's five weeks away and she fears that's too far in the future. Can she explain the stone noises to a computer? With the young man sitting beside her? Her resolve shrinks. No. She's going to have to lie. If she tells Justine she's dying, she believes her granddaughter will come to her. Especially if she mentions land.

Justine first visited as an active eight-year-old, who loved village life—the novelty of climbing down to River, the ring games in the square, the unfailing sunshine. By then, the construction of Miss Pauline's stone house was long in the past, and she believed her living circumstances were all anyone would want, until she heard Carol whispering to Justine in her new American accent, It's only for two weeks. I know there's no piped water, no TV, and that disgusting outhouse. Just hug it up. Family is important.

Lamont says, Signal not good, so not using video. Miss Pauline doesn't know what he means, but then she hears Justine's twang: Gran? What's happened? You okay?

No, she says. Me is sick. You can come here? Soon?

Come to Jamaica? Now? What's wrong?

Me not long for this eart', chile. Me need to talk to you about ma house. About ma land. Before—

Miss Pauline stops, glares at Lamont. Less people know her business, the better. He shrugs and leaves, a bounce in his step.

Justine looks to one side, as if someone has walked into the faraway room with her. Her lips move, but Miss Pauline doesn't hear anything. She looks around for Lamont, but he's gone. Then she does hear her granddaughter, Before what, Gran? I don't know if I can come there right now, air fares are expensive this time of year. But tell me what's going on. We haven't spoken in such a long time. And I haven't visited in forever.

Miss Pauline hears reluctance, even irritation, from her granddaughter and wants to make a suitable retort, but suppresses it. Nuh worry 'bout money. Me buy you ticket, me give you cash when you get here. U.S. dollar cash.

Justine's face peers closer to the screen. She drops her voice. This is about land, you said?

Just come. Send me a telegram wit' you flight. Do this for me, Jussy. Me will mek it wort' you while.

Okay, Gran. I'll be in touch in a day or so. Let me see what's possible.

The computer makes a squeaking noise. Miss Pauline sits back in the chair. A pattern of moving squares comes up on the screen. Justine has gone, her attention grabbed by the mention of land, possible sickness ignored.

Miss Pauline knows land is like honey to a bee. A drug, stronger than weed.

# Chapter 5

Her legs tremble at the top of the library steps. She's not sure she can make it home, at least not without a longer rest, and she's not sure she wants to go home. She follows the narrow veranda around the building, hand on the railing, looking for somewhere to sit. There's a low, rough bench against the rear wall, the kind farmers used to sit on to milk their cows. She eases herself onto it, knees popping, hoping no one will see her there. This side of the library is shaded by a poinciana tree, and she leans her head back, closes her eyes, already regretting the Skype call to Justine.

Suppose her granddaughter does come and hears the noises? She'll refuse to stay in the house one more minute. But suppose she hears nothing? Miss Pauline will then have to face what she does not want to confront—that it's all in her mind. Pure old age foolishnis or some new nighttime 'fraid. No. Maybe it *was* the earthquake and its aftershocks that made the stones seem to scrape against each other. Stone is not dawg, she whispers like a mantra, but she believes buildings hold the stories of those who lived and died within their walls and keep their secrets. *Her* secret. She's afraid because the stones know what she did all those years ago.

Her stomach gripes. All she's had today is a half cup of mint tea. She can't stay here. She pushes herself to her feet. As she makes her way to the center of Mason Hall, she thinks: Same old rough road, same birdsong, same sunhot. And: Where me is to go, if me don't go home?

A large square stone, the size of the back of a dray cart, sits on a rise in the middle of Mason Hall's triangular center, which everyone still calls the square. The stone has been there all her life. When she was young, the heart of the village was the post office, Miss Pearl's wholesale, and a rum shop, with plenty of space in the middle for ring games, football and cricket. A wooden signpost with arrows directed travelers to other places, the names long forgotten. The three old buildings are still there, but now the square is crammed with small businesses, some failed. An open-sided shed where young men she doesn't know sell car parts, Miss Lora's cookshop Niceness, Miss Bridget's bar simply called Bar. Several derelict structures, now filled with garbage, a collapsed stone wall, a triumphant clump of hibiscus, blooming year round. Parked cars and taxis. Much less space for the games of children.

She walks over to the rock. She likes that it's older than she is and more mysterious—no one knows how it came to be there. Kingston heritage people came to see this rock, once, in the sixties. Couple years after independence. Miss Pauline was in her backyard, weeding the kitchen garden, when Zepha walked around the side of the house. Paulie, she said, a whiteman in the square. Lookin at the big stone.

A whiteman? Here? What him want?

Me nuh know. Him not alone. Come, nuh?

She went over to the yard pipe and washed her hands. That

damn big road, she said over her shoulder. Me did know it going bring outsider to Mason Hall.

They ran to the square together. A boxy car was parked next to the center rock and three people stood beside it. A short man, wearing a peaked cap like a policeman, a young woman in office clothes and the whiteman, eyes hidden behind dark glasses, wearing a wide-brimmed hat like a cricketer. The short man—Mus be the driver, Zepha whispered—walked over to the shade of the guinep tree and sat on a root.

Men walked out of the rum shop and so did the postmistress. A group of boys kicking a soft football disappeared into the lanes, spreading the news. A whiteman in Mason Hall. The villagers gathered under the tree, standing shoulder to shoulder in a row. Legal, Mason Hall's unofficial lawyer, hastily dressed in a white shirt and suspenders. Farmers, old and middle-aged, wearing work clothes and broad-brimmed hats, women in aprons with patch pockets, a new Sunday school teacher in a white dress. Bare-chested boys squatted in front. No girls. Pauline stood with Zepha, watching the three strangers. The young woman was athletic in build, maybe a sprinter or a netballer, hair creamed and styled. She carried a clipboard and pen, and stood beside and slightly behind the whiteman. Pauline exhaled. Not police or army.

Me nuh trust Kingston people, said Legal.

White people going want sumpn, agreed Maas Pooku, one of the farmers.

You tink them going find out, Paulie? Zepha whispered.

Find out what?

You know.

Not if evrybaddy keep them raasclaat mouth shut.

The whiteman took out a carpenter's tape and measured the rock, calling out the dimensions to the woman who wrote them on her clipboard. He was foreign and hard to understand, but Miss Pauline's time with the old librarian had exposed her to speaky-spokey standard English.

An exact square, down to the centimeter, said the man.

Is that someone's initials? asked the woman, pointing.

Fossil. Common in limestone.

Then they walked over to the people watching from the shade. How did this get here? the man demanded, nodding at the stone. No one answered. No fuckin *broughtupsy*, muttered Miss Pauline, loud enough for the strangers to hear. The woman looked at the ground.

The whiteman removed his wide-brimmed hat, pushed his dark glasses onto his head, caught and held Miss Pauline's gaze. He had short no-color hair, sunburned ears, and his blue eyes had crinkles at the corners, as if he spent a lot of time outdoors. He wore a beige short-sleeved shirt, no tie, ironed khaki pants and leather boots she once would have wanted.

You, he said. What can you tell me about this stone?

Always right yah so, she answered. From Whappie kill Fillup.

I beg your pardon? the man said. I don't understand you.

It just mean a long time ago, explained the woman at his elbow. It's how country people talk.

Miss Pauline bristled. From time immemorial, she snapped. The villagers snickered.

The man returned to the car and tried to open the door,

which the driver had locked. Dixon! he shouted. Bring the key, man. Why'd you lock the car? We're not on Orange Street.

*Facety* an outta order whitey, Legal said. Mussi from Eng-lan.

Is only the rockstone them come here to see, Maas Pooku said, and the people of Mason Hall began to drift away.

The whiteman fetched a camera from the car and took pictures of the stone from all angles. When he had finished, he returned to the smaller group of people under the tree. This stone has been quarried, he said, speaking slowly. Worked. Carved with considerable skill. Transported here somehow. Is there a great house nearby?

*Backra* house. Miss Pauline breathed in. The full and truthful answer was: Not anymore. The villagers shook their heads, which was also the truth.

How to get the whiteman to leave before he looked around, before he saw other things to catch his interest, other stones? Miss Pauline's mind raced. Then he cleared his throat: St. Mary parish has a place in the history books, he said. You people know that, right? You know about Tacky? The leader of Jamaica's longest slave rebellion? He and his men set fire to the great house at Frontier, but there's no possibility this stone could have been brought all the way from there.

*You people.* The remaining villagers murmured and kissed their teeth.

But hear dis now! said Maas Pooku. Di whiteman come here to tell *we* about Tacky!

Legal detached himself from the others. He glared at the whiteman. You tellin we 'bout Tacky? You nuh even sey who you is, just walk up here like you still own the place and start measure up tings you will never unnerstan. You is a *eedyat*, whiteman, you, wit' you book learnin. Legal spat at the visitor's feet.

The whiteman took a step back. He pulled his dark glasses down and replaced his hat.

My apologies, he said, and his voice shook a little. You're right, of course. I was just excited to see this stone—I've not seen one like it anywhere on the island. My name is Sutherland. Robert Sutherland. I'm on secondment to the Institute in Kingston, doing a report on Jamaica's cultural and historical heritage. An independence project. We heard about this stone from road surveyors. And you are? He held out his hand.

Legal ignored the outstretched hand. Me is Maas Everton St. George Prince and you is in the township of Mason Hall, parish of St. Mary. Like Miss Pauline sey, we right yah so since time im-orial. From Whappie kill Fillup. We nuh have nuttn to sey about the *backra* stone you so interest in. But if it quarry and carve and move like you sey, is *we* ancestor who do it. It. Belong. To. We. An it better for you if don't mess wit' St. Mary people, livin or dead. He stepped closer to the whiteman.

Robert Sutherland dropped his hand. Sweat shone on his cheeks. The Kingston woman pulled at his arm. He beckoned to the driver, who got slowly to his feet. Well, we'll be back with a team. I'll be recommending further study and a proper sign. Tourists will want to come here—it will be good for Mason Hall. Good morning to you all.

Mout' mek to sey anyting, Miss Pauline said, dismissing

the whiteman's promises, full relief flooding her chest. The Kingston people were only interested in the big stone and knew nothing of *backra* house.

Now, dusty buttercups bloom around the base of the central rock and grass grows at the roadsides, tall and seeding, some with sand-colored tassels, others with pale round puffs, still others with tiny white flowers. Grass quits make clicking sounds. Her father had once shown her a nest—a vertical, oval shape of woven grass. Bird can fly straight in, he had said. Living things make shelters. She thinks of her grandmother's wattle-and-daub hut at the edge of the forest. As a child, Pauline ran the words of her name together in her mind—Granenid. Her grandmother's world cracked with malevolent spirits. Are the nighttime sounds a message from Granenid's duppy? She died alone in her hut when Pauline was eight and was buried there under her favorite pear tree.

Then, she remembers mother's two-room rented house, where she slept on the floor, sometimes with her sister Lyn, sometimes with her brother Troy, the open-sided shed in the yard used as an outside kitchen, the iron stove and coal pot for roasting yam and breadfruit, the bowls of water for washing on a rough wooden table. The smell of woodsmoke. The eye-watering reek of the zinc-sided outhouse, the cockroaches that scurried away as she squatted to do her business; later, the chair with the seat cut out which allowed them to sit. Her father's shack at the edge of his *grung*—this little patch of ground long returned to the soil. The concrete nog house with the leaky galvanized zinc roof, where she first lived with Clive and their children until they built the stone house. *Backra* house, the slavery ruin in the forest, where people, her people, her ancestors, toiled and died—no, were murdered—yet became a sanctuary for her. All shelters of one kind or another, all with their own story.

She puts her hands on the rock, letting it take her weight. The sun lies down on her head and her vision darkens as it had on her veranda. Someting wrong. Wit' her.

Her hands seem to shimmer and become transparent, and for a moment, she thinks she can see right through them to the rock beneath. Then her knuckles morph into hills, her veins rivers, and her skin becomes the brown, thinning soil. The stone turns cold, and she knows this is impossible, here in the mid-morning sun. She stands there, head lowered, eyes closed, focused on the stone, asking it for an explanation of the noises she's heard in the night. But it is a stone. Nothing more. She thinks about right pathways and wrong choices, the place where she got the stones that built her house, and the sinkhole the smallest room was built over; the hole into the rock, its edges smoothed with fire bricks. There was no stone of this size there, at least not back then. This central stone has been here all her life, more than ten years before she went into the forest.

Now, people rarely go to the square rock in the triangular center of Mason Hall. There's no longer a weekend market. When the works crew built the first road from the coast to the hills in the fifties, Mason Hall began to spread out, becoming a district, rather than a village. The history of the village is written by its dwellings in various stages of decay: the earliest huts, made of bamboo strips and clay, roofless and abandoned now, the structures built with hand-cut boards from felled trees. The houses sitting on blocks of limestone, some with walls of wood, others made with concrete nog, most with galvanized zinc roofs, now rusting, some half covered with tarpaulins. Then modern cement and steel homes with flat roofs and flower beds. Now, there is a whole new category, the houses built by returning Jamaicans, large and full of boasyness, bristling with columns, balconies and even turrets, although Mason Hall attracted very few of these.

It's time to get out of the sun. Miss Pauline lowers herself to the same root the driver of the heritage people sat on all those years ago and leans back against the trunk. Half hidden by the thick grass, rows of wooden carvings are laid out on a blanket under the tree. Somebody still hoping to sell a few items. Maybe there is a walking stick, and it will help her up the hill to her house. She'll soon take a look. Her eyes feel full of sand and she shuts them, just for a moment, remembering when she could run like Arthur Wint, skip over and between two ropes twirling at the same time. Reliving what happened after the Pastor's invading, bloody fingers.

# Chapter 6

She bolted headlong from Pastor Slowly's schoolroom. Her uniform skirt, worn four inches below her knees, caught between her legs, almost bringing her down. Avoiding the square where the market was in full swing, she sprinted down one of the many narrow lanes between houses until she found a faint trail used by men and boys to get to their fields or to bearing fruit trees. When she was sure she could not be seen by anyone in the village, she stopped, bent double to catch her breath, chest heaving.

She was in a shallow dip in the land, probably once a cultivated field, now in ruinate. The sky was low and overcast. Tears and sweat mingled on her face and she wiped them away with the back of her hand. Which way? Back to the village? Not yet. She followed the trail upward, until she could see where she was. She crested the small hill and directly ahead, faced a much thicker band of vegetation, and behind it, the green wall of the forest.

Was this the way to Granenid's hut? She wasn't sure, but she remembered her grandmother's many words of warning about the forest: First and commence, Ol' Hige live in there. She the worst. Worse than Rolling Calf. When you hear one owl, it mean death. The old woman's face had been too close, and her breath smelled of sickness. Pauline had pulled away. Listen me, pickney. If you see a owl, stone it. Then you is to shout out loud, You mumma an you puppa, you brute yah.

What that mean? Owl can unnerstan word?

Is one insult, to show you not afraid. Bat is bad too—will suck you blood while you sleep. Snake will strangle a baby. She held Pauline's face in her papery hands. If me see you inna the forest, me beat you raw, you hear me, pickney? An don't go near any cotton tree—*backra* massa did hang slave from cotton tree, bury them body underneath. Pure duppy an spirit live there.

Out loud she said to the landscape, You brute yah. She would not be afraid. Not of owl, forest, tree or man. She headed toward wildness along an uneven ridge. Had anyone from Mason Hall been here, apart from the unknown farmer who cleared a field?

As she approached the tall bush, the ridge widened. Through the thin soles of her school shoes, she could feel the earth was solid and tamped down, different from the crumbly, stony terrain she had just navigated. She squatted and parted the plants at her feet and saw a narrow whiteish rut made of crushed stone. Guinea grass and flowering weeds grew taller on each side of it, and then as she cast around, searching at the roots of the vegetation, she saw a parallel rut. It was a track made by an old-time buggy or a dray cart.

She stood. The outer, thinner trees of the forest were straight ahead but the track seemed to curve away, skirting the trees. She did not use words like east and west for direction, nor for that matter, left and right. There was home and there was away, there was near and there was far, there was yard and there was bush. What if bush was safer than home?

She began to follow the track.

The going became solid underfoot. Her legs brushed against the sharp blades of guinea grass—they would itch for a while. The steady breeze dried her face, and she heard the tinkling songs of kling-kling birds, the knocking of a wood-pecker, jabbering crows quarreling in the distance. Away good, she decided, out here under the arcing sky. Alone, she was strong. Defiant. And her rage was an ally.

But then the track turned and headed straight into the forest and she stopped. The light was flat. If she went into the trees, it would be dark. Scary. Out loud she said: Owl an bat don't hunt in daylight. Ol' Hige is jus' a story for fraidy pickney. She strode on.

At first, the trees were spindly, far apart and familiar— guava and common mango and starapple. She picked a cluster of starapple leaves, admiring the coppery color of the un-derside against the dark green of the upper surfaces—it was a two-tone leaf. A starapple tree was a thing of light and shade all by itself, not needing the sun to cast shadow, nor the wind to seem to move. She thought of her farmer father's words about the St. Mary soil: *If me plant you, you will grow.* What you want to grow to be, Puss?

A starapple tree, Dadda.

He had died of something called lockjaw when she was ten, after a careless, self-inflicted cut with his 'lass. All her life, her father was bleeding and voiceless in her dreams, trying and failing to warn her of something, the cold white of his shin bone revealed.

The trees were closer together now and bigger, but the leaf-strewn forest floor was springy and welcoming underfoot. Then the dappled green light faded. Never mind duppy or Ol' Hige, she could get lost, never find her way out again. She needed to mark her path through the forest. She looked around for a sharp stone, left the path, and was suddenly disoriented. She turned in a circle. The track had vanished.

She brushed against a tree with a reddish, flaking trunk. Was that the low cough of a patoo? In the day? The rustle of a snake? 'Tap you damn foolishnis, she cried. You don't gone far. Owl and snake come out at nighttime. Use you brain. Is the livin you need to fear, not the dead. Human, not animal.

The track was covered with fallen leaves and dirt and hard to see, but it would not be hard to feel. She tied her skirt in a knot to one side and dropped to hands and knees, searching for the hard ruts she had discovered earlier. She found them easily and knew which way to go. Then she searched for and found a chalky white stone, stood, and began to mark the trees as she went by, to make sure she could find her way out. It was a long track for a cart—who had made it? Where did it start and where was it leading to?

The track curved through trees and outcrops of stone. She scratched her irritated skin and her steps slowed. She was annoyed with herself for running away. Then the track narrowed and straightened and led deeper into the murk of the thickest forest, between two stone pillars.

She stopped. Were these gateposts? One of the pillars was level at the top, the other crumbled to half the height of the other. Dislodged stones had retained their square shape and were scattered on the ground. Man mek this, she thought.

Small ferns and mosses grew in the cracks of the pillars and she touched the plants with her fingertips, looking around. The remnants of a low stone wall curved away on the right, becoming lost in the tangle of bush, and she remembered her father's words: *Stay away from* backra *tings*. Who else would build a stone wall in a forest?

She smelled rain. She was parched.

What you doing, girl? she argued with herself. The sound of her own voice made her feel less alone. Go home, tek you beatin. Forget 'bout education, avoid fuckin Pastor Slowly. *Me and you, our time will come.* She knew what his words meant—they were a threat for the future. Cyah hide from him forever. So find out from the herbalist how to bring on you monthlies, in case of worse. Get a weapon, learn to use it. Mek him be sorry him ever put him dutty hand on you.

She heard the swish of a band of rain approaching and then it was overhead, but the forest canopy was so thick only drops got through the leaves, not enough to quench her thirst or wash her face.

She felt beaten. Time to go home. Then, as she turned to retrace her steps, she saw an enormous tree off to the side, and for a few seconds thought snakes were hanging from its branches. She pushed down the urge to run again and wiped her eyes, peering through the gloom. It was a banyan, the tree itself sprouting tendrils, which grew downward from its branches. Some were thin as *wis*—vines; others had rooted in the soil and thickened into ropes, on their way to making new trunks. A good shelter, if the rain came harder. A place to rest. Making sure she could find the last mark she made on a tree trunk, she fought her way through the undergrowth.

She collapsed on a thick mat of leaves, leaning forward, her head in her hands. She was just a girl: hungry, thirsty, angry, unimportant.

Soothed by the sound of the steady rain, she leaned against the banyan's trunk, eyes closed. She thought of the book learning provided by Pastor Slowly. It was something she wanted. Needed. In childhood, she had spent time with her mother on her return from school each day. Miss Glad wanted to see the letters she had learned, and they used to sit together at their small table, one side tied with *wis* to strips of wood nailed to the crumbly walls of their house, the other side on unstable, removable legs. It was their time, maybe their only time, without harsh words.

If she refused to go back to Pastor Slowly's classroom, schooling would never be hers. She would be dark, ignorant, dunce—insults she had heard hurled at the children who couldn't read because they had to spend some days in the fields or selling at market, instead of in the schoolroom. Her anger rose again at this man who had power over both her mind and her body. She cried out in frustration, and a flock of parrots exploded above. No. She would not surrender herself to anyone, not now, not ever. The Pastor did not own knowledge. She would take his books and deliver a threat he would notice. In her mind, she saw his bloody fingers and the mix of lust and revulsion on his face. The diaper strips in her underwear were sodden.

She got up but as she cast around for the last trunk she'd marked with the white stone, she glimpsed the largest cotton tree she had ever seen; that haunted, forbidden marker of torture and death in slavery time. She swallowed hard, reached for defiance and found it. The threats of today were more important than any in the long ago.

She went straight up to the cotton tree. Touched it. Rough, knobbly trunk covered with irregular, whitish circles, almost like splashes of paint, some kind of fungus. Strange, flaring roots supported the main trunk, which did not branch until very high off the ground—almost impossible for a person to climb. Granenid said slaves were hanged from cotton trees, but this particular tree seemed designed to make that difficult. Perhaps the branches were lower when it was younger. Or maybe that was just another story.

The tree loomed, a silent, enduring presence. She sensed no peril. Water dripped from high above. She walked around it, her fingertips touching, taking its measure. This was a living thing. Like her. A survivor. The Pastor would not get away with what he'd done to her. She turned to begin the long walk home, when in a flash of peripheral vision, like sheet lightning in a night sky, she saw a massive structure almost hidden by the trees and undergrowth. *Backra* house, she whispered. This was where the track led—from Mason Hall, across the undulating land, through gateposts, to this place. Her chest tightened. Dadda, she whispered. But her father was dead. Refusal to feel fear was going to take practice.

She stood, looking up, tiny beside the bulk of *backra* house. It was unimaginable as a home; a miraculous construction of uneven stones, fit together seamlessly where they could be seen, but most were covered in greenery. Absent windows like blindness. Tree roots snaking through the walls, as if trying to pull the building apart. Festoons of vines. No veranda at the front; the roof fallen in. A large doorway with a single plank of wood hanging half off a hinge. Two wide stone steps leading to the door. Darkness inside. Her breathing began to slow. Should she enter? She thought of the warnings of the elders about *backra* tings but she felt no fear of an abandoned building, no matter who had lived there.

The forest noises hushed. A leaf wafted into the under-growth. The dull light was fading. Blood trickled down one leg, and she wiped it off with her fingers. It was the present that mattered. Today. She untied the knot in her skirt and let it fall, checking behind her to see if it was bloodied. Her skirt was clean, except for a few leaves and dirt stains from where she had sat under the banyan tree. She brushed the leaves off. Duppy know who to frighten. Old house cyah do nuttn to me. The cotton tree at her back was a beacon, and from there she could find the track that had brought her this far. Not 'fraid of *backra* house, not 'fraid of cotton tree. And she was not 'fraid of *fuckin* Pastor Slowly.

What you doing, Miss Pauline? Lora says. You drop asleep out here?

Miss Pauline wakes with a start, unsure where she is for a moment.

You still outta road? You really nuh look good. You aw-right? You find Lamont?

Miss Pauline nods, wiping her face with her kerchief. Jus' takin a rest. Sun hot. She points at the blanket. You know who mek the carvin over suh? Tinkin to buy a walkin stick.

Jeremiah. Ras Thabo's grandson. You memba him, right?

Ee-hee. But nobaddy is here.

Chuh. Mek us go look, still. Him not going mind if we tek it an leave the money.

Miss Pauline shakes her head. How we will know how much to leave?

Mek us look. Lora holds out her hand. She has Zepha's warm brown eyes. Oval, like the grass quit's nest turned on its side. Miss Pauline accepts her helping hand.

Three walking sticks are displayed on the blanket among wooden bowls and carvings of faces. Two are the wrong height, but the third seems made for her, with a swirled, round top which fits her palm as perfectly as her 'lass. It's stained orange with faint green lines, along the grain of the wood. That bwoy is a artist, Miss Pauline says.

Tek it. Me see him evry day. Me find out the cost an pay him. You pay me back. Tek it, Miss Pauline. Look like you need it. Lora gestures at the basket on her head to avoid Miss Pauline's displeasure. You want a few naseberry? Me takin some to Miss Doro. Tree over by Maas Jonas have plenty.

Come over by me after Doro, nuh? Me will make some mint tea. Me tek a few naseberry, yes.

Sound good, Lora says. You have honey? You voice soun' scratchy, Miss Pauline.

The walk back to her house is much easier with the walking stick and soon Lora will join her in the stone house.

# Chapter 7

Miss Pauline cleans the small bedroom where her children once slept; her granddaughter will arrive on the weekend. Although two weeks have passed since they first spoke on Skype, she still hasn't settled how to get Justine from the airport. Too many tourist get extort by badmind taxi drivers. Or worse.

She knows it won't be a low fare, but she has money. All her life, she's been careful with what she's earned: she throws partner with only those she trusts and that has never included banks; she hides cash in various places, including buried underneath the house. She's made her mistakes, like when the currency changed from pounds to Jamaican dollars—she still has a stash of the old money, no use to anyone, but she keeps it in the cedar chest as evidence of her history, the things she's seen, what she's lived through.

She has not heard the strange noises every night, but she lies awake expecting them, ready to run. To fight. And now she's tired to her bones.

It takes her hours to clean the one room to her satisfaction. It's a pleasant enough place to spend some time, she thinks, one of the new box spring beds from Courts, a white chenille spread with red tassels, the mosquito net tied back, a wooden rocking chair, small table covered with an embroidered tablecloth made by Zepha in her sewing years, an enamel basin and pitcher on the top. And a window that opens to the trade winds. She remembers the windowless alcove in Peanut's house where she and Clive slept for years—he wanted the door closed but she needed it open. Sun have to find you a mawnin time, she insisted. Clive. He used to stroke the back of her wrist with his thumb, back and forth. She wishes she could hear his whistling, the sound of her pet name in his voice. Lina. Why not, if stones can move?

She arches her back, feeling less stiff now that she's moved around. She wants to feel joy at the thought of Justine's arrival, but it's smothered by lingering fear. By shame. Apart from the question as to what Justine will hear from the stones, she's afraid she'll see herself in her granddaughter's eyes—mad old ooman. Madness she fears, but not death. She's long rejected religion, but she does value two verses in the Bible—the one about looking toward the hills from whence cometh help, and the other about dust and ashes. She believes help does come from the eternal hills and she's happy to become dust. Duppy know who to frighten, she reminds herself. And that is not me.

Justine was a teenager when she last visited Jamaica in the nineties. Then, Miss Pauline had specific worries about her granddaughter's safety—the threat presented by men to all females, which she knew firsthand; the kind of random accident that had killed her father, dengue fever. But Jamaica is different now and dangers abound. Gunmen. Politics. Gangs. She decides to consult Lora about the airport trip. She pats the made bed, puts away her mops and dusters and goes into her bedroom to tidy.

She stands in front of Miss Glad's mirror, one of two on the walls. It had been given to her mother by her father only a few months before he died, now smoky, pockmarked and cracked in places. It used to be hung too high for her to see herself but over the years her face was revealed—broad forehead, tawny, defiant eyes, rounded nose and cheeks, and finally her determined mouth and cleft chin. The mirror is almost too high again—she has begun to downgrow. She believes the mirror stores her image as a young woman, even if she can't see it herself. She doesn't look at Clive's mirror. She settles her headtie, leaves the 'lass under the bed, scowls at the walking stick by the door and goes out into a *bleaky* morning.

Lora's cookshop is closed. She must be at her home. Damn fool. Shoulda brought the walkin stick. Like the remembered contours of her own face in Miss Glad's mirror, the village of her childhood hovers behind what it has become, as if the past is waiting to judge the present. To bear witness. She starts her walk to Lora's house, glad of the scudding clouds, the threat of rain.

There's little street life, until she gets to a cluster of rum and betting shops just before the road branches again. Four older men sit around a rough wooden table under a straggly tamarind tree, playing dominoes. Young men, boneless and vacant, slouch on benches outside the rum shop, smoking weed. Ganja. Her crop. She stumbles on the uneven ground and catches herself.

Hi! Elder! Mummi! says a male voice. She turns with

caution. It's Lamont, who helped her make contact with Justine. He's wearing oversized pants around his hips, an outline of a handgun is etched into in his hair, and a loose vest shows tattoos on his neck and arms. He pushes a new kind of motorcycle—she thinks it's called a yeng-yeng. You call to me? she says, lifting her chin.

Ee-hee, he says. What you ah do out inna di sunhot? Whey you going?

Miss Lora.

Whoy, that not so near. You want a lift, Mummi?

She regards him, this youngster she believed had hardly registered her existence at their previous meeting. You going carry me?

Ee-hee. He leans the motorcycle in her direction, nodding at it. Get on backa mi. Not even two minute on di bike, you see mi?

She laughs. He turns the bike around, straddles it, and remains standing. Get on, nuh?

Miss Pauline wonders if her newly weakened legs will allow her to mount the bike. How much you charge? she says.

Mi sey anyting 'bout money? He kisses his teeth. Get on, Miss Pauline.

She tucks her skirt between her legs. She used to squat with ease to wash clothes at River. She gets her leg over the seat of the bike.

Hold on to mi, Lamont says. Tight-tight.

She hasn't been this close to another human being in a long time. She puts her arms around his waist, feels his springy, young man muscles, suppresses the urge to lay her cheek between his shoulder blades. Lamont kicks at something near the ground, the motorcycle roars and they're away. She smiles. Whola heap better than a walkin stick.

Miss Lora is not at home, front door locked tight, curtains pulled, no response to Lamont's shouts, or her own knocks. She sits down on Miss Lora's front steps. Mummi? says Lamont. You awright? Mek mi tek you home, nuh? You nuh have a phone?

No phone, she says. She wonders if she should seek the advice of this worldly young man. In her mind, she sees her son Alvin as a baby, lying in the space made by her crossed legs, staring up at her. His dependence on her for every aspect of his life had rendered her breathless, undeserving of his steady, trusting gaze, certain she would make a fatal mistake. Despite her doubts, she remembers how babyhood was easy in comparison to the early childhood years, when she and Clive struggled to put food on the table, and Alvin's small face grew pinched. They did their best to hide their worries about money from both their children and often went hungry themselves, but once she found him searching the chicken coop for uneaten corn, even though both the rooster and the hen had long been killed and eaten, and any leftover corn would have been as tough as gravel.

Mummi? says Lamont. Wey you waan go now? You house?

Tek time wit' me, she says, and he leans the yeng-yeng against its kick stand and waits, standing astride.

Maybe she should just leave it to her granddaughter to find her way to Mason Hall—she's a big woman, after all, living in a giant, tumultuous American city. Surely she has already overcome much, enough to get from an airport to a rural village in a tourist island?

Mummi? Lamont says again. Mi gots to—

She blurts out: How me can get ma granpickney from Kingston airport to Mason Hall?

The same one wi Skype wit'? Big ooman?

Yes, same one.

When she comin?

Sat'day. Tek me home an me show you the telegram.

Telegram? Why she nuh send you a text? Ohh, he answers his own question. No email. No phone. You have to get wit' di program, Mummi.

Tek me home, she says again. He turns the bike around and this time she gets on easily, deciding she could get used to a yeng-yeng. She likes how it parts the warm air and makes her eyes water with the speed. She doesn't like the noise, but they leave it behind.

He parks the bike at her house, helps her off—she pulls her arm away from him—and he bounces up the front steps. Dis is one of di old stone house-them, nuh suh? he says, walking inside. Nice an cool.

She joins him, glad of his presence. Old-time walls keep inside cool, she says, watching him walk around, even touching her things. His watchfulness has gone and she senses his curiosity, his interest, his youth. She knows nothing about his background but feels no impulse to caution. Stay here, she tells him. Me get the telegram. Then she wonders how well he reads. He uses a computer; he must be able to read. But maybe a computer relies on pictures.

Lamont takes the flimsy paper and glances it. Sat'day comin. From New York, American flight, eight o'clock, she nah reach Mason Hall 'til midnight. Mebbe later. No problem, still. You want me ask a bredrin? Good yout'. *Krissas* car. Him look after you granpickney. Not so cheap to come from Kingston to Mason Hall, still. You can manage?

She glowers at him. You tink me woulda almost reach ma fuckin century if me couldna *manage*?

Hush, Mummi, mi no mean nuttn. You miserable bad. He takes out his phone, taps the screen and holds it up, walking around her home, talking. What her name? he says, over his shoulder. Puppy get her. Him make a sign wit' her name an evryting. He names a price.

She nods and Lamont goes on talking, rapid fire Jamaican, with slang words she doesn't know. She feels a small sadness at this but knows that language changes as much as anything else.

Tell me you bredrin real name, she says to him when he's finished. You want some fresh soursop juice?

Puppy him name. Me no drink dem ting. You have a Red Bull?

Soursop juice or River water, them's you choice, she says, and Lamont laughs. He goes to her kitchen table, pulls out a chair and slouches into it. Dem sey you di biggest ganja farmer in St. Mary back inna di day. Ah true?

She purses her lips. You smoke, yout'?

Of course. Evybaddy smoke.

Me never like it.

So you sell it an don't use it? Mi never know ooman grow ganja, not in old-time day.

She sighs. Foolishnis. You ever hear 'bout Hurricane Charlie? Nineteen fifty-one?

Mi granny talk 'bout it, ee-hee. No disrespeck, Mummi,

but old people love talk 'bout tings inna di long ago. What hurricane have to do wit' ganja? He leans on his elbows, chin in his hands. He's close enough that she can smell his stale breath. How much should she tell this young man she's only recently met? Why is he interested in her story?

That hurricane mash up Mason Hall back to dirt, she says, deciding to risk the truth. We almost dead for hungry. She looks away, remembering the hours of the storm, under the bed with Clive and her two children, the floor awash, the howl of the wind and the screeching, tearing sound of the sheets of zinc on the roof being torn away. She says to Lamont: That storm like a leggo beast. Like a mad dog or bush pig. Like it want to *nyam* we.

The aftermath is as clear in her mind and lasted longer than the storm itself, she and Clive walking around in a daze, silenced by the damage—the uprooted trees, bare branches turned to kindling, the decapitated houses, crops trampled by a rampaging weather giant, the bloated corpses of animals, the acres of mud, a slush of leaves torn away and piled against rocks and buildings.

There was no shortage of water, because it poured for days afterward, but nearly everyone was without shelter. The parish banana crop was destroyed. Landslides erased roads and pathways; River was a torrent of mud. The village of Look Out, where her sister Lyn lived by then, was flattened and for weeks, she did not know if she and her family had survived. Clive's best friend, Lammie, was dead, crushed by a fallen beam of wood and Clive dug his grave in the rain. The sides of the grave fell in, and she watched Clive's bent back, his arms shoveling, shoveling, his face hidden. Miss Pearl, who ran the small shop in the square where everyone bought flour, sugar and tinned goods, was missing and never found. Pastor Slowly's replacement, the white missionary, disappeared—the rumor was to Kingston, extracted by the Mother Country. The house Zepha and her baby father, Jiwan, lived in was one of few left more or less intact.

Mummi? You okay, Lamont asks.

She nods. Just remembrin.

Why a hurricane mek you decide to grow weed? Mi nuh unnerstan.

She meets his eyes. Brown, deep-set, shadowed, and again she senses hidden damage, like a building with a faulty foundation. Seen more than he shoulda for a yout'. She continues, Two tings come outta Hurricane Charlie. Me start grow food. Yam first. Then me hear 'bout ganja an me decide to try grow it. So the first ting is: me tun farmer. Second ting: me want a house mek of stone. She nods at the walls around them.

He wrinkles his brow. But you cyah eat weed?

She laughs. You nuh hear 'bout money, yout'? Weed sell. For plenty. Even tourist want weed. An money can buy any kinda food you want.

He smiles with her. So you just ups an grow ganja? Jus' like dat? You nuh 'fraid of solja an police?

Cunnin better than power, yout'.

He raises his eyebrows, wrinkles his nose. Wha' you mean?

What words can she find to describe those shattered months after the hurricane when desperation broke every rule she held to? Does she even want to try?

She looks away. Is a long story, yout'. Me not sure me want

get into it right now. Mebbe we talk some more. Me want hear you story too.

Lamont stands. Nex' time mi will try dat soursop juice. An you tell me 'bout dis stone house.

She follows him to the front door and watches him run down the steps. At the bottom, he turns and makes a mock salute. She sees his wariness return, like rising, murky water. His face for the world he knows.

She doesn't move until the sound of the yeng-yeng dies away.

Nex' time, she thinks, and her spirits lift.

# Chapter 8

That night, she sits alone on the glider, drinking mint tea, a plate of dry crackers beside her, avoiding her bedroom. The conversation with Lamont has stirred up the past and she thinks of the first time she saw Clive, stroking his mule's ears under the guinep tree at the center of Mason Hall. He was a stocky man with a haircut so close he was almost bald and a trimmed, ginger-colored mustache. He drove a mule-drawn mail cart. She wanted to speak with him, this man from another place. Once a week, he arrived in the village, left the cart in the square, unharnessed the mule and tied it out in the shade. Then he took the *Gleaner* newspapers and the mail to the postal agency, hailing everyone he met along the way. She was sure such a man must already have a woman, but still, she waited behind a clump of crotons, hoping he might teach her how to drive a mule cart, take her to the coast and beyond. Almost eighty years later, she remembers her pounding heart, the way her body quivered at his approach like fence wire strung too tight, her dreams of them lying together and living together, having children. That restless, churning longing.

Summer, 1938. Labor strikes on the sugar plantations.

Turmoil, but elsewhere. Her mother was long gone, Lyn already walking out with a blacksmith from the nearby village of Look Out, Troy had run away, and she heard he was mining river sand. She planted a vegetable garden at the back of their rented house and struggled to make enough to feed herself and pay the rent. She took in sewing, but despite Zepha's tutoring, her stitches were uneven and too big, the thread constantly knotting and breaking. She refused to wash or clean for anyone else. Often alone and hungry, she did not know what to hope for.

You like him off, don't? Zepha said. Her friend was pregnant with her second child; a stick figure with a low belly and hopelessness in her eyes. She refused to speak of her firstborn's father. Given her own experience with the godless man, Pauline believed it was Pastor Slowly who had impregnated her, but no amount of questioning received a straight answer from her friend. Nor would she say who had fathered this baby, still in her belly.

They sat on a bench outside Miss Pearl's shop, fanning themselves with day-old newspapers, Zepha sucking on her favorite food, sugar cane.

Like off who? answered Pauline, but she heard the lie in her own voice.

The mail man. Mr. Clive. Me see how you wait for him.

She nodded. Clive was her choice. To share their life's *grung*, till it, plant it, weed it, reap its bounties. Cry together over its losses.

Them say he involve in the riots. Them say he runnin from the police.

Good for him, Pauline said.

Zepha groaned and shifted on the bench, which rocked away from the wall.

Tek time, Pauline said to her friend, steadying her. Mind you drop. Go lie down, nuh?

Too hot. At least some breeze out here.

Zepha still lived with her mother. She worked as a live-in maid for a family at Brimmer Hall, looking after white children. She saw her son, Wilful, every other weekend. She did not talk about her work.

The mule nosed at the grass in its usual spot, a bucket of water nearby. Had the mail man gone himself to River to carry water for his animal up the hill and through the village? Pauline thought about what this would mean about him as a man, and her desire bloomed.

When he returned, she led him to the guinep tree and they sat together in the shade as the afternoon waned. He was born at Roebuck Hill in Westmoreland, he said, near to the Frome sugar estate, where all the men in his family labored, and yes, he had joined the riots. As the authorities began their arrests, his mother told him to leave for the east.

So you go from one end of the island to the odda?

He nodded. Me like moving around. They sat without touching, but she felt the heat of his body.

What happen to you mumma and fadda?

Clive looked at his hands, his jaw clenched. Ma fadda get arrest. Him did hurt in the confusion, them never send for a doctor, an him die in jail. Ma bruddas, dem scatter. Ma mumma still in Roebuck Hill. When me can, me visit, tek her money.

She leaned closer. What the riot was like?

Noise and confusion. Bloodshed. Me want hide from it. He sighed. Ma mumma sey, coward man keep sound bone. You, you waan coward man?

Me waan you, she whispered. Ma Granenid sey evry broom have him stick a bush.

He smiled, turned and laid his forehead against hers. It became one of their marks of intimacy. Me is for you and you for me, he said.

They rented a house from Peanut, just after her twentieth birthday, and moved in together. It was a one-room concrete nog house with a rusted, leaking zinc roof. They slept in an alcove on a rough wooden platform barely softened by the thin mattress Clive bought in Port Maria. The floor was made of reddish tiles, easier to clean than wood, and there were also fewer insects inside. The roof had gutters that sent brown-tinged water into a wooden drum. The mule, Benjamin, was tethered to a stringy mango tree near the outside latrine and kitchen shed.

In their early months together, Clive was often gone for days at a time, delivering mail. He returned on weekends, full of stories of his travels; she loved to hear the names of the places he had visited—Kellits, Wait-a-Bit, Nonsuch, Alexandria, Sturge Town, Cold Spring, Endeavor, Frontier, places closer than those in her books, but still far enough away. Treasure Beach, on the south coast, which he said was like going to a different island. When he came home on Friday evenings, they sat together on the front steps, his arm around her shoulder, delaying the moment when they would go inside and lie, hot skin sliding against hot skin. She was wanton and knew he loved her for it. When he left her to travel in those early days, deprived of his touch, his mouth, his fingers, his cock, she felt her body dried out like dogshit in the midday sun.

You nah breed yet? *bufutu* Miss Martha taunted when Miss Pauline saw her in the lanes of Mason Hall. You is a mule like the one tie out under the mango tree, gal? You nuh see you fren Zepha soon have baby number two?

Mind you owna fuckin business, Pauline said and took a step toward her.

You is ignorant an fool-fool Pauline Sinclair, sneered Miss Martha over her shoulder. Tink sey you is better dan evybaddy. You don't even finish school.

All you know to do is run you mout', Pauline said. But Miss Martha's words struck home.

You ready to have baby? she asked Clive the next time he was home.

Baby will come in its time, he said. He licked her fingers and she trembled.

They had two years alone together before she missed a period and awoke with a ravenous and escalating hunger for food and for Clive's body. Stay home wit' me, she said.

Need to work to eat, he said, tracing the brown line emerging from her navel to her pum-pum. Baby need you to eat good food.

Despite her earlier desire to see other places on the island, she went with him only once in the mule cart. He was going to Look Out, and she intended to visit her sister while he did his business, but the lurching and swaying of the cart made her feel sick. Stop, she said, and he pulled up Benjamin, helped her down, and walked with her along the track, his arm around her waist, his face turned to the sun. He whistled and she thought: Now that is music.

Hurricane Charlie, 1951. Alvin was eight, Carol six. Red flag at the postal agency, Clive said. Storm comin. Together they collected and bought what food they could—tins of mackerel and bulla cakes from Miss Pearl, almost ripe bread-fruit and green bananas. Miss Pauline carried water from River, knowing it would become churned-up by the storm and be undrinkable for a time. Clive found a few battered sheets of ply and nailed them over the windows.

The waiting was hard. The sky was dirty and filled with flocks of birds. Them know what comin, she thought. It was difficult to breathe and her temples throbbed. The roar of the approaching wind was a relief. The rain pounded on the roof like a cascade of stones and in minutes, the house was flooded. We going lose the roof, Clive said. Mek us shelter under the bed. She held her son, Clive soothed Carol. The children were too frightened to cry, and although they were all drenched by the rain, they slept. Half of the roof was torn away, but the area over the sleeping alcove held. She never knew how long the storm lasted.

Afterward, Clive wanted to leave Mason Hall. Many roofs, including their own, relied on tarpaulins to keep the worst of the rain out; there was no money or materials to rebuild. School had not reopened, and food remained scarce. Their family was better off than many, because when Clive went to other places on the island in the mule cart, which he had kept even after he had been given the mail van, he brought home tinned goods and powdered milk supplied by foreign countries to churches and community centers.

Big road comin, he said to her eight months after the hurricane. Road worker get good pay. We get light too when road done build. He had never been this thin. Her children whined and begged for food she did not have. A letter from Lyn said that due to the hurricane, she had left Look Out for Kingston and promised to write when she was settled.

Maybe Clive was right: they should leave Mason Hall, but then she would be like one of the trees uprooted by the hurricane, cast down but unable to rest where she fell. She wished she could imagine other places, and believed Clive could think of leaving because he had seen them. Should she travel with him in the mule cart, leave her children with Zepha? Or take them? There was no school, no crops to tend, and soon May rains would come, and they would sleep under meager shelter, kept awake by the sound of water plopping into tin buckets.

Clive salvaged damaged zinc sheets blown against a fence and nailed them to the roof's rafters. Thin beams of sunlight came through the holes, the tarpaulin covering one section of the roof flapped and cast a blue light. One day, he found stale bulla cakes in Port Maria, and her mouth watered for them, but they were for Alvin and Carol. She remembers the anger she felt toward her own children, how she wanted to box the food out of their small, grasping hands, out of their mouths. Hungry will mad you, she said to Clive then, her mouth full of saliva.

The mule died, his ribs like a giant birdcage covered in hairy skin, and the wheels of the dray cart disappeared one night, leaving it flat on the ground, a useless box. Clive chopped it up for firewood. Peanut refused a rent reduction. The money in the Milo tin under a loose tile was almost done. Lyn wrote to say her daughter had died of polio, which Pauline had never heard of. Troy was with Lyn in Kingston, her sister wrote on lined paper torn from an exercise book, but had taken up with bad company.

And then Clive got the road construction job and was gone. They did not know when he would return. She allowed herself to cry for him once, on his first night away. She sensed this separation was different in quality and duration. Then she dried her eyes and held her sleeping children close, her brain churning.

# Chapter 9

December. Friday night. Justine arrives tomorrow and Miss Pauline is ready. She stays awake on the veranda as late as she can. A dance is keeping in Mason Hall and she feels the bass line in her chest. Surely whatever sounds the stones might make will be drowned out by the DJ. Her eyelids droop and eventually she pulls herself to her feet and goes inside.

Lying in Miss Glad's bed, she feels imprisoned, interred, the stones conducting funeral rites. Home, she insists to herself. This is ma home. But her breathing doesn't settle, her mind doesn't clear. How long can an old woman go without sleep? She closes her eyes and tries to think of a story she loves, but this just reminds her of the books she took from Pastor Slowly's schoolroom and the stones of *backra* house. Her thoughts tumble like River over rocks. Sleep not someting you can war wit'. Sleep is someting you have to welcome. Invite inna you body. She thinks of Clive's light touch and lets herself feel him close.

She wakes with a start. Near dawn, she judges, but there's no light creeping under the door, no grayness through the shutters. She can't see the bedposts or the chair. Then she hears the sound of a saw through wood, back and forth, followed by the thud of a piece of wood falling as the saw cuts through. Terror rises in her chest. Run run run, she thinks, but she forces herself to lie still, listening. She waits for the saw to begin again but all she hears is Maas Garland's rooster. Must be near dawn for true. She will stay in bed until the night retreats.

When she puts her bare feet on the ground, groping with her toes for her slippers, she feels grit. She had cleaned the whole house that morning in Justine's honor—there should be no dirt in her bedroom. She turns on Alvin's electric light and sees a scattering of white dust on the floor. Her eyes lift to the wall opposite the bed. The stones now stand out of plumb. She runs her fingers over them and a thin strip of mortar falls, she hears it, light but ominous. Heralding weakness. Time come, she thinks. Just the day to get through now. She goes for her broom and dustpan, relieved to be facing something tangible. Just some dust from an old house. But she knows she lies to herself.

She waits up for Justine, sitting on her veranda, sipping cocoa tea, enjoying the rich, earthy taste. The drink will keep her awake. She pushes the second glider with her foot and the springs squeak. Lamont told her the earliest she can expect her granddaughter is midnight, three hours away. The stone house looms at her back.

There's a small, high moon, just past full, the edges hazy, and she gazes at a landscape gilded with silver. Tiny lights of *peenie-wallies* flash on the wire fence that marks her property, and she remembers trying to catch them in childhood, hoping to keep them alive in glass bottles which would shine in the dark. She had caught a few in a makeshift net, but they died quickly in the bottles. She wondered then if they knew they had been trapped.

A patoo coughs, fruit bats swoop in the night sky, she rocks and sips. She shouldn't have lied to her granddaughter about being ill. She supposes it wasn't a lie, exactly, but sickness wasn't the reason for her request. She'll tell the whole truth once Justine arrives and accept the judgment she deserves. The night rustles and creaks with the sounds of the bush but the stones are silent. For now.

She rubs her fingers together, remembering the texture of the dust on her bedroom floor that morning. Dust is one thing, noise another. What could cause the sound of wood being sawed? And what will happen if Justine does hear the noises? Miss Pauline is sure she will refuse to stay in the house. Yet, if her granddaughter doesn't hear them and they continue, she'll have to face she's hallucinating. That it's her own mind telling her there's atonement to be made. She remembers the desperate screams of the whiteman that have echoed through her dreams for thirty-odd years, and she pulls her shawl close.

She drains her mug. It's not a lie to believe she's ill; the pain in her belly is spreading, her fingers tingle, her limbs are sluggish, her back aches, food revolts her, she's often dizzy. She'll tell her granddaughter that she wants to die with a soul at peace. She doesn't know if Justine is religious, but it's likely given Carol's love of church, and she hopes her granddaughter will accept a near-death epiphany from her atheist grandmother.

She might be sick. She might be crazy. But the dust on the floor was real.

Lack of sleep has made her wilt like callaloo in August. Too tired for 'fraid, she thinks. *Nuttn can be undone but mebbe me can set tings right before ma time come.*

She rocks, thinking of the first time she heard the stones, and her certainty that she wouldn't live to see her hundredth birthday, now less than a month away. Her only experience with a hospital bed comes to mind—waking in the St. Ann's Bay hospital, after Carol was cut from her belly. She hates the idea of a deathbed in any location. She doesn't want to meet death inside a room, however well known, however comfortable. She'll die outside, perhaps under a night sky like this one, maybe in the embrace of the cotton tree's roots, the one near the site of *backra* house, the one that bears witness to her defying Granenid and her father's warnings. *Cotton tree fulla duppy. Stay away from* backra *tings.* The tree still stands, and she smiles at the thought of curling up between those flaring, supportive buttresses, maybe she'll even lie naked, her skin in intimate contact with the earth. Dust to dust. Does the cotton tree judge her for what she did? Surely it has seen worse? How to evaluate crimes, one against the other?

She touches Clive's ring strung on a ribbon around her neck. Feels her solitude this night. She's lived alone since he died, Carol gone to foreign that same year, Alvin in Kingston until he too died, the house she built too large for her but still her shelter. She'd taken lovers as it suited her and, safe behind recaptured stone, locked them out when they flexed their muscles. Zepha and her children lived with her for a time after tragedy hunted and caught her old friend. Yes, they mourned together, and the time was full of tears and pain, but she had also loved the noises of children in the house. She's been alone at many stages of her life, but rarely lonely. As she waits for her granddaughter, she wonders at the meaning of loneliness. It has always seemed like a transplantation. Being torn away. Or confinement. Like the *peenie-wallies* in the glass bottle. But maybe it's also about no longer having a life witness; someone who saw it all with you, faced it, shared the burdens and transcended all that came. Old ooman always end up alone.

Clive. It wasn't that they spent every night of their lives together. When he drove the mule cart, he was on the road three weeks out of four, she in Peanut's ramshackle house with two small children, reading library books by the light of a kerosene lamp, rainflies and moths trying to get through the glass to the flame. Then, after Hurricane Charlie, and against her wishes, Clive took the road construction job and was gone for just over a year. She never knew when he would get a weekend off and in some ways she liked that—the possibility that each sunrise could bring him home. When it was rumored that the road was almost at Mason Hall, she went with others to look. She remembers the black streak of it curving like a river, smelling of burning oil. It seemed to move but was also lifeless; manmade, not real, but somehow all too real. Peanut wondered aloud if the road would come right through the village, dividing it in two, and if they would have to move their houses.

Coulda never, said Miss Mazie, the herbalist, arms akimbo. Pauline was not so sure.

Around a corner, she saw the men working, heard the growling, grinding sound of the machines farther away and when they fell silent, the shouts of men. They sounded exultant. She remembers thinking: Him soon come home.

And the road did bring Clive home, walking, carrying a worn-out bag, his skin shades darker from the sun, his hair unkempt, hands gnarled and scored with dirt. His touch was unfamiliar to her, and on his first night home she had to close her eyes to reduce her sense of strangeness. He smelled of unnatural things she couldn't name, but he took his time, lying on his side, tracing the line of her nose and mouth and the cleft in her chin with fingers rough as tree bark. When he kissed her, the remembered taste of him softened her body, and the dormant pull of desire rose. She opened her mouth and parted her legs, and he slipped easily inside. They rocked together and she wrapped her legs around his waist. The sounds of whistling frogs and croaking lizards receded.

Me learn 'bout buildin tings, he whispered.

We is growin tings, she replied.

# Chapter 10

A week after Clive left for the road construction work, she decided to plant yam on her father's *grung*. Her children were at the new school a female teacher from Port Maria had started under a tent. She ranged the bush with the 'lass Clive gave her and cut the straightest sticks she could find to hold up the yam vines. She thought of the wound that killed her father and she built her skill. Her hands blistered and healed and blistered again. She used the last of her savings to buy bulgy yam heads from Maas Pooku. She settled them against her house, covered them with banana trash, dug a trench to guide water away and taught Alvin and Carol how to sprinkle the area with just enough water.

Carol whined and complained about getting her hands dirty.

Farmin not for girls, agreed Alvin.

'Tap you nonsense, she hissed at her children. Girl can do whatever boy do.

She feared for Carol. At seven, she was scared of lizards, duppies, cockroaches, rain flies, mayflies, horse-flies, ticky birds, jabbering crows, John crows, the rooster, *peenie-wallies*, rain, wind, thunder and the Jonkanoo dancers who came out at Christmas time. She hated being dirty or sweaty; preferred being inside to out. She started to call her daughter Princess even though she knew Carol hated it. You 'fraid like puss, she said to her, and Carol cried.

The yam heads sent out spindly green vines and she coddled them, turning them the right way up so they began to seek the sun. Then she and Zepha dug the hills, rooted the sticks and planted the yam heads. They would reap in the rainy season, which was not the best time, but she could not wait any longer. Six, maybe seven months before they would have some food, before they could sell what she had grown and buy staples. Rice. Soap. Cooking oil. Maybe even toilet paper.

You nuh 'fraid smaddy tief them? Zepha asked, as they washed the dirt from their hands at the outside pipe.

No, she replied to Zepha. Them laughin after me. Them tink woman cyah grow yam. Them not going come over here.

She planted a few faster growing crops at the edge of the *grung*, skellion and Scotch bonnet pepper and thyme, salad tomatoes, callaloo. She scraped whitefly off the leaves with her fingernails and searched twice a day for caterpillars. Her family lived on barely ripened roast breadfruit—she had no oil for frying—but Maas Pooku was still burning coal from all the fallen tree branches, so she used the coal pot, instead of the wood stove.

She had to find some way of making money.

Maas Pooku sold every last piece of her yam crop in Port Maria. She bought corn oil and white rice and chicken neck and back, and she cooked with her daughter and Zepha, who brought six ripe plantains and a pitcher of lemonade, sweetened with her own cane juice. The two families filled the small house to bursting—herself, Alvin and Carol, Zepha's new baby father, Jiwan, and Zepha's three children, each from a different father: Wilful, Stedman, who everyone called Steady, and the baby, Lora. Only Clive was absent. There were not enough chairs for everyone, and the children sat on the floor. Together, they ate every grain of rice, sucked the chicken bones dry, fought over the last piece of fried plantain and licked the plates clean.

She would plant again, but it would be months before she could reap.

We need a crop that grow faster, she said to Zepha while they washed the plates outside.

Talk to Jiwan, Zepha said. Him growin ganja. It soon ready for drying.

What is ganja?

Talk to Jiwan.

Them call you Coolieman, nuh so? she said to Jiwan. He sat on the front step, watching Zepha's boys throwing a ball he had made out of a feed bag, stuffed with grass and bound with string. He had long, straight black hair tied back and smooth skin with a grayish cast.

He nodded. But my name is Jiwan Sirjue. His accent was different. Educated.

Which part you hail from?

He gestured at the step beside him, and she sat. My family spread out all over. Some in Portland, some St. Elizabeth. We followed the cane. My great-grandfather came here from India after slavery. Indentured, they call it. My mother said he was a time-expired Indian.

What is that?

After his time of work, he was free. Free to go back to India, free to stay here. He took money instead of land. A mistake, I think. Jiwan stared into the distance. Long time ago, he said. Too long to think about.

Zepha say me must ask you 'bout ganja.

He turned to face her. You've been friends a long time, then. She trusts you.

We is *sistren*, ee-hee.

What d'you want to know? he asked.

Evryting, she replied.

Everything. Well, I can give you seed. You find land in the bush where nobody goes. You clear it. Don't use fire—will bring the soldiers. Leave some bush and trees but the plants need sunlight. Plant and mulch and fertilize like any crop. I use cut grass and chicken manure. Takes a lot of care in the first three months, weeding and watering. Not so much after that.

It need plenty water?

It needs enough. At the roots. In the beginning.

So how you water inna the bush?

Hey, stop that, he shouted at the children. Wilful and Steady were shoving each other. He went over to them and bent down, calming their tearful explanations. He tossed the ball a few times and then came back to her.

You know roof gutters? Same idea. I cut bamboo and bore some holes in the bottom. Sink it beside the plant. Fill it with water. For the days when I don't get there. But St. Mary has rain—the watering is not so difficult. When it rains, you have to shake the water off the plants afterward, or they get mold. If a storm is coming, you have to reap.

How long it tek?

From seed? Five, six months.

Still slow.

He nodded. Farming takes time. Patience.

Patience mek a sick man drink water an sey it is food.

He laughed. That may be so, but you can't tell a plant to grow faster. It grows in its time.

They talked yields and prices. He told her she should dry her own crop, but he sold to a Kingston man who bought from all the farmers in the area. You get a little less, but it's easier than selling it yourself, he said.

How you learn 'bout this?

Ras Thabo showed me. You know him? I started with his plants. He told me it's God's herb. Gad-ja, he called it.

You smoke?

Sure. You should try it.

They watched the boys, still thin, but full of energy and play. Zepha sat on an old blanket spread on the grass. Lora slept in her lap. She my heart baby, she told Pauline who understood Lora was the first of Zepha's children who had not been conceived in rape. Zepha had still never spoken the name of Wilful's father but eventually told Pauline about Steady's father, Alphanso, who sold snow cones to school children. He had come across Zepha at River one day and enticed her into the bushes with talk of the sweetest custard apples, pushed her against the rocks, and after, told her he loved her. Him jus' hol' down an tek wey, Zepha spat, her face rigid, her eyes like holes. Alphanso left Mason Hall before Steady was born and had never met his son.

Miss Pauline? You listening? said Jiwan. If we're going into a partnership, I could germinate the seeds for you—make sure no female plants. Give you the seedlings. Shorter time then. We need to build a shed for drying. But you know it's against the law, right? Soldiers, police, if they catch us, we're going to jail. Sometimes people steal the plants while they're drying. Fights blow up over ganja. Killings. It's a dangerous thing, ganja.

Starvin more dangerous, she retorted.

She went to see Jiwan's field, his plants just coming up. He planted in rows, but she resolved to let the land guide her where to plant. She studied his bamboo watering system, leaned down to touch a plant. Look almost like a fern, she said.

Much stronger than a fern, Jiwan answered. You want to try a draw?

Spliff you call it, nuh so?

He nodded, held it out to her and she smelled its sweet smokiness.

Take a deep pull into your lungs and try hold it.

She did as he said but bent over, coughing.

No man, you just kept it in your mouth. Breathe it in. Right down.

She tried again and this time her throat burned and her chest expanded.

Good, Jiwan said. Now wait.

She took another draw and waited, the sun on her head. What supposed to happen?

You feel smooth. Easy. Restful.

The smoke made her feel sick. She shook her head and handed the spliff back to him.

Me no feel different.

He smiled. Maybe you need practice.

Where you cut the bamboo? Miss Pauline said.

River. Upstream.

Miss Pauline ranged River's banks looking for clumps of bamboo, marking their location in her mind.

Where would she plant? Somewhere no one would go.

Of course. *Backra* house.

She found a sloping piece of land on the other side of the forest around the ruin, hidden by a steep, rocky cliff, the white limestone showing through. She cleared the land alone, leaving a few trees and taller shrubs in place at the edges. The swing of the 'lass and the sound of her breath coming hard drove out doubts. Fuck rule an law. Starvin kill you faster than solja, she chanted. In all her years of visiting *backra* house, she had never seen another soul.

She liked the focus of physical labor, the simplicity of it. Clearing the land took almost three weeks, her muscles ached and strengthened, her skin darkened in the sun. She dragged the cut and drying bush into the nearby forest—she knew sometimes the British soldiers looked for ganja with helicopters, although everyone was still focused on recovery from the hurricane.

Getting the cut bamboo stalks to her field was difficult, especially given the need for secrecy, but she paid Wilful to pull them through Mason Hall at night. He left them piled up for her at the top of the slope and she tumbled them down to her field. She learned a new, more subtle way of wielding the 'lass to slice the bamboo for the watering system. Then she made hillocks for her plants, as she had for the yams, selecting natural hollows where the soil was thick and dark and crumbly. She remembered her father smelling the earth of his *grung*, holding it to her nose. Dat is fertile soil, he said to her. You smell it? And she had smelled the life in the dirt her father held.

Then, in the nearly sheer cliff that shielded her from observers, she found a small but deep cave and the ground was covered in bat shit. This gave her a source of fertilizer and suppressing the old fear of bats planted by Granenid, she worked it into the hillocks with her bare hands.

Jiwan came to inspect her field. You alone did this? he marveled.

Me one.

I told you they don't need hills like yam.

Me know. Is just how me want to do it.

Where will you get water? Climbing down that hill is murder.

Me know where to find water, she said, and he didn't press her.

I think you're ready, he said.

He gave her the seedlings with their off-center, star-shaped clusters of leaves, and she nestled them into the earth, one to each hillock. Then, she went to *backra* house. She tied a long rope to a bucket and dropped it into the sinkhole she had almost fallen into when she began to explore the site in teenage.

At first, she struggled with the bucket down the cliff to her field, spilling most of it, until Jiwan helped her set up a system of ropes and pulleys over the branches of a tree growing out of the limestone rock. He refused to go anywhere near the ruin. Those places are wicked, he said.

In time, she learned to plant within waste tires, which were good at retaining the soil and less work than hillocks. Rain came at just the right time for her first crop; the sun beat down and the plants grew tall and green.

Jiwan, Zepha and Pauline built an open-sided shed for drying. The plants have to be separated on the rafters, Jiwan said, or they get mold.

Miss Pauline decided "weed" was a good name for ganja—it grew just like one. The plants put out modest, spiky clusters of buds, and she smelled their green, resinous smell. She watched the sky for rain and searched for insects on the plants. She stripped most of the leaves at the end of April and hung the stems and buds from the rafters in the drying shed. She never tried smoking it again.

Jiwan dealt with the Kingston man who bought the buds; she did not want to see him, or know anything about him. And cash came in. U.S. dollars. Every morning, she sat down with her family to a breakfast of cornmeal porridge with brown sugar and a splash of cow's milk from Maas Pooku's herd, and while they ate, she packed school lunches of bulla cake and tinned yellow cheese for her children in tiffin containers.

Dadda soon come home? Alvin said.

Soon. She was not sure what Clive would say about her new occupation, but she saw the plump cheeks of her children and the light in their eyes.

She began to think about a second field. The aftermath of Hurricane Charlie had kept the soldiers away, but that wouldn't last forever. She imagined her crops burning at the hands of whitemen in uniforms, her children in an institution in Kingston, herself lying dead in the dirt, bleeding from the throat, gurgling. Cunnin better than power. They would not catch her.

After Clive returned from the road construction, they spent one of their longest stretches of time together every night, months, until he began to seek new work. He was hired to drive a red country bus between Oracabessa and Stony Hill Square and was gone again, often spending every other night in Stony Hill.

What it like? she asked him, stroking his face.

Nuh like anyting. A room. Toilet down a passage. Food from a cookshop. Early start. Me is for you and you for me. She never wondered if he had another woman.

On the night he died, a late-season rainstorm hammered the roof of the stone house and sheeted off the land in muddy torrents. She was alone with Carol and Alvin, both asleep. The island was under a declared state of emergency and the rum shop talk was of politics, communists and the CIA. She stood in the doorway of the stone house, gazing out at the loved and familiar view, now hidden by the lashing gray rain, and wished Clive was home, hoping that wherever he was, it was not pouring like this. She imagined him running up the path, he would be soaking wet, and she'd help him off with his clothes, and they would eat together in lamplight, then go to bed, her head on his shoulder, his fingers exploring her body, stroking, teasing, withholding, until she begged. Then she saw a figure hurrying up the path, and she remembers that moment of pure, upwelling joy. Relief. Me will meet him, we get wet up together in the rain, me and him, and we going laugh like we is pickney again and he will sey ma pet name: Lina. She went down the steps into the deluge and the figure was not Clive, but a man she did not know, wearing a hat and raincoat. And then she knew the man she had loved for eighteen years, the man who stood in the shade of the guinep tree near to Mason Hall's center, stroking his mule's ears, showing her his gentle heart, Clive, the father of her children, the one who whistled through the rooms of the house they built together, that man was dead.

She's awoken by a car door slamming. She's fallen asleep on the glider. Why is she out here? Then she remembers. She struggles to her feet and reaches for her new walking stick, to take her down the front steps to meet Justine, getting out of the robot—unregistered—taxi. Her granddaughter drops her shoulder bag and opens her arms. Gran. I made it. That road, though. My God.

Miss Pauline is surprised at her granddaughter's height. How old you is now? she asks. She knows her granddaughter's age, of course she does, but right now the numbers dance just out of reach, like rain flies around the kerosene lamp at dusk. Puppy makes a noise of impatience and Justine turns to pay him. Miss Pauline tries to intervene, but Justine waves her off. She picks up her suitcase, shoulder bag and smaller bag that rolls along behind her on wheels and gestures for her grandmother to go ahead of her.

Looks the same, Justine says, after Miss Pauline turns on the electric light.

You mus be tired. You want anyting?

Just some water. Miss Pauline fills a glass from her jar and leads Justine into the guest room.

That night, for the first time, she hears the low, slow sound of drums from the stones, feels percussion in her chest, like the bass line from the dancehall. She lies in the dark, her heart pounding in time with the drums. Then, as the drums fade away, comes the wail of the whiteman's voice, and she can't fight dread any longer. *Story come to bump.* Hidden things are revealed. She waits to see if what she hears rouses Justine, but her granddaughter does not emerge from the spare room.

# Chapter 11

Miss Pauline sleeps late the next morning; it's after eight when she opens her eyes and hears Justine moving about. She's felled; an ancient tree whose roots have finally released their hold on the earth. The light is dim behind the curtains, but she can see new shifts in stones and mortar, more white dust on the floor. The noises had invaded her nightmares, but not brought her to full wakefulness. She's at some force's mercy and it's toying with her. She smells coffee, which Justine must have brought with her because she's not herself a coffee drinker.

There's a soft knock on the door, and she hears Justine say, Gran? You okay in there? Justine has the same almost-American voice she remembers of the white American man, Turner Buchanan, who came to Mason Hall all those years ago. The man she must now speak about to her granddaughter.

Comin, she calls out.

She stands, testing her newly unreliable legs. She shuffles over to the basin, pours water from the jug, washes her face, and slips her housedress on over her nightgown. She looks into the second mirror that hangs in her bedroom. Clive's gift on the first night they slept in this house. Oval, with a wooden frame carved by the crippled carpenter in Portland who made the shutters for the windows and the locked cedar chest, still in the corner of her bedroom, keeping her secrets. Clive's mirror reflects an ancient woman with drooping eyes, the whites yellowish, the amber irises faded, the lids swollen by sleeplessness. The flesh of youth is gone. Her skin seems barely to cover the bones of her face and falls into wrinkles and pouches, and there's an irregular black patch on her cheek, larger than the last time she gave it any attention. Her eyebrows are thin and gray, the sparse hairs long. As she looks from mirror to mirror, she sees the girl she was, the woman she's been, the elder she is. She fingers the threadbare ribbon she wears around her neck holding the ring Clive gave her after Carol's birth, made by her sister Lyn's baby father, the blacksmith, along with the key to the cedar chest. She never wore the iron ring on her finger because it chafed when she worked her plants.

She stares at her reflection; Miss Glad's mirror, then Clive's. Her face seems to flicker and dim, shadowed by something behind her. But when she turns, there's nothing.

Her chest is brittle, as if breathing might crack it open. Will Justine have heard sounds in the night? And if she has, how much will she reveal to her granddaughter? Will they sit on the veranda while she tells the story of Turner Buchanan's visit? What will she then see in Justine's eyes? Maybe the only story she should tell is about what happened to *backra* house. Definitely nuttn about stones louding up. Yes. Me an she will tek a walk over suh. She pushes away the thought that she will simply not be able to make it.

She goes into the living room. Justine has opened up the house and is cooking something on the stove. The small table near to the kitchen is set and there is even a jar of fresh thyme in the middle. A wash of emotion sweeps over Miss Pauline, and she yearns for someone to carry her burdens. To take them away. To absolve her. She smells frying plantain and her stomach clenches.

What you cookin, Jussy? she says. Should be me doing that for you. She steels herself. How you sleep last night?

Like a baby.

Her granddaughter turns, wearing the apron embroidered by Zepha. Never known you to be one to sleep so late, she says. Now, let me look after you.

Miss Pauline considers pointing out that they've spent very little recent time together, so Justine doesn't know her sleeping habits, but it seems unkind. You never hear anyting in the night?

Anything like what?

Noise. Mason Hall noisy sometime.

I remembered. Brought earplugs with me, Gran. Justine turns back to the stove.

Miss Pauline pulls out one of the chairs around the table, thinks: Fuckin ear plugs. She sits. How you mother?

Justine sighs. Miserable. She's in a home now, Gran.

A home? What you mean? You did live 'pon the street?

Justine gives a nervous laugh, her attention on the frying pan. A home for old people. Sort of, like, a hospital.

Miss Pauline has heard of such places but has never encountered one.

I cut some callaloo from out back and you had some saltfish in the food safe, Justine says. That okay for breakfast, with some plantain?

Whoy. You memba how to cook Jamaican food?

Of course. At least, I hope it's callaloo. Maybe you should check.

Miss Pauline laughs, gets up and looks into the pan. Callaloo for true. Me don't feel to eat too much these days, still.

You *mawga* down for true, Gran. Jamaican echoes in Justine's voice. Miss Pauline wants to drink her tea outside before she eats anything more substantial, but she doesn't want to reject her granddaughter's cooking. She resumes her seat at the table and waits for Justine to join her.

The callaloo is overcooked and the plantain too ripe, but Miss Pauline eats it all. She hopes she won't regret the unaccustomed amount of food. Justine makes noises of appreciation as she eats. So much better than American food, she says.

Miss Pauline regards her granddaughter. Nearly forty, but looks older, hair creamed and styled, no sign of the ear piercings Miss Pauline remembers from her visit in teenage. Hazel eyes, a color she has only encountered in books. More green than amber. Faint vertical lines edge her lips, as if she spends time pouting or smoking. Her nails are painted blue, and she wears a gold bracelet that looks like seashells. Not short of money.

Standing at the two-burner gas stove, Miss Pauline removes the breakfast pans, and sets the kettle to boiling, tearing mint leaves off a sprig she keeps in a small glass jar on the windowsill. Now that this moment is upon her, she doesn't know what to say to Justine. On the Skype phone call, she had told Justine she was ill, dying, and needed her help to sort out the family land. That the trip would be worth her while. She had wondered at the time if Justine's ready willingness to visit was motivated by greed. She well knows what land ownership can do to people.

Come, she says. Mek we sit outside while me drink ma tea. You did bring coffee wit' you?

Yes. I remembered you didn't drink it. But I was going to clear up the kitchen first.

Do it later, she says.

They sit on the glider together, looking out, listening to the morning sounds of Mason Hall—motorcycles and coaster busses and cars—smelling burning leaves. People are going to work, mostly in hotels on the north coast. Very few still farm, and Miss Pauline is long out of the ganja business herself.

Mason Hall is so different, Justine says. Plenty more houses. More trees too. You still have only tank water, though.

When last you was here? Miss Pauline says, although she remembers.

Hmm. Nineties? Justine lowers her gaze. After I had the abortion.

Miss Pauline doesn't react to what she had suspected but wasn't mentioned at the time. Carol had merely said Justine needed to be "straightened out." The nature of the crooked path was never fully explained but had something to do with an unsuitable crowd. A taxi had collected her granddaughter from the airport at Montego Bay—she doesn't remember now how that was organized—and a surly teenager entered the house. She had the family eyes and prominent ears, each pierced with four silver rings. That never hurt? Miss Pauline had said, pointing.

Of course it hurt. Her granddaughter thrust her chin forward. Are you going to, like, give me a hard time about everything too?

Chile. You welcome here an me have no intention to run you life for you. Back innna the day, you be a mother already. But hear me now—me is no maid. You help out, you tek you turn cookin, you mek you bed, you wash you owna clothes, you leave you shoe-them at the door. You sleep here a night-time. Mebbe we talk, mebbe not. Mebbe you find some roots here, mebbe not.

Roots in a backward village on a backward island? Justine sneered in her foreign voice. I don't think so.

Mebbe you learn sumpn 'bout what is true backwardness, Miss Pauline replied.

One night, she heard Justine sobbing and went to her. She lay curled up on the spare room bed. Hush, Jussy, she said, sitting beside her, expecting words of rejection. But Justine sat up and threw her arms around her, buried her wet face in her neck. The girl's chest heaved. Miss Pauline waited. Eventually Justine quieted. Me bring you some mint tea, ma girl. Evryting look better a morning time.

Mm-mm, she says now to Justine, deciding not to delve into the abortion. You right. Evrywhere different now, don't it? She sips, the mint tea comforting her belly, calming her. Justine's visit in teenage is too long ago to matter.

Catch me up, Jussy, she says. Tell me about you life. You married? You go college? What work you do? You like New York? Me woulda hear if you had baby, right?

No children, Gran, Justine says, looking straight ahead. Except—She doesn't finish the sentence. She rattles off the details of her life, her words falling over themselves, her American accent causing Miss Pauline to lean closer. Not married, but just ended a long relationship, and glad to leave New York just now. Went to nursing school, graduated, but didn't like looking after people. I wasn't cut out for it, she says. She turns to meet Miss Pauline's eyes. Mama said my heart is hard. Like yours.

Miss Pauline kisses her teeth. Ma heart not hard but ma spine strong. Sometime folks mix up them two tings.

Justine looks down at her coffee cup and a beat of silence throbs between them.

Miss Pauline drains her own cup and puts it on the floor. So. What you do after you stop nurse?

Different things. Reception in a doctor's office—that was okay. Waitress for a time, but my back hurt from all the standing and customers were so rude. Telephone operator, but then phones started having recordings. I work in a lawyer's office now, mostly filing. But I'm thinking of, like, studying to become a paralegal. Except, Gran, I never really liked book work, so I don't know. She lifts her hands in a gesture of uncertainty. Maybe it's too late.

Never too late, says Miss Pauline, but she's not sure this is true. So where you live?

Lived with Mama all my life. You know she divorced, right? New York is expensive; not so easy to afford an apartment on your own. We live in the Bronx. Lots of Jamaicans there. But maybe a year or so ago, Mama started to forget everything, leave the stove on, go outside in her night clothes, saying she was going home. Even in winter. Justine looks away again. It was hard, she says.

Musta been. Then what happen?

I'm going to get more coffee—

Miss Pauline holds Justine's arm, stops her from getting up. Finish you story first.

Okay. Well, I took her to the clinic. A Guyanese doctor said dementia, maybe Alzheimer's. That's a big thing in America. He told me about the place where she is now. It's not an official place, we could never, like, afford what they call assisted living over there, but it's a group of Jamaican women, about my age, two sisters. Their mother left them a brownstone in Queens, and they got together with others and started taking in old people. One of them, Jackie, went to nursing school with me, she's what they call a geriatric nurse. Anyway, the people at the home look after Mama, they cook the kind of food she likes and talk to her about Jamaica, organize morning devotion. You know how she is about that.

Miss Pauline scoffs. What me know of you mumma, she never love Jamaica. Lef it easy.

I guess so. Back then, anyway. When I was young all she wanted for us was to be American. It was cool to be Jamaican in school, but she said she would beat it out of us. Now, she talks about the seventies a lot. And her childhood. She's gone there in her mind. Where you're born is home, right?

Pauline makes a sound of agreement.

What went wrong between you two? Justine asks. She says you didn't like my father. Says you were rough with her.

Miss Pauline purses her lips. Is true me never like Evon Marshall. Too *stoosh*. Hoity-toity. Me never trust him. And me was right—how long them marriage last? Not even five year. She takes a breath. But me and Carol, you mumma, we rub each other wrong from she was young. You ever stroke a cat fur the wrong way an it spit at you? That was me an her. Me not even sure why. Tings was hard. Me was too different, mebbe. Never fit in wit' odda people, never in ma whola life. Never want to. Then she got religion an—

She stops, hearing the tremble in her voice. She picks up her cup, rises and goes into the kitchen. She puts the cup in the sink and leans on the counter, thinking of her labor with Carol—she can still hear the low howl coming from her own throat, hopeless, like an animal in a trap, but remembers nothing of the trip to St. Ann's Bay hospital in the night or of the cutting of her belly. Alvin, two years older, had slid out with ease and she herself had planted his navel string right beside hers, under the same Julie mango tree. But Carol. That labor felt days long and ended in darkness.

She does remember opening her eyes in the hospital, Clive beside her in an unfamiliar room, holding her hand, his thumb stroking her wrist, tracing a lifeline, back and forth. Is a girl, he said to her, and his voice brimmed with unshed tears. She good.

Where she is?

Them have her, don't fret.

What 'bout me? she replied. Her belly was impaled to the bed.

Clive blinked. You good, Lina. You in the St. Ann's Bay hospital. You soon get to see the coast, like you did want. When them let you out.

The doctor was a whiteman, balding, with a big nose, peeling skin and ghostly blue eyes. Solid as a building. Not at all like the maggot she imagined when her father warned her about white people. She thought the doctor was too old and could not possibly know anything about birthing babies. He had a strangled way of speaking she could barely understand and wore a white coat with black trim and an instrument of some kind around his neck. Good morning, he said to them both, then ushered Clive outside, joking with him, man to man, about his refusal to leave her side. Good thing the ward was pretty empty yesterday, the doctor said to Clive, walking him to the door.

I'm Dr. Sterling, the whiteman said, returning. You gave your husband quite a fright. Baby was a breech birth—you should have been brought in much earlier. You had a cesarean section—do you understand?

She didn't but said nothing.

The doctor sighed, fiddling with a clipboard he held. We had to cut you to get the baby out. You'll have to be careful for a while. You already have a son, I understand? I'm afraid—aah—you will not be able to have any more children.

How you know that? she snapped. After you is not fuckin God.

Language, Mrs. Armstrong. I'll thank you to keep a civil tongue. You had a hysterectomy. We had to stop the bleeding, or you would have died. We—aah—we took out your uterus. Your womb. Your baby girl is healthy and strong, though. You should thank God for that.

She had been drifting elsewhere, sick, only loosely tethered to herself, but at the doctor's words, she inhabited her body fully, felt the sheets on her skin, harsher than they looked, her hair itching, her throat sore, her breasts aching and leaking. The sharp pain in her belly which throbbed with each beat of her heart. She would not groan or wince, not in front of this man. She felt invaded, violated, gutted. Decisions had been made for her, without her, and she wanted to howl her outrage at this male stranger. Whiteman. Tief.

Ma name is Pauline Sinclair. *Miss* Pauline.

The doctor raised his eyebrows, and she felt his judgment. I thought you were married to Mr. Armstrong, he said. Let's have a look at your incision. Nurse!

Do not rass touch me, she said, but he ignored her.

A high color young woman wearing a white apron and cap came up to her and began to ease the gown off one of her arms. Me don't want him here, she said to the nurse.

Hush now, the nurse said. Dr. Sterling saved your life.

She remembers the sight of the rough, reddish-black gash bisecting her abdomen. Her pum-pum had no hair. The cut was unevenly stitched together, and there was a new cavity at her core. The sight of the gaping cut on her father's leg flashed into her mind—maybe he would have lived if he had got stitches.

No more children.

No sign of infection, Nurse, the doctor said, peering down. They stood on either side of the bed and spoke of her as if she were absent. Good thing we got that penicillin last week. These people—

Bring ma daughter to me, Miss Pauline demanded. And her fadda. Now-now.

The hospital threw away her daughter's navel string and she raged at the nurse. Me nuh expeck the whiteman to know, but you suppose to know navel string to plant!

She knew then her daughter's life would unfold elsewhere.

And then there was the journey home from the hospital, her close-up view of the sea for the first time, Clive driving the new red Royal Mail van by then, whistling, a warm wind gilding her face through the windows, Carol sleeping in her arms. The baby was named for Clive's favorite time of year—Christmas—even though she was born in April. Me never see blue like that, she said to him, nodding at the sea. He pulled over. You want get out? he said. Long time you want come here.

How you get gas for the van? she asked him. Gas rationing was still in place because of the foreign war.

Me been storin gas.

He took her hand. You want us married, Lina? You an me? So you nuh get no *facetyness* from the likes of that doctor man?

Married? For what? After me nuh set foot inna church since—

Can get married legal. Don't have to be in church.

The baby whimpered. Me no care 'bout married. You want know what me want? Me want ma owna house an land.

He was silent.

Me never see blue like that, she said to him, nodding at the sea.

He pulled over. You want get out? Me hold the baby.

She shook her head. From the hills of Mason Hall the sea looked like sheet metal but here its vast, unceasing motion unsettled her. Clive put the van in gear and they drove on.

Baby Carol rejected breast milk and they had to buy formula. Pushed away her mother, lifted her arms as soon as she saw

Clive. Carol, a child, sneaking out to Sunday school, dressing for church, reading her Bible, lips moving, insisting on prayer at meals, blaming her mother for the risking of her immortal soul, hanging a crucifix in her room. Finally some money from ganja to pay for her schooling, Carol a teenager, crying over bloody panties, refusing all sports, wanting the things her classmates had, a transistor radio, a record player, finding stations on the radio that played ska, and rock steady, and then the music of Bob Marley. Hating Mason Hall. Backward, boring, stupid place, she shouted at her mother. Dear Jesus, deliver me from this. And yes, remembers Miss Pauline, me did hit her right across her face. More than one time.

Are you crying, Gran? Justine walks up behind her.

Miss Pauline is surprised her eyes are wet. Just tinkin of you mother, that's all. Don't like it that she is being look after by stranger.

You were hard on her, she was hard on me, Justine says. I call it sins of the mothers. I was angry with her for a long time, but it's hard to be angry at someone who needs you, someone who's helpless. Anyway. When are you going to, like, tell me what I'm doing here? Something about land, you said? That you're sick?

Miss Pauline thinks: Sins. She exhales. Me going tidy ma room an get dress. Then we talk. She glances down at her granddaughter's sandals. Put on decent shoe. An pants. We going to walk. Me want show you sumpn.

Where are we going? Is it a long walk? I'm not sure you can—aahm—She stops.

Miss Pauline kisses her teeth.

Over Justine's objections, she leaves the walking stick in

her bedroom. If she can't make it to the site of the ruin, her hiding place, her sanctuary, her crucible, the source of her strength and her shame, she might as well find that place between the cotton tree roots and go to sleep forever. She settles her cutlass in its scabbard hidden by her long pull-up skirt. She still takes it with her whenever she goes to *backra* house.

It's the best time of year for a walk in the bush, although early morning would have been better. Miss Pauline loves the golden end-of-year light and the poinsettia plants beginning to turn their deep red; the euphorbia bushes looking like snow, which she knows exists but has never seen, will never see. The site of *backra* house is no longer forested, although the two sentinel trees—cotton and banyan—still stand, and the view the house commanded is fully revealed, sweeping down to the coast and all the way to the horizon. The land has been cleared as far as the eye can see, a few places are planted with crops by people who don't live in Mason Hall, but most of the land is in ruinate. Ganja fields no longer need to be hidden, in theory, but the growers need licenses which they mostly don't have. Still, the Jamaica Defence Force doesn't seem to have much time for ganja anymore, although it's rumored that this is just a matter of the right payoffs, and in other parts of Jamaica, the plants are often burned.

Me ever take you to see where you great-grandfather bury? she asks Justine, having shaken off her steadying hand.

I think so. Not sure.

We go there first. His name was Winston Sinclair. Ma father.

How did your father die?

Lockjaw.

Tetanus. Nobody dies of that anymore.

Back then, we believe it come from a rusty nail, if you step on it. Country people always barefoot. Him die young. Me was only ten.

That's rough, says Justine. He died at home?

No. St. Ann's Bay hospital, where me had you mumma. Them took him in too late. They walk in silence for a while and then Miss Pauline says, Him use to call me Puss.

Her father's grave now has a marble headstone—with the year of his death, his name and only two words—*Father. Farmer.* Miss Pauline paid for it with her first big ganja crop. She sees the grave with her granddaughter's eyes, so randomly placed, next to a rock and a medium-sized guango tree, which casts a generous, soothing shade over grave and rock. There has long been no trace of her father's meager shack and she's glad Justine won't know how he lived.

She lays her palm on the tree's rough bark. Me plant this tree, Miss Pauline says. Justine is looking at her phone, muttering about the poor signal, and when she notices her grandmother's eyes on her, snaps a picture of the grave.

This don't matter to you? demands Miss Pauline, hands akimbo.

Justine looks embarrassed. Sure, Gran. Lovely headstone. Did you go to his funeral?

Ee-hee. Me memba the drummin at the graveside by Maroon Titus, an how mumma mek me t'row dirt on the coffin. She doesn't tell Justine that she prayed for sickness to take the herbalist who treated her father's wound and how she waited for her father's spirit to say a final farewell during his nine-night, when he would say goodbye to those who loved him, perhaps to impart wisdom or direction, but she was not able to stay awake and he did not come to her. She says: Ma fadda a good man, way ahead of his time.

You never talk about your mother—I don't even know her name.

Gladys Cameron. Miss Glad, they used to call her. Bawn 1900. You can believe that? Miserable ooman cyah done. She holds up her hands. Mebbe me is like her. She take up with a new man when me tun fifteen an them remove to Orange Bay. She die after Hurricane Charlie, get wet up an dead in hospital. Me did hear she raise more children, not sure if her pickney or the man own. Never saw them, don't know them name. Blood don't always hold strong.

So you lived alone from you were fifteen?

Miss Pauline nodded, remembering the weight of responsibility for her younger brother and sister, the day in, day out search for food and money for the few things they had to buy, the miraculous gifts that appeared on her doorstep from the villagers. A trussed-up live chicken. A pound of rice. A full pot of stew peas. A bunch of guineps. A pair of second-hand shoes, which fit none of them.

I guess you spent most of your life alone, Gran?

Not alla it, she says, swaying on her feet. She needs to sit. She walks the few steps to the nearby rock, noticing that she can no longer pull herself up into the small sink where she has often sat remembering Winston Sinclair. She says, Me okay alone.

You're sweating. Are you all right? This walking about in the sun is a bad idea. We could be sitting on your veranda right now, drinking lemonade. Is this it? What you want to show me?

Just catchin ma breath, Jussy. Come, sit beside me. See, this a good place. She pats the rock beside her, feeling a welcome breeze on her face.

Justine pulls herself onto the rock. She sighs. If we're doing family stories, didn't you have a brother?

Miss Pauline knows she's being humored. Ee-hee. Troy.

What happened to him?

Tell you the truth, me don't even know. Him left home from young. Last me hear, long time now, him in Kingston, takin up wit' bad company, but Miss Bridget over at the bar, you know them call her Radio Jamaica, she tell me sey him use to involve in lottery scam in Negril an him in jail from long time.

Wow, that's serious, Gran. Lottery scamming.

Me don't even know what it is an me nuh want know. She stares off into the distance.

But he must be—ahhm—old too?

Miss Pauline nods. Ninety-odd.

Can't, like, still be a criminal.

Me nuh know. From him young, him refuse to go school. Leave Mason Hall, sey him a sand miner. Him sey nuttn in Mason Hall for him.

Justine puts her arm around her. Miss Pauline jumps at the unexpected touch and stiffens for a moment, then thinks: Fambly. She softens. Me memba how him eyebrow did fulla dust when him visit, she says. Him the one that teach me how to cuss badwud. Mebbe him dead for thirty year or more. Mebbe him in jail wit' no trial, or in poor house, or one of them people inna hospital the government sey is abandon by them relative. Mebbe him livin on a gully bank, or garbage dump, or a piece of open land.

That's sad.

She nods. Sad, yes. What about you brudda? Wey him is? You and him is close? Jacob, right?

He calls himself Jake now, says Justine, fanning her face with her open palm. Thinks it's more, like, American. I don't know if we're close, exactly. He was closer to our father and spent time with him when he was a teenager. He moved to Chicago after the divorce.

You brudda or you fadda move?

Both of them. Jake, he's in financial services. A hedge fund manager. He's done well for himself.

Him is a gardener?

What? Justine laughs. No, a hedge fund manager is—well, I don't even know what it is, but nothing to do with gardening. He looks after other people's money.

Him married?

Yes, twice. Second one is recent, maybe last year. Jamaican woman. At least her parents were, I think she was born in the U.S. Not sure. They got together at some tech conference. I only met her at the wedding. Nice woman. Arlinda. Rootsy. You'd like her.

Him have pickney?

No, not for the first wife, but just before I came here, he emailed me to say Arlinda is pregnant. I haven't even told Mama yet. Justine slides off the rock, dusting off her jeans. Shouldn't we be going, if you're determined to do this walk? It's not going to get any cooler.

Miss Pauline stays where she is. And you fadda? Him still alive.

Yes. Not in such great health, you know he was a smoker. He has a live-in girlfriend now. Sheila. Quite a bit younger. If you think he was *stush*, you should see her!

Miss Pauline thinks of Carol, being looked after by strangers, hungering for the place she left without a backward glance, Jamaica to be beaten out of her children, in ignorance of another grandchild on the way, and her heart twists in her chest. She slides off the rock, looks over at the grave. Once, she would have pulled the weeds. Once, she would have brought a handful of buttercups to lay on her father's grave. Mek us go, she says.

She leads Justine toward the two big trees in the distance. The cotton tree is more trunk than leaves, but the banyan is all canopy, branches, leaves and vines sweeping to the ground. Now, there are several paths, some wide enough for a vehicle, others made by men on foot. Miss Pauline goes straight to the old cart track she found the day the Pastor grabbed her. The grass grows more thinly there, and she can still feel the tamped-down crushed stones through the soles of her boots. This is the way *backra* came, centuries ago. She's glad the hidden track survives. Sweat trickles into her eyes.

What about grass lice? Or ticks? asks Justine, walking on tiptoe.

Long as you stay outta the cattle pasture, you good.

Why don't we take the path over there? Justine points with her phone in hand. Why are we walking through the grass? Where are we going, Gran?

This. Ah. The. Way. Me. Go.

Okay, okay, Gran. Don't get upset.

They walk in silence and the sky clouds over. John Crows ride the rising hot air, circling. Granenid once told her they were important birds, because they ate the dead, returning flesh to earth. Miss Pauline thinks of forces that work to bring down even stone, slow ones like rain and wind. Lightning-fast ones, like the recent earthquake she had not felt. Hidden ones, like the work of insects. Like Pastor Slowly's worming fingers. Well, she'd sent him a warning. She remembers the walk back to Mason Hall after her discovery of *backra* house, using the marks she'd made on the trees to guide her way.

# Chapter 12

The market was long over when she entered Mason Hall and the sun was setting. She slowed her pace, nodding and greeting her elders.

Afternoon, Miss Pearl.

Afternoon, Maas Bernard.

Forgot one of my books, Miss Linda.

Politeness and a long skirt were good ways to be underestimated. She would ask Zepha to lengthen all her skirts. She opened the door to the schoolroom, where what happened only that morning seemed long in the past. Her righteous rage burned again. And she reached into her underwear and removed the saturated cloth rags, given to her by her mother, and she smeared Pastor Edmond Slowly's desk with her clotted menstrual blood. She left the rags right there, sure he would be repulsed anew. And frightened. Blood is powerful, female blood especially. That is for me an evry odda girl you ever put you nasty, dutty hand on, she whispered.

*Bloodclaat.* Her brother Troy's favorite swear word. Now she understood it. She was almost satisfied. She looked around the room and saw the shelves of books, hardly ever taken down or read from. She reached up and took the five at one end, held them close to her breasts, and left. She was never going back to that schoolroom.

She walked quickly down the lane to Zepha's house, trying to keep her legs together. It was twilight and she met no one. Her breasts bounced and she hated them. She stopped behind a clump of guinea grass to see where Zepha's mother was— she wanted to avoid her. The door to her friend's house was open but she couldn't see who was inside. She hesitated, then heard a flapping sound. She tiptoed around the house. Zepha was taking sheets off the clothesline.

Without preamble, Pauline said, Pastor Edmond touch me too. Him—her voice caught—push him finger inside me. Him tear at ma breast. Me just start bleed too. Nasty fuckin evil man.

Zepha turned to face her, dropping her eyes to the blood on Pauline's leg. Me did tell you. What you going do? Pauline put the books on the ground and reached for one end of a sheet.

Lef' ma blood on him desk. Tief these books. Me want kill him, Zeph. Fuckin pastor, wit' him goody-goody holy man self. Me hate him.

Not you alone. They folded the sheet together. But if you kill him, is you going end up in jail. Mebbe God punish you too.

God? Pauline was scornful. No God was in there wit' me an him. You tellin me him mus just get away wit' it? Next time, him going try rape me! Him was *strong*, Zeph. Me fight, but him heavy like rockstone. An me did shout out one time, but nobaddy hear me. Why me never bawl out more? Why me never bite him, kick him inna him seed bag?

Zepha reached for her hand. Paulie, listen me. You nuh

know this is how the ting set? Pastor, teacher, farmer, politician, Kingston big man—it nuh matter. Them want pum-pum
from young girl an them feel them can tek it any time.

That man rape you, Zeph? That nasty bloodclaat pastor
man who sey him is teacher—what him do to you?

Zepha turned back to the clothesline.

Lef the fuckin washin. Talk to me. Why you nuh angry?

Over her shoulder, Zepha said, Me angry, yes. But for
what? You tink police will listen to the likes of we? Not even
you owna madda going believe you.

No. Me cannot stand it. Me want bawl out. Run. Get 'wey.

Get 'wey an go where? Someplace wit' no man? No place
like that. Put down some cow bawlin if you want, if you will
feel better, but it not going change anyting.

Should she tell Zepha about finding *backra* house? No.
That would remain her secret.

Zepha's face was somber in the dying light. Nuh mek
sense you talk up, hear wha' me sey. You going home
now? She nodded at Pauline's leg. You want me find you
some rags?

Zeph. If that man is rapin you, you going breed.

Zepha did not reply.


Next morning, Pauline did her daily tasks and dressed as if
for school, the books she had taken hidden in a cardboard box
under the house. She walked with Lyn to the schoolroom.
Me hungry, her sister said.

Pauline was hungry too. She had taken Zepha's advice
about not telling her mother, but should she warn her sister
about Pastor Slowly?

Not going school today, she told Lyn. Mebbe never. You sit at the back. Evry day. Nuh do anyting to cause detention.

Her sister stood in front of her, hands on hips, giving her cut-eye. There was insolence in her stance. A testing. Pauline was glad to see it.

Gimme you lunch then. Although they had the same mother and father, her sister had lighter skin and was admired for it. Her eyes were light too, but more gray than hazel. Pauline handed over the two slices of dry, hard dough bread she had taken from the bread box for lunch.

Here. Learn evryting you can. It nah last long. She remembered her mother's warning and repeated it: Nuh mek no man nor bwoy fool aroun wit' you. But Mama me had no choice! she thought. Why you never tell me that?

# Chapter 13

Justine has stopped ahead to let her catch up. Miss Pauline is panting now and tries to hide it.

I've no idea what we're doing out here, Justine complains when Miss Pauline is within earshot. She's breathing hard as well.

Soon see a gatepost. We left one to remember.

We? Remember what?

Jus' wait. We soon reach.

Miss Pauline touches the one remaining gatepost as they go by, now in the direct sunlight, bare of vegetation. They're not at the highest point yet. There's no sign here of the remains of *backra* house and the bush has grown almost four feet high. She reaches under her skirts for her 'lass and hefts it. She begins to swing it, clearing a path for them. They climb.

Boy, Gran, you know how to use that thing! *That's* what you keep under your skirt?

Me a farmer all ma life, girl. Me know how to clear a field. But her arm is leaden, her palms have softened with the years, and after a few strokes, she stops. Once her tool was the 'lass, now she knows she should've brought the walking stick.

They emerge from the bush and stand in waving tall grass,

facing a strong sea breeze. They can see all the way to the blue line of the horizon. The island's green shoreline dips in and out, curving away into the distance, the coast road hugs the land far below, the hills are steep and forested in some places, grassy and gently sloping in others. The colors of the sea range from turquoise to deepest indigo and surf breaks white on underwater reefs. The reddish, rusting roofs of Port Maria cling to the edge of a sweeping bay with a steep, circular green island in the middle.

This is so gorgeous, says Justine. I guess this is why tourists visit Jamaica. She turns. Are those graves over there?

Ee-hee. Three graves are just visible through the grass.

Whose graves?

Can't tell. Name wear off long time. Then she says, The white people, them took the good places.

What d'you mean, Gran?

Jus' look. High up. Breezy an cool. All the colors. She sighs, searching for the right words to introduce *backra* house. You ever tink about it, Jussy? How we come to be yah so? How a whiteman jus' pitch up in Mason Hall an decide sey this is him land an him going build a house? Mek Black people wuk or die, an mek himself rich?

What whiteman? But no, Gran. I don't think about it. Too long ago to matter. Sick of the whole slavery argument. Mama says it's just an excuse Black people make for the bad things they do. Justine wipes her forehead. It's so hot. There's a tree over there. She tugs at Miss Pauline's arm.

You believe that?

That it's an excuse? I don't know. I just—I just want to get out of the sun right now.

Miss Pauline stays where she is, looking out to sea. Well, me tink about it. That man, whosoever him be, him find him way up here, an him decide sey alla this—she lifts both arms to embrace the landscape—alla this belong to him. Well, me tink it not so long ago an me tink it matter still an me tink that man do pure wrongs. An not only him, she thinks.

Justine fidgets and looks over at the small African tulip tree that does give some shade. Can we just, I dunno, get out of the sun?

Awright, Jussy. We nearly reach. Me did jus' want you to see this place.

She leads her granddaughter downhill, back into the bush.

Awright, she says again. We here. She takes the cutlass and parts the weeds to show a line of stones at her feet. This is the room me come to when me want hide, she says. When me a teenager.

What room, Gran? says Justine. There's nothing here! I'm really worried about you now.

There's very little shade left. One trumpet tree has grown tall over where the kitchen used to be, but it's not a good shade tree. The site of the ruin has been taken over by saplings reaching for sunlight, fallen leaves and patches of bare soil. Miss Pauline hears the exasperation in Justine's voice. She thinks she's going to faint and she looks around for somewhere to sit. The 'lass falls from her hand.

Gran? Lean on me—look, see a rock over there. For God's sake, let me help you!

That rock too near the sinkhole, says Miss Pauline. Next minute, you fall in.

What sinkhole? I don't see anything.

Bush grow over it. Me put some wood down a while back, but maybe it rotten out. Help me to the banyan tree. We talk there.

Banyan tree?

See it there! She points with her mouth and leans on Justine's arm.

Miss Pauline collapses against one of the tree's aerial roots which connected to the earth a long time ago. She holds up her hand, asking Justine to be quiet.

Are you okay. Gran? I knew this was a bad idea. I don't know why I let you talk me into it. Can you make it home?

She opens her eyes, sees her granddaughter sitting awkwardly on one of the tree roots of the banyan. Me good, Jussy. Just need a likkl rest. Of course me can mek it home.

For God's sake, tell me what we're doing here? It might rain. Things are biting me. Let's go home and you tell me what this is all about. You too damn stubborn, Gran.

Jus' give me a minute, Jussy. She bends over, putting her head between her knees, and silence falls between them.

Justine stands, takes a few steps away. This is a strangler fig, not a banyan, she says. Look, see how the roots grew down and squeezed the original tree to death. You can just see the old trunk. Come look.

Justine is trying to get her to stand. Miss Pauline lurches to her feet and peers into the tangle of roots and trunks at the tree's core. During all her time in this place she's never noticed that there's an almost hidden trunk of some other tree, right in the middle of the banyan's outward advance. *Backra* house was lost in the forest, until she found it, and she thinks of all that is hidden and how it might be revealed. *Story come to bump.*

Listen me, now, she says and begins to speak to her granddaughter.

Well. One old slavery time ruin was right yah so. *Backra* house, where the massa did live. Me come here as a young-ster, time an time again, says Miss Pauline. Nobody find me when me is here. Ma hiding place. Me learn to read here, to be alone, to find strengt'. Not to be afraid. Me cyah explain too good.

What are you talking about, Gran? What slave house? Learn to read in the bush?

Miss Pauline feels Justine's uncertainty, even worry. How much of the story will she reveal? Sit down, nuh? she says.

In the dirt?

See a nice flat root beside me? She pats it and Justine sits on the edge.

Miss Pauline decides to begin with the books. Me steal some book from the schoolroom. Five of them. Me hate the pastor, so me decide not to go school anymore but me never tell ma mumma, so me start walk in the forest in the daytime. One day me find this place. She looks around. Me did like it here. Me never see no duppy, never feel no danger. It always feel like me belong here, like it build for me.

Okaaay, says Justine, scratching her neck. So there was some kind of ruin here. What happened to it?

How to capture her granddaughter's interest? Miss Pauline remembers taking Clive to see the small rocks she used to mark the place where she wanted to build a stone house after Hurricane Charlie. He had stared at them. You cyah jus' tek it, he said. Land have to own.

Why? she demanded. The whiteman did tek it.

*Land have to own.* She thinks about all that land is made of—its shape, the rocks and soil, the roots of trees, a host of busy, unknown life, water held underground, the gravel of riverbeds, the sand used in building, the minerals that men and women desire. Limestone, holding the tracings of history. The strange square stone at the center of Mason Hall, too large for the strongest men to move without modern equipment.

To Clive she said, A hurricane tek evryting from we. *Evryting.* Listen me. A stone house nah blow down. *Ever.* We going tek the stone from *backra* house.

Three people—herself, Clive and Lizard from the road crew—began to pull the ruin down, using chisels to ease the stones apart.

Limestone a soft rock, Lizard said. We have to tek time with it.

Cyah be soft, objected Clive. It last from slavery time.

It soft. Need to move one-one. Look how them fit together so close? Di man wha' build dis know wha' dem a do.

Miss Pauline had watched them from one of the low steps, remembering how she marked the trees when she first she visited the forest, so she could find her way home. Put a number on them, she called out. To show this stone go next to that one. Use a piece of coal.

Back then, the stones were shades of pink where the sun caught them; in shade, their colors passed through grays, reds and oranges, to the brown of the St. Mary soil, some stones flecked with the relentless green of tiny plants. Scraping out the mortar was slow work, but it was soft and came away easily. They piled the numbered stones on the flattish area which Clive agreed was once a barbecue for pimento, and the pile grew. They bought a rusty wheelbarrow from Maas Pooku to transport the larger stones from where they fell to the stockpile. When they began to take down the room where she had spent so many hours, she stopped them. Leave two wall, she said.

For what? Lizard demanded.

To memba, she replied.

Lizard knuckled his brow. You a di boss.

Zepha often came with her to watch and soon began to bring roast yam and saltfish for the men at lunchtime. She sat beside Pauline and they ate their share of the salty, filling yellow yam together. Woulda be better wit' some margarine, said Miss Pauline.

You have margarine? Zepha challenged, knowing the answer was no.

People upset you doing this, enuh. They stood together, looking at the pile of stones.

How them know about it?

You know Lizard love him white rum. Him talk.

Which people upset?

Church people. Some Rasta. That loudmout' herbal woman—the one that put honey an orange peel 'pon you fadda foot when him did chop it. What she name again?

Miss Maizie.

Ee-hee, she same one. An Babu, you know him? The obeah man son. Him vex too.

Miss Pauline kissed her teeth. Pure badmind. *Kass-kass* don't bore hole inna ma skin. You watch, them going want stone for them owna house too. Ants follow fat, don't it?

Zepha smiled. Paulie, you well know how some people

stay. Always have sumpn to sey. Them sey you wake up demon-them, rolling calf an blackheart man. Them sey you bring fire an brimstone an murderation down 'pon we. Some sey you a disrespec' the ancestors. Them sey you to leave *backra* house wey it is mek the bush tek it over. Some want it bun to the ground.

Talk is ear food, Zeph. Mason Hall going be a stone village. You watch.

Her friend shook her head. Me hope you know what you a do.

Maroon Titus was the first of the Mason Hall men to make his way to *backra* house. Miss Pauline watched him walk around the site, parting bushes with his 'lass, lifting and replacing the smaller stones, touching the remaining walls. He stared at the pile of dismantled stones. When he neared the sinkhole, she called out a warning: Watch you step! He stopped in front of the cast iron sink which had been part of the kitchen.

Dis is my own, he said, tapping his chest, and she did not argue.


Gran? Can we go? Seriously, it's going to rain and whatever you want to tell me about whatever was here—

Miss Pauline says, Jus' listen. When me an Clive decide to build a house because of the hurricane, me tek the stone from here suh. Me did want a stone house—cool inside, hurricane nah blow it down. Me tek the slavery stone to build ma house, the same one you sleep in last night. Odda people do the same ting. You never notice how many building mek outta stone in Mason Hall?

Never really paid any attention, says Justine, holding a palm out. I felt a raindrop.

Anyway, me tek—some sey tief—the stone from here an that is what me want to make right.

Justine meets her eyes then. She makes a sound of utter disbelief. You make me fly here, spend over four hundred U.S. dollars, *U.S. dollars*, not Jamaican dollars, Gran, over some old rockstones? No, man. That cyah be the whole story! Her American accent has vanished.

Miss Pauline sighs. Is not the whola story, you right. But is what me want tell you right now. Me is sick, chile, me feel it. Me know it. Me don't have long. Hear me now. She slows her speech, emphasizing each word. A man come here one time, in the eighties, me forget the exact year. Him sey is him own ma land. Me want you find him fambly. If you find them, me deal with the rest. You don't have to know all the ins an outs of it. You can do that, Jussy? Find him fambly?

Justine wrinkles her brow, shakes her head. A man came here? What man? What do you mean? You're not making sense, Gran.

A whiteman. American. He come here to Mason Hall. Him find me. Thas it.

A man came here, a stranger, and said he owned your house and land? More than thirty years ago? And you want me to find him?

Ee-hee. An him fambly.

What on God's green earth for?

You lef that part to me.

No. You tell me *exactly* what this is about. But back at the house. Come on, Gran, get up. Right now.

Miss Pauline hears a scatter of rain on the leaves of the banyan tree. Big drop rain, she thinks. Trouble set up. More comin. Her granddaughter is right. Time to go home.

The rain holds off, but the air is dense with stored moisture. The walk back to Mason Hall takes much longer than the outward journey and Miss Pauline allows Justine to place a firm hand underneath her elbow. Her feet are numb, and she can't feel the buried path through her boots anymore, but Justine steers them to one of the dirt tracks where the going is easy. The cutlass under her skirt is heavy, dragging her down, and she knows she's stooping, as if her spine wants to assume the curve of a baby's body, nestling in a mother's arms to nurse. Her vision flickers yellow and black circles.

On the edge of Mason Hall, they encounter strangers— three men, wearing khaki clothes, carrying instruments. One of them greets Miss Pauline and asks her if she felt the recent earthquake. He speaks in standard English and calls her Miss.

Me feel it, she answers, wanting this to be true.

The man inclines his head and looks a question at Justine. I wasn't here, she says.

What about tremors since then? the man says.

You is who? says Miss Pauline. Police? Army? What you want know about eart'quake for?

The man smiles. I'm Dr. Campbell. Professor Campbell, actually. We're from the university. There's a big fault near here and we're—

Fault evrywhere, says Miss Pauline and turns her back on the men.

\*

When they get back to the house, Miss Pauline stands looking up at the four steps to the veranda and thinks: Me cyah do it. She's not sure if she means climb four steps or complete the confrontation she's set in motion. The toes of her boots peek out from under her pull-up skirt, and she thinks of her aged feet, the nails thick and yellow, the troublesome corn on the right big toe, the cracked heels. She supposes her feet have served her well and if they are now signaling their inability to carry her any farther, well, it's time. Long past time.

Gran? says Justine, and Miss Pauline hears the tension in her voice.

Me okay, she says. Jus' need a minute. She leans against Justine and smells her sweat, foreign lotion and unease. She breathes to the bottom of her lungs and puts her foot on the bottom step.

An hour later, she's recovered, sitting on the glider, drinking her third glass of River's water, assuring Justine that her weakness was just the heat and the long walk. Never used to be this hot, she says, not even in summer. This time a year, we used to build fire at nighttime an sleep late under blanket.

What about some lunch? Justine says. What you have in the fridge?

You go look. Me good wit' a panganat—two inna bowl on the table. You memba them?

Too much work to eat, says Justine, referring to the many tiny seeds of a panganat. And anyway, you have to eat more than fruit! Are you still killing your own chickens? I heard them out back this morning. I saw some eggs in the fridge. Maybe we could have an omelet. I could show you how to make it.

Justine bustles inside. Miss Pauline rocks and the land exhales its hot breath.

After they've eaten and Justine is washing the dishes, Miss Pauline goes into her bedroom, pulls the ribbon around her neck over her head and fits the key into the cedar chest's lock. She can't remember the last time she opened it. The key sticks and she jiggles it, feeling resistance. Maybe some things should not see the light of day.

The lock scrapes open and she raises the heavy lid, noticing how tightly it fits. She sees the carved face of the Portland carpenter who made the chest and remembers Clive's joy when he brought it to her on a handcart on her fortieth birthday. The rich cedar smell is gone now. Old air rolls out. Inside, she sees Zepha's embroidery, handkerchiefs, table mats, hand towels, all folded neatly, the white fabric turning brown at the edges, the intricate stitches in bright colors, made with her friend's hand. Miss Glad's blanket, now much too heavy for use, her father's 'lass, never sharpened after his death, the handle still holding an echo of his palm and his pain. A shoebox, softening in the humidity, containing the few photographs she owned—she had hoped to fill it to the brim. The single artifact of slavery she found at *backra* house—a manacle for a child's leg. She reaches for it then lets it lie, afraid of what she might feel if she touches it. And then, at the side of the chest, the document she was given by a stranger so many years ago, rolled up and tied with a black ribbon. She takes it out, leaves the chest open to air out and goes into the living room.

The title's heavy paper resists the unfurling. Justine gets

some cups from the cupboards to weigh down the corners and they spread it on the small table. The cedar wood has kept the insects at bay, but the document is spotted with mildew. It still seems wrong to Miss Pauline that this piece of paper conveys ownership of land.

The whiteman who come sey this is proof him own the land.

Oh. A land title. What was the name of this man? Justine says, leaning over the document.

The lettering has faded over the years. See it at the top there? Turner Buchanan. Just find them for me. Him fambly. Please. Who else me mus' ask, Jussy?

Justine looks at her. You know I could have done this from New York, right? Didn't need to come here?

Cyah really sey me did know that. And mebbe me just want see you, chile, one more time. Want to see you right yah so.

Justine's face is serious. She straightens up and folds her arms. I wanted to see you too. But listen. I'll look for this Turner whoever, on one condition, Gran. If you're sick, you're going to let me take you to the doctor and you're going to do what he says.

Miss Pauline considers this. After Carol's birth, she'd been to doctors reluctantly; once for a cold that never got better and was said to be bronchitis, another time when a red lash of pustules circled her waist, causing her to cry out in pain— a disease with the strange name of shingles. The time one of River's stones turned under her foot and she fell against a rock and broke a rib. When she took a young lover—Ralston? Alton?—and her piss burned after a weekend when they almost forgot to eat. She has always resisted the release of her autonomy to anyone else. Still, if going to the doctor means she needs to make no further explanation to Justine, that she doesn't have to describe Turner Buchanan's visit or what happened afterward or speak words about her own house now dismantling itself, the stones emitting that once-heard wail, yes, fine, she'll go to a doctor.

Awright. Me will do that, Jussy.

And we're going to do that before anything else, Gran. Like I said, I don't have to be here to use the internet. This man that came, it could be some kind of scam. And if I do find him or his family, I want to know what you're going to do with the information.

Miss Pauline points to the words at the end of the letter which accompanied the title.

Justine reads the letter. American. Brooklyn address, she says.

If me memba rightly, him sey his parents go to England in the fifties. Them die young. Dunno how he came to be in America. Dunno how him fambly came to be yah so.

Modern times now, Gran. People move around. Did he tell you his profession?

Miss Pauline tries to remember. She shakes her head.

And you never heard from him again? After this one visit?

Him come back one more time.

And after that?

She shakes her head again.

Did you consult a lawyer?

Ma sista talk to one. Icylyn. Lyn. You an she never meet. She move to Kingston in the fifties, after the hurricane. She know plenty people. We never see eye to eye about Turner Buchanan but is she tell me to start pay the property tax.

What d'you mean, never saw eye to eye?

Miss Pauline sighs. Nuttn cause people to fight like land, Jussy. Lyn tink me should sell to the whiteman. Share the money. She struggle her whola life, them house in Look Out mash up in the hurricane, her baby father was a blacksmith and nobody have horse to shoe anymore, them go Kingston an the daughter die of polio. Lyn have it hard. But me ask her, so what she have to do with ma stone house? She never find the land, she never move the stone, she lef Mason Hall long time. Miss Pauline looks down. Me shame how me handle ma sista.

How did you have this fight? She was in Kingston, you were here, right?

She come home. Sit at this same table. Me show her the title. We have hard words. After that, we nuh speak for month 'pon month. But then she talk to one lawyer friend an write me a letter to pay the property tax if me want make a claim for the land.

And did you pay the taxes?

Evry year. Miss Pauline remembers the trip to Kingston to the tax office, the long lines, the scornful glances directed at her country clothes, the way people moved away from her, fanning their faces, the disdain of the cashier as she counted out the crumpled bills she handed in, one at a time. She's ashamed that she only visited her sister once in Kingston where she lived within two rooms at the side of a derelict house.

Wait. The man was offering you money for the land? I thought you said he owned it.

Him sey him compensate me to leave.

How much?

Not enough.

They lapse into silence and Miss Pauline senses Justine's deeper interest. Land. Inheritance. Money.

Suppose I find this man—he could still be alive—or his children? Or other relatives? Then what? You're going to tell them the land is theirs? This doesn't make any sense, Gran. She leans forward. You're definitely keeping something from me.

It hard to explain, Jussy. Me just tink history important. What happen before. How anybaddy come to be wey them is. What is home. Who build what. Who own what. She shrugs. If you don't find them, me rest easy. Me cyah explain any better. Do this for me, Jussy.

Okay. We have a deal. Doctor first, research next. Who's your doctor? I'm phoning him right now.

Her, says Miss Pauline, although she's only been to the young doctor with the locs and the level gaze once; that time when her piss started to burn. She name Dr. Shillingworth. In Port Maria.

A private doctor?

What that mean? How a doctor can private? She work inna the health clinic.

Justine taps her phone. Man, the signal up here is terrible!

Go library. Ask for Lamont. Him set me up to talk to you on the computer.

Doctor's appointment first. Justine's thumbs tap the small screen she holds.

*

Miss Pauline thinks about the meaning of land. She knows it's not eternal. If it can be owned, it can be stolen or sold and new owners can do as they please with it, excavate it down to bedrock and deeper, lay it to waste. Even weather wages war against land, land can shake and rend and tear itself apart. And once people arrive, land ceases to be itself. It becomes the place where human events unfolded, it becomes its memories, ghosts and tragedies. Here is where it happened, in this very place. Borders are constructed, naming is done. But she has no sense of herself if she is not grounded. She's as much part of the land as the lowliest worm, the most insignificant pebble. Land give, she thinks, remembering her father's shelter at the top of his sloping, stony *grung*, where he watched over his crops day and night, catching a few hours of sleep on animal feed bags laid on the dirt. She thinks of the food she grew and her ganja crop, and her father's swollen leg, chopped with his own hand, wielding his own tool. Land give an it tek too, she whispers. Land is *dangerous*. Her mind feels fuzzy and thick, like her mother's horse blanket. She wants to avoid the days and nights ahead. Her rejected religious instruction comes back to her, and she whispers: Let this cup pass from me.

That night, the stones crackle, like static from a radio. Behind the sounds, a faraway voice reaches for words.

# Chapter 14

That place too hot and untidy and the internet is slow as molasses in winter, Justine complains, returning from the library. She's disheveled and sweaty and holds a folder.

You have molasses in New York? Miss Pauline says.

What?

Nuh mind. You find him?

Who, Lamont?

No. Turner Buchanan!

Sort of. He's, like, dead. Did you know that?

Miss Pauline faces her granddaughter. No, she lies. The symptoms of illness surge in her body—her stomach roils, her chest tightens, a band of pain squeezes her temples. The stones mutter. No. Not in broad daylight. Justine doesn't appear to hear anything.

Tell me what you find out.

Miss Pauline pours them both glasses of lemonade and they sit at the table inside. Justine drains her glass. I'm not sure I could manage summer in Jamaica anymore, she says, fanning herself with the folder she holds.

Hotter now for true. But smaddy can used to anyting. Tell me what you find, nuh?

Wasn't hard, Justine says. Newspapers are online these days and Turner Buchanan is not such a common name. He came here in 1987 and went missing. You must have known that, right? Looks like he came to Mason Hall with a taximan, didn't drive himself, and the taximan killed him. His body was never recovered, though.

*Sey what?*

Yeah. That's what the *Gleaner* story said. A taximan was found with some of his stuff, his suitcase, documents, even family photos. He got stopped by the police in a roadblock, and they searched the car. He was convicted of murder. He got a twenty-year sentence. So that's that, Gran. There's nothing you can tell Turner Buchanan now.

Miss Pauline reaches for her glass of lemonade. Her hand shakes, and she knocks it over.

Careful, Gran, Justine says, grabbing the papers out of the way. She goes to get a cloth. You want a refill?

Miss Pauline shakes her head. Nuh-uh. Nuh fret about the lemonade. Come back. She hides her trembling hands in her lap. A *taximan*. This man, Turner Buchanan, him have a fambly?

Justine wipes the table and sits. Yes. His wife came here more than once after he went missing, until Hurricane Gilbert hit in '88—they wanted him declared dead, I guess, so a will could be probated or something, I'm not sure about that part. She kicked up a big fuss, accused the police of covering things up. She got his story in the papers and I suppose the police, like, worked harder on it than they might have otherwise. But then she couldn't get them to do whatever paperwork was needed to declare him presumed dead. The police just kept saying the matter was under investigation. The wife—Sandra Buchanan—even wrote to foreign news-papers. Told tourists Jamaica was too dangerous.

Miss Pauline purses her lips. There's a dark tunnel with no exits in front of her. How had she missed this story of the taximan?

What 'bout the taximan?

What about him?

Him have a name?

I didn't focus on him. Why d'you want to know?

What him name, Jussy?

Why're you fixated on the taximan? Okay, okay, let me look at my notes. Justine thumbs through the papers in the folder. Ellis something. Or Elliot. Here it is. Elliot Gardner, also known as Slide.

How old?

Justine looks at her notes. Never wrote that down. He was someone the police were looking for after the government changed in '80. One of those gang leaders, don men, I guess you call them. Left Kingston, holed up in somewhere called Gayle. Started running a charter taxi service from Ocho Rios to the airport in Montego Bay. I wrote down that he had a daughter. She said her father was a thief but never a murderer. What is she to say, though? I think I have her name somewhere. You don't want to know about Turner Buchanan's family? I thought that's what you were interested in, not some random taximan. Oh, here's the daughter's name: Bernice Gardner.

Yes, me want know 'bout Turner Buchanan. Gimme a minute to catch ma breath. You want anyting to eat? Me cook some chicken soup for later, but Lora bring over some grater cake, if you hungry now.

That sounds good. You know you can even get grater cake in New York now, Gran? Any of that lemonade left?

Ee-hee. You finish it.

You want anything?

No, chile. Me don't feel to eat right now. She remembers one of Granenid's sayings: Rest me down easy, for me is a cracked plate. She's cracked, like carelessly excavated stone.

While Justine is in the kitchen, Miss Pauline stares at the beige folder and the white papers and thinks of crimes reduced to records. Lists. Newspaper stories. The word "prison" beats in her mind, but she can't imagine the details of such a place. She knows some of the slavery houses had dungeons where people were chained up, underground places, with no light or fresh air, but she's never really thought about modern places of incarceration.

She thinks then of Granenid's stories of slavery, the old woman's face solemn. My mama bawn into slavery, she recited, as if she had said the same words many times. She was roun' six at Emancipation an she memba one mass of people in Spanish Town square on that August mawnin.

Same age as me, but me soon be seven, the young Pauline always replied.

She a bawn yah, but she did talk 'bout them that came on the ships, them that dead on the way an throw inna the sea, them that work the land until them cyah work no more.

Who throw them inna the sea, Granenid?

The white *backra* massa. Same as who beat them an kill

them. Tek them from Africa. Sell them. See this island? Is them—we—who build it. Never figet that.

Me hate white people, said Pauline.

Granenid sighed. Them powerful, still. Them is like the forest, fulla secret an evil an hurtfulness. You stay away from *backra*, you hear me pickney?

Me know. Dadda tell me.

Yet despite all the warnings, *backra* house was never a haunting to her. She sees herself, a young girl on the edge of womanhood, returning a week after Pastor Slowly's assault, wearing her school uniform, so as not to arouse Miss Glad's suspicions. She walked through the open front door of the slavery-time ruin, carrying the books she had taken, and set them down. Astonished at the number of rooms of unknown function, she explored. Empty windows were trimmed in rotting wood, the remnants of a staircase led to a second floor. She laid her hands on the stone walls, cool to the touch, immovable. She thinks of her books—all, except one, with plain red covers and black writing on the spines, as if they were part of a set. The authors' names were unknown to her. *Tarzan of the Apes* by Edgar Rice Burroughs. *The Wind in the Willows* by Kenneth Grahame. *Just So Stories* by Rudyard Kipling. And a farming almanac. Inside were pictures of the moon, waxing and waning.

She climbed the partly rotted wooden staircase to the upstairs floors. On the second floor, she stared out through empty windows to the green sea of the forest, uneasy at the height.

There was no furniture left, of course, and she wished she

could see what kind of tables and chairs the white people had owned and used. She daydreamed about the shoulders, arms and hands of the craftsmen and carpenters, Black men, who made the furniture, along with their tools.

Who was the woman in charge of this house? Did she look out at the captured land with appreciation or loathing? Was she afraid? Did she have a choice as to whether she accompanied her husband? What were all the various rooms used for? Why had they built here? How had they found the site?

A walkway made of partially sunk stones led to what must have been an outside kitchen, with a massive cast iron sink set into a wall. Over the front door, there was a broken stone, bigger than the others, green with moss. She thought she saw faint letters, perhaps an A. Maybe she could pile up loose stones so she could reach it and see what was written there.

She claimed a half-covered room on the ground floor. She brought a pile of crocus bags with her, taking care to shake them out each time she visited to dislodge scorpions and centipedes, and for her remaining teenage years, she lay with her books, an unmapped country, and she made her way through them, building word upon word, idea upon idea. She dreamed. She imagined the physical selves of the builders of the house she sheltered in, she learned to masturbate in that room, and it made her laugh out loud. *Backra* house. Fuck him. She made it hers.

Justine returns with a grater cake cut in half. Have some, Gran? she says, holding out the plate. Miss Pauline shakes her head. Elliot Gardner, also known as Slide. A taximan.

Believed to be the last person to see Turner Buchanan alive. Had the taximan died in jail? Where were prisoners who died in jail buried? Who was he? Why hadn't she seen the story of his arrest in the *Gleaner* at the time? Justine had been able to find it, so it must have been published. Perhaps it was buried in the back pages—stories of crimes against tourists were often suppressed. What had happened to his daughter, who insisted he was a thief but not a murderer?

Miss Pauline has wished for death only twice in her life— during the final hours of her labor birthing Carol before her trip to the hospital, and the night she climbed down a rain-slick ravine to the crashed country bus Clive was driving to look at his body lying crooked in the undergrowth, his neck broken, all that he was extinguished. Forever. She wishes for death now, this moment. Not merely before her hundredth birthday. She wants any reckoning taken out of her hands, and she understands the impulse to appeal to any god, to surrender her life to the almighty for judgment. For absolution. Or sentencing.

Justine puts the empty plate on the ground. Gran, she says. I'll be gone in a few days. Are you listening? I already set it up with Puppy and he'll take me back to the airport. What're you going to do with the names of these Buchanan people? You going to write them or what? I don't think they're going to care about your moving some stones or even this land. They've probably never even been here.

Miss Pauline feels foolish and doesn't answer. It now seems like a ridiculous quest, bringing her granddaughter here to find strangers on the internet. What's done is done, she thinks, but she knows what's done is never done.

Me sorry to drag you here, Jussy, but me nah lie, me glad to see you, glad to have this time wit' you. Write down what you find 'bout the people. If you find phone number, address, workplace, whatever. Leave it wit' me. Me see the doctor an do the blood test to mek you happy, but chile, me not going spend ma last days in any hospital. One time in ma life me lie in a hospital bed an me not going back there. Argument dun.

Justine smiles. I'm glad to see you too, Gran. And, you know, happy to remind myself what this place is like. My roots, and all that. But tell me the truth now—why are you so interested in this man, Turner Buchanan? It's not about the stones you took, is it? I mean, who's going to care about that? She clears her throat. Is it because you're going to leave this house to any of us? Or were you thinking about leaving it to him, if he was still alive?

Is that a flash of greed in Justine's eyes? Or apprehension?

Miss Pauline is astounded. *To the man Buchanan?* she says. But how me coulda *ever* do that? You mad?

Then what? You're leaving it to us, and you're worried about what? That it won't be legal?

Miss Pauline sighs. Dead lef can bring pure trouble to a fambly. Me know—

Wait. What's "dead lef"?

What a dead person leave to the livin. You know how much people in Mason Hall fight over land? Die over it? To this very day? Not even a year ago Peanut grandson, Hector, chop up Miss Daphne and her two girl children over one half acre of precipice that cyah even grow grass. Land is what bring the white people here an what mek them capture the Black people an force them clear it an plant it. Bury inna it. *Dead lef.* Mm-hm. She stops.

Justine looks confused. Are you talking about an inheritance? Are you wanting to make a will, Gran? If you don't have a will, you should make one.

Miss Pauline bites her lip, turns to face Justine. Mek me ask you sumpn, Jussy. Is who really own the land this house build pon? Me? Or Turner Buchanan? Him give me that paper, a title, you see it, an me know the law sey is him land. But then him—ahhm—disappear, you sey him dead, an is me pay the property tax since that time. Me dunno for sure how him ancestor get to own the land, but him is a whiteman. *Backra.* Them people just tek the land. Tief it. Ma ancestor—your own too—get capture, bring here, work the land, mek the white people rich. Some of us dead before we even reach, throw inna the sea for shark food. Me is *here* 'cause some of them an them pickney survive. This house build 'cause them was here. Them tek from we, me tek from them. You tink a whiteman capable of building a house wit' him owna two hand? No, sah. Them is helpless people. So. Who own this land? she repeats. Me? You an ma odda grands, even the ones me never meet? Or Turner Buchanan pickney an them grands?

Justine raises her hands, palms open. Gran, you need a lawyer. This title is a legal document.

Miss Pauline shakes her head. Me nuh need no lawyer. Me jus' need to know what is *right.*

The light turns molten and the bush rings with birdsong. Miss Pauline thinks: Christmas breeze. The holiday has never meant much to her, but she's always loved the weather;

hurricane season over, dry time not yet come. The exuberance at grand market, the garish decorations. She loves the food too—rice and green *gungu* peas, sorrel with ginger and rum, Christmas pudding, but it's a long time since she's made it for anyone, not even for herself. Maybe she'll make herself a goodbye Christmas dinner.

Justine says, You know what was interesting about the family tree? Not so much Turner Buchanan's descendants, but his whole line of ancestors is there as well.

Miss Pauline's attention leaves the flare of the waning afternoon and returns to the veranda. Ancestor?

Yes. The people he is descended from.

Miss Pauline shakes her head again. Me don't believe. Nobaddy can find out them tings, not now.

They can. They have. I focused on his children, like you asked me, but the website has his ancestors too, going way back. He or one of his children must have put it all together. But Gran, it was such a long time ago.

Ee-hee, long time, Miss Pauline says. But so what. Them bawn yah?

The ancestors? A lot of them, yes. I mean, I don't remember it all, but yeah. Born here. Most left. Like Mom did, I guess. God, I'm hot. Do you have an extension cord for that fan? We could bring it out here.

Sun soon set. The ancestor, them was slave owner?

Justine shrugs. Can't tell. An online family tree, it has names and dates, maybe an occupation, maybe where the person is buried, but that's about it.

Them bury here?

I didn't really study it, Gran. But it's there if you want

to look. I thought you were interested in his children. She stands. I think I'll have a wash-off.

Miss Pauline says nothing more, but she remembers how she, strong in the limb and heart of youth, roamed the bush around *backra* house, looking for traces of the dwellings where enslaved people lived. Nothing was left. She thinks of the smallest room in *backra* house, the last one she cleared, with the uneven hole in the tiled floor, lined with red fire bricks. She threw a rock into it and heard a faraway splash. A sinkhole. *Inside* the house. And in her mind she sees the three graves she eventually stumbled upon, at the very top of the hill, the names erased by the centuries. No name *backra*, one of thousands. For the first time she understands that maybe a particular whiteman, Turner Buchanan, had roots in Mason Hall too.

The doctor's appointment is tomorrow. Lamont has arranged for Puppy to drive them, and the price has been negotiated. She's worried the doctor will diagnose her illness and pre-scribe treatment, even an operation, and Justine will want her to agree. She feels the house tremble again and knows tonight the stones will be loud. Maybe after Jussy goes to bed she'll take a blanket outside. Rest under the breadfruit tree. Wake with the dawn. No one will know. 'Tap you stupidness, Pauline, she admonishes herself. Sleep on dutty *grung* when you have a good-good bed?

That night, she hears the man's voice again. Hollow. Despairing. When she lays her palms against the walls of her bedroom, they are slimy like the trails made by slugs.

Her hands are sticky and she rubs and rubs them, but the slime clings. Her sense of foreboding grows and she thinks of crawling, relentless forces. She scrubs her hands in the basin until they are sore. In the morning, she checks for water on the floor but it is dry and there is no new dust.

# Chapter 15

Dr. Shillingworth has a low Afro hairstyle, intricate hoop earrings and a calm but serious demeanor. The young doctor launches a raft of questions: Miss Pauline's age, her place of birth, whether she lives alone, what medications she's taking, why she has come to see her this morning. Miss Pauline describes her thirst, nausea, stomach gripes, back pain, chest tightness, fatigue, dizziness. Is that everything? Dr. Shillingworth says, with a level look.

The doctor's office is small, painted white, framed certificates on the wall, as well as a large wooden carving of the shape of a pregnant woman. Interesting, isn't it? the doctor says, following Miss Pauline's gaze. It's just a slab of wood—that shape was already there. Strange what nature can do, don't you think?

The doctor is no fool. Miss Pauline understands the meaning of her probing questions, but she can't speak about moving, wailing, sawing, weeping stones here in broad daylight, in this modern building in a coastal town, the sounds of everyday street life coming through the open window. Certainly not in front of Justine. She sits in silence and Dr. Shillingworth opens the folder on her desk.

Your blood pressure is appropriate for a much younger

woman, Miss Pauline, says the doctor, looking at the results of tests already taken by the nurse when they first arrived. Nothing in your urine. You're on the thin side—are you eating well?

She isn't, says Justine and Miss Pauline curses under her breath.

Dr. Shillingworth turns to Justine. Would you mind waiting outside? Miss Pauline here seems more than capable of speaking for herself.

Right, the doctor says when they're alone. Please get up out of that chair. Don't use your arms.

Me can still chop ma way t'rou the bush, Miss Pauline says, but she complies because she's grateful to the doctor for sensing her need for privacy. The doctor asks her to touch her toes, and when she's done that easily, to take off her shoes. She examines Miss Pauline's feet, murmuring about a toe fungus. The doctor's dry, strong hands on her feet are soothing.

Dr. Shillingworth straightens up. No glasses, Miss Pauline?

Never. Ma eyes fine.

When last you see a dentist? Teeth doctor.

Me know what a fu—dentist is, snaps Miss Pauline.

Sorry. Of course you do.

Long time. Me lose a tooth for ma second child—Clive pull it out with a pliers. That was anodda night of plenty blood. Maybe four years gone me get a filling an them tell me about braces. Fu—damn foolishnis. Ma teeth fine.

You're in remarkable health, the young doctor says, but she looks unconvinced. Are you sure you're telling me all your symptoms?

Watch me now, Miss Doctor, me never want come here. Is

true me don't feel to eat, me t'irsty all the time, an me not so strong anymore. But me is *old*. What you expeck? When tiger get old, evry dawg bark after him. Me is here jus' to get ma granpickney outta ma skin. Jus' tell me what wrong wit' me, so me can go about ma business.

I don't see much wrong with you at this point, Miss Pauline, but I want to run some tests which can only be done in Kingston. I'll give you a paper for the lab in Port Maria— they'll draw blood samples and send them in. When I get the results, I'll know more. Your symptoms make me a little worried about your kidney function.

So me have to come back?

Yes, it's likely.

Miss Pauline stands, and the doctor raises her hand. One more question—how are you sleeping?

Sleepin?

Yes. Are you getting enough sleep?

Miss Pauline doesn't think she can speak another lie. T'anks, doc, she says, and looks toward the door.

Not sleeping well then, Dr. Shillingworth says and writes on her pad.

They find the lab in Port Maria and leaving Puppy and Justine in the car, Miss Pauline hands in the paper. She waits in a crowded room and eventually, a nurse takes her into a small cubicle and asks her to stretch out her right arm. Look away, Mummi, she says. She wraps a strip of rubber around her arm, slaps the thin skin on the inside of her elbow lightly and says, Looking for a vein. Mek a fist for me. Awright den. You ready? One likkl stick.

When Miss Pauline gets up, she sees the thin glass containers filled with her blood. She wonders if the test will reveal a map of all her origins, journeys and trials, or if the study of her blood is more like a photograph, showing only the here and now.

They stop to buy patties at the gas station in Port Maria before they head back to Mason Hall. Puppy fills the gas tank, and Miss Pauline asks if he wants a patty as well, which he accepts. Justine goes inside and buys them two beef patties each, in paper bags.

You can get patties in New York now, but they don't taste the same, Justine says, nibbling at hers. Miss Pauline thinks about Jamaicans in New York, eating grater cake and patties, having left the island physically, but still there in mind and heart.

Back home, Miss Pauline sits heavily on the glider. Water, Jussy. Nuh from the pipe—from ma jar.

After she returns with a glass of water, Miss Pauline drinks and drinks. When her thirst is slaked, she tells Justine she wants to hear the rest of Turner Buchanan's story.

Not until you tell me what the doctor said and eat at least one patty.

The patty tastes as if it has been stuffed with dirt. She gets through half of it and hands the other half to Justine.

You're making me gain weight, Gran, says Justine. Now the doctor.

She waitin on the test-them. She sey she no see nuttn wrong wit' me.

Hm, says Justine. She goes inside to get her research on Turner Buchanan's family.

*

That night, for the first time, the stones speak in a woman's scratchy, unused voice, first in English words, in an accent Miss Pauline has never heard. Me dig. Gra-a-ay-ve. Me. Res-s-st. Sometimes the woman mourns, her words thick like silt on the move, other times she sounds sharp like a chisel teasing at mortar, chipping away at it, beating a rhythm Miss Pauline somehow knows, speaking a language she doesn't: *Nkakat itaha ekpeme, eto akpa ayak oduñg, sia odung edi ûkú eto.* She sits up as if stung. An African voice speaks English to her. Efik, the stone woman says, which she doesn't understand. Ma-ma-mine. Then: Dead tree always-s-s leave root to start ov-over.

*Story come to bump,* whispers Miss Pauline, fear swelling. Stone know. The beat of her heart seems loud enough to shatter her ribs. The woman falls silent, and the air in the bedroom contracts, as if the house itself has taken the deepest of breaths. Miss Pauline hears a whooshing sound, like the first gusts of wind from a hurricane, before they become a roaring. Mortar shakes itself loose from the stones and shivers down, down, pattering.

# Chapter 16

Justine has seasoned a basin of chicken parts. She washes her hands at the sink, then lifts them to her face. Still smells of thyme, she says. Hope I don't excite those drug dogs at the airport. Her suitcase is packed, and her hand luggage contains a Christmas cake made by Lora, who makes the best cake in Mason Hall, soaking her fruit for a full year beforehand. Miss Pauline wants to hide her granddaughter's bags, to keep her with her until the end. She hears the sound of Puppy's taxi coming up the hill and thinks, no. Not yet.

You cook that chicken today and you eat it, Justine says, pointing at the sink. She's wearing a freshly ironed suit, high heels and an elaborately tied scarf on her head. They face each other and Justine opens her arms.

Chile, Miss Pauline says. She steps into Justine's embrace and lets her body relax. Me is grateful to you. Some of that cake is for you mumma. And you walk good, you hear?

She watches the taxi drive away, raising a haze of marl dust.

She's once again alone in the stone house with its movement and its voices, alone with Justine's file of papers, containing the names of Turner Buchanan's children. Two daughters, Nicole and Kelly. A son, Jeffrey. And the name of the taximan's daughter, Bernice Gardner.

She knows, though, she doesn't have time for letters. Now-now, the stone woman rasps each night. Re-turn. On the night after Justine leaves, Miss Pauline lies rigid, fighting thirst and fear. Me know, she says out loud, trying to comfort herself with the thought that maybe the woman who mourns and rages can be appeased. The stones swish like a cutlass through cane, a lash through skin, a shovel through dirt. They thrum with percussion, sometimes a slow marching beat, other times a complex, tonal weaving beaten out by many hands. The whiteman's voice wails and wails. The woman bawls out, exactly as Miss Pauline remembers her own voice in childbirth.

She can't just lie abed anymore, afraid, listening. Waiting. She gets up and leaves her bedroom. The noises fade but her dread clings. She goes to the kitchen table and sits in the dark.

All manner of people come here, she thinks. Have pickney. Them bury here. Some leave, some stay an some come back. The whiteman, mebbe him have a story too.

She curses out loud. Me don't interest in him story, she tells herself. Member what you has to do. Find the whiteman's pickney. Find the daughter of the taximan. You mek Jussy come here an you nuh tell her what really happen. *Eedyat* ooman.

She looks over her shoulder at the open bedroom door, as if the stone woman might walk through it. She—you—know what happen, she thinks.

She needs Lamont and yes, finally: she needs a phone. She remains sitting at the table in her living room, which still smells of her granddaughter, until dawn. Only then does she return to her bedroom to sweep up the dust and grit shed by the walls during the night.

After she's washed and dressed, drunk her tea and eaten a panganat, she goes to find Lamont. She doesn't know where he lives but she believes Miss Marcelle at the post office will have his number. She takes the walking stick with her.

You nuh have a phone, Miss Pauline? says Miss Marcelle. That yout', be careful of him, me hear sey him inna pure badnis.

Miss Pauline kisses her teeth. That man who was here? You get rid of him? Him nuh inna badnis? Don't is you send me to Lamont inna the first place?

Awright, Miss Pauline, sekkle down. Me just hear tings, thas all. So what? You want me call Lamont for you?

Miss Pauline nods. Me know it not my business, but man like that, them never *ever* change.

Miss Marcelle taps the phone and does not reply.

Ten minutes later, Lamont shows up on his yeng-yeng. He leans it on its stand and bounces into the post office. Miss Pauline sees Miss Marcelle's interest in their conversation, so she leads Lamont outside into the heat of the day. Standing at the side of the road, Miss Pauline tells him what she wants—a cell phone, and the contact information of four strangers. When she's made her requests, agreed the phone should be smart, and negotiates a price with him, she asks, You have fambly, yout'?

He shrugs and looks away. Mumma migrate when mi a baby. Never know ma fadda. Mi grow wit' ma granny until she dead. Mi rent a room from Miss Bridget, di ooman who run di bar wit' di TV—you know her? Mi is okay, Mummi.

You eat Christmas dinner wit' me, then, she says, surprising herself.

He looks down at his hands. Long time since mi have Christmas dinner still, he mumbles.

That is bare fuckery, Miss Pauline says, and he laughs.

Mek mi ride you home, Mummi. Too hot to walk. Gimme you stick.

She smiles. Another ride on the yeng-yeng.

Next day, he returns with a phone in a box. Pauline is astonished by its small size and complexity. If her eyesight weren't so good, it would be useless to her. Lamont starts to tell her what he's doing but she holds up her hand: No sense tryin to explain to me, yout'. Come, mek us sit inside. You going have to work it. When you done, just show me how to phone smaddy. Start with you.

Signal here better than over suh, he says, walking around her living room, holding the phone aloft.

Justine complain it was bad.

Bad compare to what she used to. Good compare to what mi used to.

He sits on the dusty old couch, taps and swipes at the phone, hunched over. *He* might need glasses, she thinks. After a while he says, Gimme di name-dem you want mi look for.

She pulls up a chair to face him. Nicole, Jeffrey an Kelly Buchanan. Bernice Gardner. Bernice probly here. The rest in America.

His thumbs fly over the phone. Nuh-uh, he says eventually. Bernice an Kelly, di two of dem right here suh.

She tells him he's wrong. He turns the face of the phone

to her. See? Here is Bernice. She work inna hotel in Ocho Rios, not far. Mebbe forty-five minute, mebbe a hour, depend on who drivin. She looks, but before she can take in the picture, he swipes the phone and the image of a middle-aged woman with an over-wide smile and a name tag on her dress disappears.

Wait—Miss Pauline says and Lamont laughs. It not gone anywhere, Mummi. Soon bring her back. He taps and swipes and turns the phone to her again. Dis is Kelly Buchanan.

She takes the phone. She sees a fair-skinned woman with a thick cloud of dark blonde hair, a broad forehead like her own. Unsmiling, forty or so, wearing a flowery dress and lace-up boots. Several strings of beads around her neck and on both wrists. The woman stands in front of an airplane tail with the words WELCOME TO NORMAN MANLEY INTERNATIONAL AIRPORT painted on its side.

How you know when that taken?

Posted last month. Cyah tell when it taken.

Then she might come and gone, don't it? Maybe she just a tourist—come for a likkl while, lie on a beach, go home.

Lamont shakes his head. She have nuff recent picture on Insta, Mummi. Kingston, Highgate, Oracabessa, Portie. Recent pics in Treasure Beach.

What is Insta?

Instagram. A different social media site.

Miss Pauline remembers the way Clive talked about the south coast, as if it were a different country. Maybe social media is like a different country, one without borders or shoreline. There's so much she doesn't know, won't ever know.

Lamont takes her hand and shows her how to swipe with

her fingers and she sees the recent Jamaican life of Kelly Buchanan scroll by. Most of the images are of plants, but occasionally she stands beside others, mostly Jamaican women. Miss Pauline decides they are her servants—she refuses to use the new word "helper" believing it obscures and softens the truth of the relationship. She's not going to like Kelly Buchanan.

Lamont demonstrates how to find his number stored in the phone and call him. Mi put it on speed dial, he says. She practices. He explains that there's only a certain amount of money on the phone and she will have to do what he calls "top up." Post office can do it fah you, he says.

She smiles at Lamont. The outline of a gun in his hair is beginning to grow out and his hair is picky-picky. His clothes are faded, torn and too big for him. He will welcome a meal, long before Christmas.

You ever shell *gungu* peas? she says.

He wrinkles his forehead. No, Mummi. Never.

You ever grater coconut?

He rolls his eyes and doesn't respond.

Today you go learn. Full belly tell hungry belly: tek heart.

Old people full a sayin, he says.


After they've cooked together and eaten brown stew chicken with rice and peas, boiled dumplings and steamed callaloo, she reminds him of his first task—to find out how to get in touch with Kelly and Bernice. He looks sleepy after the meal during which he spoke only once, to ask why there was no plantain.

Next time you bring some come, an we fry it, she said.

She thought then about the empty rooms in her house and the young man without family in front of her, the youth who might be into badnis. She knows many would warn her about bringing him into her home and until recently, she has valued her solitude. Granenid would have said: Bad fambly better than empty pig sty. Miss Pauline thinks, Fambly come in diffrent form.

She says to Lamont, You can find phone number on the internet? Like a old-time directry?

Nah, probly no number, says Lamont. But mebbe a place to call. We start wit' Bernice; because she put di name of di hotel whey she work on Facebook. Mi look at Kelly page again, see wha' mi see. You have to track people like animal, seen? Smell dem out.

She doesn't like the imagery of tracking and capture and leaves him to it. She realizes she's eaten a fair meal herself and feels no pain or nausea. She will sit on the glider and close her eyes.

Lamont is on the new phone throughout the afternoon, mostly sitting on the front step. She dozes on the glider, letting her thoughts ripple out until they quieten. At dusk, he looks up and tells her the phone is dead. Dead an gone? she asks, straight-faced.

He laughs. Jus' need a charge, Mummi. He shows her the cord and plug, demonstrates how to charge it and tells her she must do it every night before she goes to bed. He takes his own phone inside and plugs it into a wall socket.

Returning, he says, So what you do at nighttime, all by you owna self? Why you nuh get a TV? A new radio? That radio old like you! You could watch the news, listen to music. You nuh lonesome? And why you nuh turn on some light?

She likes his irreverence, his honesty, his lack of guile. He could easily see her as a meal ticket, but so far he's made no effort to sweet her up or take anything she's not offered. Me like it peaceful, she says, jolted by the realization that her home is no longer peaceful. She goes on, trying to recapture what she fears has been lost forever. The quiet. The dark. And kerosene lamp remind me of old-time days. Ma mumma.

Not you fadda?

Inside the house don't remind me of him. Him was a man for outside. Farmer. A good man.

Mebbe this man-child, who might be into badnis, also know about goodnis.

She makes them both cocoa tea and they dip hard crackers into the foamy, sweetened liquid. The moon rises and fruit bats swoop and hunt. Mi preffa plenty people around, Lamont tells her. Dis kinda scary. Fulla duppy. He stands.

Me nuh believe in duppy, she says, although she's no longer sure this is true. You can sleep here if you want. Jus' for tonight. Will he hear the noises, when Justine had not?

He considers. You mek breakfast tomorrow?

*We* mek breakfast. You get a early start on the phone since signal better yah so.

You tough like Maroon Nanny, Mummi.

Me is no hero and duppy know who to frighten.

If you not scared of duppy, mi not scared.

They laugh together. We go in soon, she says. He sits on the uncomfortable wicker chair, with his back to the night, and at first, he fidgets, scratches his hair, adjusts his clothes, looks left and right, ducks if he sees a bat in his peripheral vision. She senses the tension in his body easing, but only slightly. He goes inside to check on his phone, telling her the time when he returns.

When you go bed? he asks.

Whenever time me feel to.

Me is tyaad now.

Inside, she begins to strip the bed Justine slept on. Lamont waits in the doorway. Help me wit' the sheets, she says. You stand on the odda side.

What you doin this fah? Sheet awready on di bed.

Givin you clean one.

He shrugs and bends to help. She puts a blanket on the end of the bed, and he says, Cold here fah true.

She shows him the inside bathroom, built by ganja at the same time as the inside kitchen, and gives him a towel. The bathroom is fed by water off the roof via gutters into an elevated black plastic tank. Me nuh have a extra toothbrush, she says, but one night nah go matter. Not so much water inna the tank, so nuh waste it.

She leaves him, washes the cocoa cups, makes sure the stove is off and returns to the glider. She's not sleepy yet.

Has she been reckless, inviting this young man with a yeng-yeng and the faded image of a gun in his hair into her house? Stories of elderly people murdered by their young relatives are commonplace. Would be a fuckin relief, she thinks. Lef the mess. Just lef it. No confession, no request for forgiveness, no reckoning with the past, no confronting the pain she caused for others.

If Lamont intends to kill her, she hopes she won't see it coming.

She thinks of smoking suddenly. She smoked cigarettes in teenage, until Miss Adina smelled it on her breath and told her she would downgrow. She never smoked again, but it would be good to sit here now with a cigarette, the red tip glowing in the dark, the feeling of alertness coupled with don't-care she still remembers. Why not, she thinks, amused. Me done downgrow awready. She wonders if Lamont has a cigarette but decides not to ask him. He's sure to have weed but that's never agreed with her, and she needs him to focus on the search for the two women.

She wishes now she could start over with both her children. She thinks of Justine flying back to New York, taking the Christmas cake to her mother. She should have sent a letter. Does Carol ever think of her, here in Mason Hall? She wants to tell her daughter that she misses her and wishes she had been a witness to her life. That she's sorry she was not kinder, more patient, more generous with her time and attention.

And Alvin, dead close to ten years now, killed in a bar fight on the waterfront. Head injury, the police said to her. Blunt force trauma. Freak accident, the man never mean to kill him. When him drop, him lick him head on a cement block. No charges ever pressed. No way of knowing why her sixty-five-year-old son would have been in a bar, let alone in a fight. Cremated at Dovecot, near to Spanish Town, a plaque with his name on a wall, no contact with the earth, the funeral a confusing mass of strangers, singing and speechifying. Sweating faces, hands pressing hers. It was the last time she saw her sister too. They did not speak.

A dog barks incessantly, probably on a chain. A lizard croaks, seeking a mate. It's chilly and the night air smells of woodsmoke. Time to face the situation in front of her. Turner Buchanan's children. And a man, Elliot Gardner. A thief, but not a murderer. The twenty years of his prison sentence have long passed—was he released from jail? Or did he die there? If he's alive, maybe she'll meet him or his daughter, but she still doesn't know what she'll say to either of them. Other dogs bark, then set up a howling at the moon, and she pulls herself up and goes inside, locking the front door behind her, knowing what she fears is already inside. Lamont won't have ear plugs. Maybe tomorrow she'll know whether what she hears is in her mind.

She lies in bed, waiting. The silence she once loved pulls the air out of the room. She tries to imagine the face of the long-ago *backra* man coming to Jamaica on a ship, but his features shift like sand deposited on a riverbank and then torn away. She imagines the whiteman seeing the island for the first time, the mountains rising up. No wonder he thought it worthy of the taking. Her last thought before she falls into sleep is of flying herself, like Justine going back to New York, like the pilot granddaughter she's never met, above the clouds in a real airplane. That would really have been something.

But still she dreams again of a jagged blue hole in the earth. She's buried, maybe dead, looking up at it. The stones are silent, and in the morning, there's no dust on the floor.

# Chapter 17

Miss Pauline is done with speculation and worry—it's time to set things in motion. To act. So me stay, she whispers to herself when she decides what to do. Puppy will drive her to the Platinum Hotel near Oracabessa, where Bernice Gardner works, according to information Lamont has found on Facebook. She's decided not to warn Bernice about her arrival, even though she might not be at work on this particular day.

She leaves a soft-faced, well-fed Lamont in the house, instructing him to make his bed, tidy the kitchen, continue his search for Kelly Buchanan on his own phone, which he will "top up" with money she has given him. He can leave the front door unlocked. They don't discuss whether he'll return for a second night. She's filled a basket with produce from her garden and fruit trees, and will pick up some of Lora's homemade grater cake on the way out of Mason Hall—gifts from country always smooth the way.

You have di phone? Lamont says as she goes through the door, but he knows the answer. He unplugs the device and hands it to her. No sense lef it inna di house, Mummi. She takes it and drops it into one of her deep skirt pockets. She wonders if it's a lifeline or a tether and if this young man thinks he can mother her.

She's dressed carefully for the first time in years—her most colorful tie-head, given to her by Zepha, made by a batik artist in Kingston in the seventies. She hardly ever wears it—keeps it wrapped in tissue paper to remind her of her childhood friend, and it smells of mildew. A plain white blouse with a high neck—pressed with the old iron she heated on the stove, normally used as a door stop. Her long gray skirt with the embroidered trim around the hem, now with a loose waistband. She uses a large safety pin to make it fit better. She wears her only pair of leather shoes and leaves the cutlass under her bed. If any chopping is necessary, it won't be by her.

When Puppy's car drives up, she refuses his help with the basket. Me can manage, she retorts.

The drive down the hill feels like escape from her house. She doesn't think Lamont will find Kelly Buchanan—how to even begin a search for a single visiting white foreigner? This drive, though, this journey to seek out the taximan's daughter, to confess to her, *this* journey is the one that's critical. She's committed a crime against her own and sitting in the front seat of the taxi, which smells of the pine air freshener hanging from the rearview mirror, Kentucky Fried Chicken and motor oil, she doesn't know what to hope for. If she doesn't find the woman, she will at least have tried, but a mountain of painful words will stand, undiscovered and unspoken.

As they navigate the winding, potholed road, she thinks about the ways people die. What to choose, if she could. To die in her sleep, that would be best. It was not too late for a violent death of many kinds—gunshot, strangulation, stabbing, chopping. She could fall, break her neck, end of story. But suppose she's sick. Going mad. Like Carol. She inhales sharply and rejects that fate. Not too late to drown. She's never been afraid of River, although she can't swim, but what would it be like to drown, at the bottom of a well, say, with only a faint light from above, scrabbling to find handholds or footholds, calling out, shouts becoming screams, then sputtering gasps, the dawning knowledge that no one is coming, that this is where it will end? When the time comes, however it comes, will she be relieved to finally *know* that here is the end, here is the manner of it, that only darkness remains?

Puppy brakes sharply to avoid a skinny, limping dog and she thinks: Maybe a car accident like Clive. Maybe today. She's shouldered more fear during the past weeks than she has in all her life and she's ready to put it down. *Rest me down easy, for me is a cracked plate.*

There's a guardhouse and red and white barrier at the entrance to the hotel. The uniformed guard is on his phone and doesn't end his call when the taxi drives up. He waves his hands at them as if to direct them to a different entrance, but another car is now behind them. The guard ends his call and strides over. Dis nah di right gate fah taxi! Sas crise, he hisses, raising his hands in an appeal to the almighty. Wha' do you, man?

How you know sey di lady not checkin in? demands Puppy.

The guard is skeptical and reaches for a sheet of paper. What her name, if she checkin in?

Miss Pauline understands Puppy's bluff has been called. She gets out of the taxi. Being an old woman is an asset in many situations. She hunches her shoulders and limps over to the guard, just as the driver of the car behind them starts blowing his horn. Mawning, sah, she says. We never know the right entrance. Sorry for that. Me is here to see ma—aahm—granpickney—is her birt'day. She work here. If you let in the taxi, him just turn around an gone.

The guard is mollified by her deference but still suspicious. What di name of you granpickney?

Bernice Gardner.

Oh, Miss Bernice! Never know is her birt'day. He lifts the barrier, glares at Puppy and points him to an exit at the rear of the hotel. The car behind enters; the driver waves at the guard and does not stop.

What you name, Mummi? the guard says, holding a phone to his ear.

Beg you—don't call her. Is a surprise.

Me have to write you name inna di book, but for you, me nah call her. What you have inna di basket?

She knows what's being asked. Green banana. Ripe plantain. Some green *gungus*. Lemme see if me find some for you.

Put it inside, Aunty, the guard says, indicating the guardhouse by pouting. Don't walk up di front step of di hotel; dem don't like that. See di walkway over suh t'rou di flowers bush? Go straight to di end, don't turn off, you hear? Look for a door sayin HOUSEKEEPING. If she not in dere, smaddy will know which way she turn.

She tells him a false name, thanks him and shuffles up the driveway, exaggerating her frailty. She sees Puppy's car ahead, parked off to the left under a poinciana tree near the exit gate. She walks up to the window, pays him, and tells him she'll call him on her new phone when she's ready to return to Mason Hall.

She's never been to a hotel before. The air is heavy and wet, different from the hills. She's not given hotels much thought—she hadn't realized how big they are. The main building is three stories high, painted white, with scores of balconies. She can just see the blue line of the horizon between other, smaller buildings, and she remembers the first time she saw the sea with newborn Carol in her arms, Clive beside her in the mail van, when she told him she wanted her owna house an land. She's never seen such a tended garden—a flat green lawn, almost no fallen leaves, mulched and weeded flower beds, and a profusion of unknown blooms. At first, she sees no people, but she can hear a reggae beat and foreign voices. A man wearing blue overalls digs a hole near to the path, presumably for a potted plant beside him. She tightens her grasp on the basket's handle and heads in his direction.

The man greets her. You lost, Mummi?

Mawnin, she replies. Nuh yet. Which way housekeepin?

He leans on a shovel, and she can see his curiosity as to what someone like her is doing in a place like this. Down suh, he says.

The flower beds disappear from the left side of the walkway and now she can see the white sand beach and the sea. It's a calm, cool day, the waves fuss at the shore and the light is blinding. She squints. White people wearing hats and sunglasses lie on loungers under striped umbrellas. She sees the radiant aqua color of a rectangular pool with black lines painted on the bottom. A white woman swims along the lines. She's never seen so much still water in one place, so clear she can't assess the depth. She's heard about swimming pools but this is the first time she's seen one and she wonders if it's fresh or salt water. A man rakes the beach. Another sits on a tall wooden seat with a sign saying LIFEGUARD, staring out to sea, talking on his phone. Women in dark blue uniforms and white aprons carry trays with drinks to the white people.

Pay attention, she thinks. You not here to gaze around. The HOUSEKEEPING door is ajar. She pushes it and calls out, Mawnin? A voice answers and she walks inside, glad to put down the basket.

Three women in uniforms turn to her. She explains why she's there. The oldest one says, Bernice cleaning Block C. Me is Miss Rubina. She nods at the others. Miss Georgia, Miss Serenity. The housekeeping women make a fuss of her, find her a seat, bring her a glass of water which smells of bleach. They won't be fooled by the birthday story, so she sticks to just being a grandmother. She distributes the rest of her produce, keeping a few pink-and-white grater cakes for Bernice Gardner.

Why it so cold in here? she asks Miss Rubina.

Air-con. You never feel it before?

Miss Pauline shakes her head. Miss Rubina, me is just wonderin if there is a place me an ma grand can talk alone?

Hmm. Old rotten bench roun' the back under the poinciana tree. If we want smoke, that's where we go. You want wait there? When Bernice finish, we send her to you?

Outside, she's relieved to be alone. Lamont, Puppy, the guard, the housekeeping women—too many new people. The bench is made of concrete, and she can see nothing wrong with it, except that the concrete has worn away in places, revealing the thick wire structure beneath. She's sorry it doesn't rock, but she relaxes in the shade, glad to be outside, away from her house. Perhaps Bernice will not come out. Maybe when she returns from cleaning Block C and hears about a grandmother waiting, she'll laugh and say she knows of no such person. Miss Pauline is still thirsty and although she disliked the smell of the water, she wishes she had asked for a refill. Her stomach gripes. She wraps her arms around her middle. No more time.

She hears a voice calling and realizes she's fallen into a doze. Disturbed nights have taken their toll. She sits up and sees a short, sturdy woman walking toward her, dressed in the same blue uniform as all the others. She has tall hair, pulled back into a ponytail. Maybe forty. Her uniform has short sleeves, and her forearms are muscular. She strides up and stands with one hip cocked, hands akimbo. So you is who now? she demands. Ma wut'less fadda mudda who lef him before him tun five an never send not even one *deggey-deggey* barrel? Or you is a scammer? You too old for dat, all di same.

Miss Pauline still doesn't know what a scammer is. She struggles to her feet and says, You is Bernice Gardner?

Das me. The younger woman looks her up and down. Nah sah. You cyah be ma grandmudda nor a scammer. You too country. Who you is an what you want?

Me come to find out about you fadda, Elliot.

Ma *fadda*? What you have to do wit' him? You an him did *deh* or sumpn?

No. Him in jail still?

But hear dis now. How you know him? You best talk up, or mi will call security.

Miss Bernice. Do, me beg you. Tek time wit' me. Me is a old ooman, me don't mean no harm to you. Just sit here wit' me a likkl bit an me an you talk like big people.

Bernice Gardner's scowl relaxes slightly. Ma break is half hour. Mi give you twenty minute. Sey what you come to sey. Start wit' who you is. She sits at the very end of the bench and turns to face Miss Pauline.

She remembers then Granenid's insistence on proper behavior, reinforced by Miss Adina, reading aloud in her speaky-spokey voice. Manners might smooth the way with Bernice Gardner. She touches her chest and begins, First and commence, me is Miss Pauline Sinclair. Me bawn an grow in Mason Hall inna the hills up suh. Me just find out you fadda gawn a prison for killin a whiteman name Turner Buchanan. This man did come to see me back inna the eighties an—She stops.

An what?

This is the moment. She hears the chatter of kling-kling birds above them, the sounds of traffic on the coast road and music; Bob Marley's "One Love," grating on her tone deafness. Lamont would dismiss this song as being from the long ago. Her long ago has caught up with her.

Me don't tink you fadda kill the whiteman.

Bernice Gardner laughs, her head thrown back. Aunty, you come to give me pure jokes today. So what? You tink is only one crime him do? Dat man have sin stickin to him soul like caulkin.

You speak for him back when them arrest him. You sey him was—is—was a tief, but not a murderer.

How you know dat?

Ma granpickney Justine. She find it inna newspaper. She sey evryting online now.

True ting dat. Well, Aunty, mi nuh know if me can explain why mi sey mi know him nuh do it. Ma fadda, him mek ma sista life a misery. From when mi leave ma mudda house, mi never speak to him, never look fah him, try don't tink 'bout him. *Ever.* Mi never even know sey him lef Kingston. Yes, him was a tief an a liar an a rapist. But ma fadda, him couldna kill a chicken or slaughter a goat. Mi never tink him a killer.

She turns away and Miss Pauline leans closer.

Trut' to tell, Bernice says, her voice shaking slightly, mi never speak fah him back den. Mi speak 'gainst Babylon— nasty police-dem. Pure lie dem tell. Mi speak 'gainst the system, Aunty. You unnerstan? Mi speak 'gainst how di ting set. Mi know dem never really have anyting on ma fadda— yeh, him did tief di whiteman tings, but dat don't mean him kill him. What you want mi sey? Mi glad him lock up an it nuh matter to me what him lock up fah.

Miss Pauline hears Zepha's voice on the day of Pastor Slowly's attack, so long ago: *So the ting set.*

To Bernice Gardner she says, Him still alive?

Aunty, mi nuh know. Him sentence dun long time. Mi never hear from him an mi nuh know which way him tun. You done wit' me now? She puts her palms on her knees and prepares to stand.

What happen to you sista? The one him interfere wit'? You have more brudda an sista?

Just di two of wi. What happen to her? Last time mi see her she line up where dem feed di homeless people inna downtown

Kingston. Mi try talk to her but she never know mi. Last ting mi do for her, is get one private doctor in Kingston to tie her tubes. You unnerstan? Doctor talk to me about consent, but once him get pay, him no badda himself 'bout dat. Mi dunno how she survive on di street, but she not alone. Plenty like her.

She turns to face Miss Pauline again. Dis island here, this *one love* Jamaica, it one terrible, wicked place, Aunty. It *dark*. But all like you, live so long, you must well an know dat.

Miss Pauline sees the shine of tears in Bernice Gardner's eyes, and she thinks of her father, his pimento and sweat smell, the squeak of the iron bed when he came to Miss Glad at night. She is sure he was welcome. To Bernice she says, Cyah blame bush an rockstone for what man do. Bad an good people is everywhere, don't it? She doesn't wait for a reply. When last you see you sista? She older or younger?

Plenty older. Bernice counts on her fingers. Mi been workin here four year, before dat, a jerk chicken place in Salem. Must be ten year now, since mi see her. Mebbe more.

So she never have no pickney?

She have a bwoy pickney for ma fadda, him that you come here about. Her *fadda*. Di adoption people tek di baby an neither mi nor she know which part him is. Bernice shrugs. She coulda breed after that, but mi nuh know 'bout anymore baby. She repeats, You done wit' mi now?

Nuttn ever over an done wit', Miss Pauline says.

True ting dat.

What 'bout you? You have pickney?

Mi? One son, yes. Him in Kingston still, wit' him fadda. Good boy, but Kingston, mi nuh know. She shakes her head. Ma break soon dun. She stands.

Miss Pauline wants more from Bernice Gardner, but more of what? Her father raped and impregnated one of his girl children. What else is there to know? She doesn't think she can ask why Bernice escaped the same fate. One more ting, she says. Why them call you fadda Slide?

Bernice Gardner laughs. Him love one old dance call Electric Slide. You know it, Aunty? So dem call him Slide. Him love a fete, use to DJ, knock out a riddim, sing in church sometime. Plenty people inna di community love him.

Rapist, thief, father, dancer, entertainer but not a murderer, convicted for a crime he had not committed. Served his prison term. Whereabouts unknown. Was his punishment just? Not me to decide that, she thinks.

Miss Pauline lurches to her feet and the hotel grounds whirl, as if she herself is at the center of a hurricane. She steadies herself on the arm of the bench. Bernice Gardner's story is not what she anticipated, but she can't think of any more direct questions. In his daughter's telling, Elliot Gardner deserved jail, but it seems too random, too neat, without cause and effect. Or justice.

She sits back down. You like this work? she asks, reluctant to leave.

If mi like it? The young woman laughs without mirth. You strange, Aunty. Mi clean floor an bahtroom. Dem pay me. Das all.

Ma first time in a hotel.

She shrugs. Pretend place. Nuttn real here. Das what money buy. But Aunty, you don't tell why you really come here. Nuh suh?

Trut' to tell, me not even so sure. She inhales and prepares her lie. The whiteman sey him own some land in Mason Hall. Then him disappear. Me want find out what really happen to him.

Wait. What land?

She meets Bernice Gardner's eyes. Just some land.

You tink me bawn behind cow batty? Cyah be some random land. Your land, right?

Miss Pauline nods. A piece of it, ee-hee.

So what, you tink is some land fight why di whiteman disappear? Nuttn to do wit' ma fadda? But who him fight wit'?

That is what me tryin to understand. Me did hope you know sumpn. The whiteman sey him own the whola village.

Bernice Gardner shakes her head. Mi don't know nuttn 'bout no whiteman nor no land, much less any village. White people, dem always ownin tings an people always in some war over land. Could be ma fadda just get ketch up inna it. She looks at her watch. Mi have to go.

Miss Pauline looks up at her. Me sorry for what happen.

You sorry him get jail? The young woman kisses her teeth. For what?

Nuh-uh. Me sorry what happen to you sista.

Bernice Gardner shrugs. Worse happen to people. Mi glad me never have a gal pickney. Anyway, Aunty, ma break dun so—

You like grater cake? she asks. Homemade.

Bernice Gardner claims her thoughts all the way back to Mason Hall. There was no need for a confession after all, no reason to speak all that she knows about Turner Buchanan's disappearance. Elliot Gardner's daughter was glad he was imprisoned. Perhaps he deserved it. She feels relief but knows her silence was cowardly. It nuh matter now, she whispers, but it is a lie.

You find who you look for? asks Puppy, swinging the taxi around corners, the radio blasting out a talk show.

Ee-hee, she says. Found sumpn. Lost sumpn too.

So it guh, Puppy says.

# Chapter 18

Her house is empty and airless. Brooding. There's a scrim of dust on the living room floor, the first time this has happened outside her bedroom. Or during the day. She longs for a human voice, thinks again about sleeping outside. She could call Lamont on the new phone, ask him how his search for Kelly Buchanan is going, but she feels like a stranger to herself; she, who has loved her own company all her life. She looks around for something to occupy her, but except for the dust, the house is clean, the dishes washed, the bed in the spare room straightened. Mason Hall is unusually quiet—did all the people leave while she was at the hotel? Is she not only alone in her home but in the village itself? Look like me turn duppy, she thinks, and goes to get the broom.

Late afternoon on her veranda, the hard light of midday easing into the glow of sunset. She nibbles at a cold patty she bought on the way home. The man who went to jail for the disappearance of Turner Buchanan deserved his punishment and she has kept her secret. Is that the end of it? She thinks about Bernice Gardner's sister and her son, a child of incest, and Bernice's baby father and their son. She had not asked for any names.

Where does her responsibility begin and end? With Elliot Gardner himself? Or with his descendants, those who were affected by his imprisonment? Was he the breadwinner for his family? Or did they celebrate that he was not coming home? How many lives were changed by Turner Buchanan's two visits to Mason Hall? Elliot Gardner could have any number of outside children, any number of baby mothers, sisters, brothers, nieces, nephews, cousins.

Thirsty after the patty, she goes inside to pour water from her jar. She thinks then of the small, calm pools created by River's largest rocks, where the water lay so still it was transparent, and in her mind she sees the ripples they created, circles within circles, and she remembers how slowly the ripples subsided. She sees herself, a girl, sitting at River's edge, creating ripples by dropping pebbles or larger stones into the water, or sometimes with her finger, writing the letters she was just learning on River's surface. She remembers the weight of carrying water—first, the rum bottle, then buckets, small to large, how the water slopped over her legs, the place halfway up the hill where she rested, until Zepha showed her how to make a circle of cloth for her head and settle the full bucket upon it.

And then she thinks about the many times she dropped stones and rocks into the sinkhole at *backra* house after she found it, and how long it took before she heard the faint plash as they hit the water far beneath her feet, and how the sound changed depending on the size of what she threw. Kneeling at the edge of the mysterious portal to the innards of the earth itself, she had never seen the surface of that water, and she never knew how long the water took to regain the stillness of metal, how long before their impact was smoothed and finally erased.

Justine had told her the online information contained not just Turner Buchanan's descendants, the ones she described, but also his ancestors. The people who came before, those who were as sharp, dangerous rocks hurled with force into hidden, quiet pools. She realizes she's spent many hours imagining the woman who presided over *backra* house, but never the man, the massa himself. Perhaps it's as important to reach back as to look forward. How strange to look for beginnings so near the end. She hears anew the warnings of her grandmother and her father—*stay away from* backra *tings*. Too *fuckin* late for that.

She walks out that night with the remnants of the patty and scatters the meat under the trees on her land, one older than she is, the others—mango, starapple, coconut, ackee, lime—planted by her. There is one dead tree nearby, just outside the fence she eventually erected—a blue mahoe, struck by lightning. Men have come with chainsaws in hand offering to take it down for her, but she sees the many birds resting there, including the owls, and she's told them to leave it alone. It's a long time since she feared owls.

The night is cool. Wispy clouds drift in the sky and she turns her face into the moonlight. It is the lightest of balms on her skin. Why hasn't she yet slept outside, as she and Clive had often done, in close embrace, while they were building their home? Surely it will be peaceful under the stars away from the stones which might know she lied to Bernice Gardner?

She trips and almost falls. When she regains balance, her breath comes short. Fear sinks its claws into her chest. Maybe she is not quite ready to die, or perhaps fear is just an unavoidable animal reflex. Too fuckin old, she thinks, too old to walk out inna the nighttime. Clive. She longs for his steadying hand, his mouth lightly on hers, his breath her sustenance.

She retraces her steps. The house looks far away, and she sees moonlight flash on the wings of an owl, hunting.

That night the stones sound the plaint of the abeng, blown by Maroon Titus at gravesides in Mason Hall, including at her father's. The Maroon is dead now and the abeng has fallen silent. The sound goes straight to her blood. The stone woman coughs, like a patoo. Then she drags out a word which sounds like "argument" and repeats it. Once. Twice. Miss Pauline realizes the voice is sounding out letters—A-G-U. Her skin crawls, because she sees those same letters every day—A-G-U—carved into one of the stones of *backra* house, now right over her own front door.

She wakes to the stirrings of hunger, fully present in her body. She runs through words beginning with the letters A-G-U but can still think only of "argument," even though the R is missing. It does seem the stones are posing an argument, seeking a response. Then it comes to her—what do men carve into stone? *Their names.* These letters are likely from the first or last name of the man who caused *backra* house to be built.

Her stomach growls. She's ravenous. Energy and purpose rises in her body. She will make Johnny cakes with saltfish and cabbage. And then she will locate her new phone, which she did not remember to charge before she went to bed, get it ready, and find out if Lamont has found Kelly Buchanan.

Lamont doesn't answer her call, although the phone makes several chirping noises afterward. She doesn't know what this means. She wishes she could speak to Justine and enters her granddaughter's number after several tries with clumsy fingers, but the call does not go through. Fuckin useless ting, she hisses out loud, but stops short of flinging it into the grass. She contemplates walking up to the library to try Skyping again, but she's afraid the uphill walk will sap her fragile returning energy. Perhaps her trust in Lamont was misplaced and he won't return, becoming just one more person she'll never see again. She cooks for herself, eats, washes up and sits on the glider. She watches shadows small-down and big-up as the day passes and remembers another one of Granenid's sayings: Trus' no shadow after dark.

She's in the kitchen at dusk, heating up the leftover saltfish and cabbage from breakfast, when she hears the sound of the yeng-yeng over the creaking chorus of the whistling frogs. Relief, perhaps even joy, wells up. She looks down at the small pot—not enough for a young man's appetite. She's sorry she didn't cook for him. She turns off the stove and walks onto the veranda. Why you no answer you phone? she snaps.

Tek it easy, Mummi! he says, still sitting on the yeng-yeng. Laad, you is like a macca bush or a wildcat, pure scratch an chastisement. Me was at the library an them don't allow no phone call. You never see ma text? He leans the yeng-yeng on its stand and dismounts. He's carrying a scandal—plastic—bag.

Text? You bring me a book?

He claps his hands to his cheeks and laughs. You sumpn else, Mummi, honestly. Me send you a text. A message. It inna di phone.

You never tell me 'bout no text.

Ah true, he concedes. Anyway, mi is here now. He walks up the steps and goes straight inside. Sumpn smell good.

She follows him. Me never cook for you. Never know you was comin back.

Don't fret youself. Mi bring food for di both of wi. You like curry goat? He takes two cardboard boxes out of the black bag and puts them on the table. Maas Amos kill one goat over by him new building site—mi get a construction work over suh. What inna di pot?

Cabbage an saltfish.

Yeah man. Share it up. Mek wi eat an mi tell you what mi find out.

The man-child sitting across from her at her kitchen table has entirely shed his wariness. He talks rapid-fire, sometimes using slang she doesn't know, his patwa dense and tumbling over itself. Tek time, she tells him.

He's found Kelly Buchanan, he tells her with evident pride. She responded to him on Facebook. She's renting the side of a house in Treasure Beach, hoping to expand a small craft charity with local women.

Who you tell her you is? Most of Miss Pauline's food is still on her plate.

Fambly, he says. Mi just tell her mi tink wi is related but den she block mi.

Block you? What that mean? You did sumpn bad?

He searches for words. Nuttn bad, but mi cyah contack her again. You not eatin?

Me eat before you come. She pushes her plate over to him. Me can go see her?

See her? Mi nuh know, Mummi. She might tink you a scammer.

Me need to see her, face to face.

He looks dubious. Mi tell her about you an she block mi. He frowns, considering the situation, chewing. His expression lightens. No disrespeck Mummi, but you old. You nuh look like you can hurt anybaddy, if she see a picture. Or lemme set up a Facebook page for you—den she can see what you post. Mebbe she block you too, mebbe not.

Miss Pauline hardly understands him. He seems to be saying she can send a message without writing a letter and taking it to the post office, put a picture of herself somewhere in the sky, capture a life of almost a century on some kind of duppy page, which is not made of paper. She thinks of the few photographs of her children and two of her grandchildren in the cedar chest. She has none of her children as babies, and she tries to remember if she's ever seen a picture of herself. Yes, there was one, she remembers, of her standing, unsmiling, in front of the half-built stone house. Who took it? How did it go from camera to shiny, stiff paper? And where is it now?

The stone house. She remembers choosing the best stones at *backra* house, her stones piled up on the drying barbecue, awaiting transport to her chosen site. At first, no one from Mason Hall would help. Nuttn good will come from dis here madness, said Maroon Titus. But men from other villages heard there was work in Mason Hall, and they arrived.

How much? the men demanded.

We pay you in stone, said Miss Pauline, standing with Clive. You take some stone to build you owna house. You help we to build my own first. We help you after.

Who decide who is to get what? said Runner, a man Clive knew from the road crew.

Me, said Miss Pauline, hitting her chest. *Me.*

A goat was slaughtered; blood and white rum was sprinkled around the foundations of *backra* house to appease the ancestors. Then Maroon Titus was persuaded to beat his Gumbeh drum at the site, the abeng was blown, and the women of Mason Hall filled Dutch pots with curried goat and rice cooked on open fires to sell to the men dismantling *backra* house. Finally, the men of Mason Hall joined in and after the argument about the type of mortar was settled, Clive bought bags of cement in Port Maria, the men dug sand from River's bed, and mixed the mortar. And then they built walls with the stones. Miss Pauline checked the numbers marked with coal to make sure they fit well, and then ran her palms over them to make sure they were laid straight.

Her house of stone rose.

After it was finished, the men from other villages left, and the men of Mason Hall carried the remaining stones into the village square, assigning a certain number to each family. They moved as a crew and one by one, the old village was transformed. Some made walls around existing houses; others pulled down wattle-and-daub, Spanish wall and plywood structures and built new dwelling places of stone. The women watched and brought water and food to the laboring men.

The men used the last of the stones to rebuild the post office and the library and then they rested.

Mummi? Why you look suh? Lamont says, touching her arm. His plate is empty, except for the bones of the goat, sucked clean.

She shakes her head. Nuttn. Just tryin to make a plan.

We go library. Tomorrow, because mi start work Monday. Mi help you send her a email. Tek it from dere. He leans back in his chair. Mi can stay here one more night? Mi love dat bed, God's honest trut'.

She can't deny the relief she feels. Mebbe more than one night, she says. Tell me 'bout the job.

After they've eaten, she knows sleep is a long way off for her and she doesn't want to go inside. The cocoa tin is empty, so they drink mint tea together, this time sitting beside each other on the glider, and it's Lamont's foot that pushes it, forward and back. Without asking, he lights a spliff after he's drained the last of the tea, and she smells the familiar, sickly smell. Funny the tings people take a set against. This herb a sin, that one holy. She holds out two fingers to Lamont and he raises his eyebrows and hands her the joint. She takes a deep draw and it makes her cough. He laughs. Whoy! Biggest ganja farmer in St. Mary cyah manage one draw ah weed! She inhales again, feels the acrid smoke in her throat, and waits for the pleasant feelings others have described. They do not come.

What kinda construction? she asks. House? Office? Road?

Me never ask. It nuh matter to me. Di sign on di gate say DEVELOPMENT.

It nuh have a picture?

Yeh. Tall buildin. Coulda be apartment, coulda be office. Mi hope dem don't want mi climb scaffoldin, you see mi? Mi nuh like height.

She can't imagine an apartment or office building in Mason Hall—who would occupy it? She says, Where it is?

Almost on di flat. Right after di deep corner by Miss Aretha shop.

The flat land close to River bend? The one them plan to build house back in the day but not one house ever build?

Ee-hee, same one. He stacks the two plates, eyes lowered.

Back inna the day, that place flood out easy.

Chuh Mummi, tings build more strong now. More engineerin.

Lamont talks more about his construction job, and how it could lead to other work, better work, and the boss, a man known as Bald Pate, says he will be part of a crew, and how he will learn new skills, he will be a 'prento, and he will earn regular money and can look for a bigger room with its owna bathroom and even kitchen. And this job will lead to other jobs—maybe in Kingston or Montego Bay, where the pay will be more, and where there's so much excitement, dancehall, round robins, trips to beaches, waterfalls. Mi will get outta Mason Hall, he exults, dropping the spliff-tail on the floor.

Pick it up, she says, pointing. Put it inna the flowers. Mek sure it out first. You want leave Mason Hall?

Sorry, Mummi, he says, bending over. Want leave? Mi is *dyin* to leave. Nuttn is here. Is a dead place. He goes over to the veranda railing and disposes of the spliff.

Miss Pauline feels his restlessness, his ambitions. Me went

to Kingston a few time, she says. Nuttn for me is there. Bare noise an confusion an gunman.

Ee-hee? You like country. That awright for you, but dis place borin as hell. All kinda ting happenin inna di worl', Mummi, but not yah suh. Not fah mi. He yawns and stretches. You nah go bed?

Not for now. You gwaan.

Lamont stands and she touches his arm. Wait, she says. He stops.

Tell me you story, yout'. You bawn an grow in Mason Hall? Where you people? How old you is? How you come to be makin you way alone in the worl'?

Her questions don't dampen his mood. He holds his arms out in a V-shape, making a large shrug of indifference. Bawn yah, ee-hee. Mi is sixteen next March, don't know exack day. Ma granny grow me, Miss Amoy, you memba her? She not as old as you, still.

She nods, remembering Amoy as a girl at River, but having no recollection of her as an old woman with a grandchild. She dead?

Lamont frowns. Why you nuh sey pass like evrybaddy? Dead sound—

Me believe in usin the right word for tings. Dead ah dead.

You harsh, Mummi. Honestly. Yes, she dead. Dem sey she get stroke. She dead inna St. Ann's Bay hospital.

In her mind, Miss Pauline sees the hospital ward where she recovered from childbirth. How old you was that time?

Mebbe eleven? Twelve?

Ma fadda dead when me was ten, Miss Pauline says. What you do after? Where you mumma? Fadda?

He shrugs again, this time without the exuberance. Mi nuh like talk 'bout dese tings. Ma mumma, she lef me. Das it. Ma fadda, me nuh know anyting 'bout him. Granny sey him from May Pen. Gran lef me a likkl money, mi don't go school after she—aahm—dead. Mi just start hustle. He yawns again, but she knows it's his way of ending the conversation. She feels the pain behind his bravado.

You Granny—she grow you good? She treat you right? You is mannersable, yout'. Don't see that so much anymore.

He turns his face away, drops his voice. Granny, she give mi her last grain of rice. Never drop lick on mi. You favor her.

Awright, yout', she says. Mek us link up now like we just bawn. Lef the past alone. Sleep good. Use the maskitta net— them bad, this time of year.

The waning moon is low in the night sky when she goes inside. Her bed, usually so familiar, so enveloping, is uncomfortable—too soft, too warm. Her bedroom is both too dark and too light. She has a standing fan now, which she only uses in the summer months; she turns it on and a few minutes later, turns it off again. She listens for the stone woman, hoping for guidance, but there's silence. Dreads the male voice. She runs her hands over her body, searching for signs of sickness, but even those have left her.

Tonight, she feels nothing—not physical pain, not fear, not anxiety. Not even sadness. She hears nothing. Maybe she's already dead and doesn't know it, maybe she's in her nine-night and soon whatever she is, whatever she was, will wink out.

She puts on her housecoat against the night air and lies on top of the bedcovers, making sure there are no gaps in the mosquito net. She revisits her time with Bernice Gardner in the hotel grounds, the life of the young woman's father a casualty of what she herself failed to do, his current whereabouts, the full shape of his life, also unknown. And his children, and their children, and Bernice's children, all entangled, not even knowing their connections. Fatherless, abandoned Lamont.

At least she knows who her father and her mother were.

She runs through all the things she does know about her own family, holding up her fingers in the dark as if checking them off. Her son Alvin is dead. Her daughter Carol is in a home in foreign, has lost her mind, but is soothed by Jamaican stories and Jamaican food. Her granddaughter seems fine. Her grandson, Jacob—Jake—is a hedge fund manager, which despite Justine's explanation, still seems to her like a gardener. She has no recent news of her other grandchildren, Alvin and Leesha's girls. Her sister is dead; she doesn't know if her brother Troy is alive or anything about his adult life. Her grandmother, mother and father are all dead. Those are the people she knows.

But there are all the others who came before. Granenid's mother, her great-grandmother, born into slavery, a line of shadowy people, leading back to Africa, their lives perhaps intersecting with the lives of Turner Buchanan's ancestors. Maybe you have to go into the past to make the present right. Maybe the long ago is demanding something of the here and now. She'll ask Lamont to go with her to the library when he wakes and she'll trace the braided tributaries of her life, all converging on a flood plain, now, at the end, and she'll follow them right back to the headwaters.

As if she has heard Miss Pauline's thoughts, the stone woman speaks. Wait-ing. Nan-an-an. Her voice becomes drowned by the harsh, tumbling sounds of what Miss Pauline knows is music but from an instrument she has never heard. Then: Zepha's nickname for her in the stone woman's mouth—Paul-ie. She shudders.

# Chapter 19

Paulie. A whiteman lookin for you over by the post office. Miss Eldora tell me. Zepha's voice was low and frightened. She stood in front of the steps leading up to the stone house's veranda. Early August 1982, the summer light harsh.

Who is Miss Eldora?

New postmistris. She just come. Zepha steps up, onto Miss Pauline's veranda.

A whiteman? By him owna self?

Ee-hee. Alone. No uniform.

The heritage man come back?

Me nuh tink so. A different whiteman. Mebbe a bawn yah, in Kingston or Mandeville. But him have a twang. Spend time in 'Merica.

How him stay?

What you mean, how him stay? Whiteman, good clothes. *Mawga*. Educated. Sweatin. Mannersable.

Him look dangerous? Miss Pauline asked.

Zepha scoffed. Cyah tell from how smaddy look if them dangerous. What you go do, Paulie?

*Do?* Me nah do nuttn.

You coulda hide. Leave Mason Hall.

Miss Pauline laughed then. Zeph. You know me from me know maself. When you ever see me run? No raas way. Post office you sey? Mek we go see what the whiteman want.

Memba Jiwan, Zepha warned.

Me tink about Jiwan evry day of ma life. She considered. Mebbe him is a tourist an him jus' want buy some weed.

Paulie. Don't chat foolishnis inna me ears. How a tourist man going get you name?

Miss Pauline nodded. True ting.

A whiteman was looking for her. Knew her name. Maybe the man was CIA, like in the seventies, finding out things for the U.S. government. Money shut mouth, whether town man, country man, soldier man or police man. And money would deal with this man too.

What Miss Eldora tell him? she asked Zepha, over her shoulder, going back inside the house, out of the billowing heat.

Zepha followed. She sey she nuh know you. But the man nuh believe it. Him sey Mason Hall a small place. Him sey him going walk 'round an see what him see.

Miss Pauline went into her bedroom, splashed water on her face from the jug, secured her red tie-head. She looked from mirror to mirror. Her hair was feathered with gray. She tucked a few spiral curls away, said out loud: Him mek a big mistake comin here. Her cheeks were still plump, her eyes defiant, direct and clear. Her long skirt will hide her puss boots and the cutlass in its scabbard.

She walked out of the bedroom. G' lang, she said to Zepha. Me deal wit' this man ma owna self.

You sure? Is no problem to follow you.

Me sure. She touched her old friend's shoulder. She was

not one for physical displays of affection, but she didn't like to think of a life without Zepha. She saw the signs of aging in her friend's face that she hadn't noticed in her own, laugh lines at the corners of her eyes, circular rings around her neck, and her face now seemed to lack mobility. How you face set so? Miss Pauline often asked. Smaddy trouble you? Zepha would laugh, her face flowing into motion, and deny that anyone had offended her. Getting old was a hardening. A rigidity. Like setting cement.

She strode to the post office, ignoring the summer heat. Hope the whiteman outside and don't have a hat. Hope him skin burn up. No good reason for a foreign man to appear in the village, asking for her.

Sekkle yourself. Mebbe him just want buy some weed. But she knew this was unlikely because Mason Hall was too hard to access from tourist areas. She had sold her weed to the brownman Jiwan set her up with. She knew little of what was done with it, but some would have been sent to other countries in myriad ways—small aircraft, the holds of ships, canned food, the luggage of travelers. Could the whiteman be a big-time drug dealer? Was there some upheaval in the chain of ganja growers, middlemen, exporters and buyers, some argument over turf? She knew how easily this could lead to bloodshed. She remembers Jiwan's early warning— ganja bring killin—and her brusque response: starving bring dyin. And there was that time when a small plane had crashed in a cane field outside Annotto Bay and the men inside vanished, their bones only found years later when a sinkhole flooded and spat them out.

The exterior of the post office had been painted white.

There was nobody inside. She banged on the counter, and called to Miss Eldora, who strolled out of the back, wearing a green Jamaica Labour Party T-shirt with the slogan, DELIVERANCE IS NEAR, referring to the general election held two years earlier.

Miss Pauline greeted her, and the woman nodded, her face unfriendly. Miserable town smaddy. Not used to country ways. Miss Zepha tell me sey a whiteman lookin for me?

You is Pauline Sinclair?

Miss Pauline shivered. The man knew her surname. *Miss* Pauline Sinclair, ee-hee.

The woman, who had not yet introduced herself, twisted her mouth. 'Bout a hour gone.

How him stay?

How you mean? Whiteman. Foreigner. Me don't tell him nuttn.

Him wearin a hat?

A hat? She kissed her teeth, showing her disdain for Miss Pauline and the man. Me nuh memba.

Miss Pauline narrowed her eyes, and the woman took a step back. Mek me tink, Granny. Yes, me tink him carry a hat.

That a pity, said Miss Pauline, who had already seen the whiteman's skin begin to blister in her mind. And me is not you Granny.

She walked the roads and lanes of Mason Hall, looking for a whiteman, who was bound to bring disaster of one kind or another, but there was no sign of him. People had seen him but didn't know where he had gone. Maybe he was a simple tourist. No. *He had asked for her by name.* Uncertain of her next move, Miss Pauline climbed down the concrete steps cut into the hillside to River. A few women still washed their clothes in River, and soap suds circled in the eddies, but mostly River had become the playground of children, who felt for rare *janga* under the big rocks and sold them at Saturday market for back-to-school money.

And then, halfway down the slope, she saw the whiteman, bare-headed in the beating sun, hat in his hand, sitting on her rock, gazing at River's mucky and depleted water.

She felt cold in the blazing heat. Her heart pounded. She collected herself. She was not *afraid*. She was Pauline, country born, self-educated, a mother, a lover, a life partner, the parish's largest ganja farmer, a respected elder, a grandmother, a woman who knew every dip and fall of the land, every ancient tree and trembling sapling, who had survived the force of hurricanes, the agony of childbirth, and the desperation of drought; had been hungry and seen her children hunger; she was a woman who built herself a house of stone from the what-lef of those who took everything from her ancestors. She would not take any raasclaat fuckery from a whiteman. She bounded down the last stretch of the hill to River, as confidently as she had in youth, setting a few loose stones clattering down to warn the whiteman of her arrival. He stood and turned to meet her.

Young, early thirties. Short-haired, clean-shaven, light-skinned. Grayish-green river eyes. He wore a light blue short-sleeved shirt with a collar, darkened by circular marks of sweat under his arms, khaki pants, leather boots with laces. He had planned to walk around the village, perhaps even into the bush. A few mosquitoes gathered around his head. He waved them away.

I hear you lookin for me, Miss Pauline said. You is who?

Pauline Sinclair? he asked.

She stared at him. He held out his hand. She ignored it.

He made a face. My name is Turner Buchanan and—

What you want?

To talk. I hear you have a nice house. Maybe we could speak there?

His voice was not quite American. He had probably been considered foreign all his life and that generated a brief pang of sympathy, quickly suppressed. He was a threat, this man— she knew it. She was about to tell him her house was for her friends, but then she considered the greater control she would have on her own veranda, instead of out here in plain view of all. And it was too hot for bad news.

Follow backa me, she said, and started the climb back to Mason Hall.

At the top of the hill, he told her that he needed to get something out of his car and asked for directions. She described how to find her house and left him.

Inside the stone house, she poured herself a glass of water, wiped the sweat from her face and neck, and waited. Her body was wound tight. As if she might need to run.

He was not ten minutes behind her. He walked up onto the veranda without her invitation, carrying a leather case. She gestured for the man to sit in the uncomfortable wicker chair. Sey what you come to sey.

He sat, took out a cloth kerchief from a pocket and wiped his face. Could I have some water, please? he said.

She nodded and went inside, worry coiling into fear. She kissed her teeth, annoyed with herself. This was a young man from far away. What could he do to her? It would be better to treat him with less hostility, to gain his confidence. She heard her father's voice in her mind: Ketch more fly with honey than vinegar, Puss.

Instead of water, she filled a glass with lemonade and chipped a few pieces of ice, bought from the ice truck yesterday and stored in a cooler. She would disarm the whiteman with hospitality. She cut up a day-old rock cake and put it on a plate.

Thank you, said Turner Buchanan, taking the glass. What's this? He pointed to the cake.

Rock cake.

Hmm. My mother used to talk about bulla. Bulla and pear. Avocado pear, that is. This lemonade is delicious—not too sweet.

From the lime tree *me* plant out back, she said.

The man drank and ate and the tension between them eased. She rocked and watched him. Clear skin, good nutrition. An educated man who had probably traveled. The mosquitoes were still with him. She could have given him some citrus oil to keep them off, but she hadn't. Wouldn't. She waited. Where had he parked his car and where was he staying?

He met her eyes. Thank you for the refreshments but I've not come with good news. This house—you built it?

Me an ma baby fadda.

What's his name, your baby father? He's not your husband?

None of you raas business. Just get to the point. Who you is an what you want from me?

He unzipped the folder he carried and took out some papers. Um, forgive me, but can you read?

She scowled at him. Yes, me can fuckin read.

I'm sorry. Didn't mean any offense. He handed her a thick document, bound together with a small triangle in the lefthand corner. She saw his name at the top in handwritten capital letters—TURNER BUCHANAN—and all the other words blurred.

I own this land, he said. All of it.

Miss Pauline held the papers, just restraining herself from flinging them at the whiteman on her veranda. She felt her dead father's cautionary presence again. She began to flip through, letting the words slide by, reading none of them.

I'm sorry—Turner Buchanan said again.

She held up her hand. Just wait, nuh.

The pages looked slightly yellowed, as if they were old, although she thought it was a copy. Sure enough, she found a stamp on the last page with the words "Certified Copy" and the date, three months ago. She didn't understand some of the words and phrases—proprietor, in fee simple, incumbrances, sub-division approval. ALL that parcel of land, she read, known as Mason Hall or Mason Manor. There was also a drawing, but she knew none of the few place names listed or the name on the final page: Earl Paisley.

Her mind fastened on the words: ALL that parcel of land...Just three capital letters, but it must be the biggest word ever spoken, ever written, when applied to land, encompassing every clump of soil, every various stone and pebble, every determined weed and cryptic insect. *All.* And then: a parcel, as if land is something that can be wrapped and tied with string to be sent somewhere else via the post office.

She went back through the three pages. What is "sub-division" approval? she said. Who is this Earl Paisley?

He was my father. He sold some of the land to build houses. The flatter part down the hill, but although they cleared the land, no houses were ever built.

The land by River's bend, where Lamont would soon be employed.

You fadda, she said, putting the title on the glider beside her, resting her hand on it. She knew the power of paper and writing and official stamps, and he would not be getting it back.

That's your copy, he said, nodding at the title. Yes. My father. I'm not sure, but I think he hit on hard times after the war, so that's why he sold a piece of it. A big chunk. Good land. Probably why they applied for a title. But he held on to the rest. Still a large area—almost a thousand acres. Includes most of Mason Hall. He looked down at his hands. My parents were born near here, but they migrated to the UK in the fifties looking for work. They divorced when I was a baby, my mother married an American, Mike Buchanan. He adopted me, which is why I have his surname. I'm an American citizen.

Clive's voice: *You cyah jus tek it. Land have to own.*

My father always told me he still had land in Jamaica, the whiteman went on, that our family had been here for a long time, and he would come back when he retired. Died too early though. Left the land to me.

She sensed no real sadness in him. So, what, you—you going move here? she scoffed. You, wit' you accent an nice clothes an white skin? *Nuttn* is here for you.

He met her gaze without flinching. No, I have no plans to move here. I'm going to sell the land, and it'll be easier if there are no squatters. As I said, the land takes in much of the village too, so that's a complication. I'll probably have to do some more sub-dividing. I came to you first because you settled on the largest piece. And I heard you're an elder, that people respect you.

Settled? she demanded. *Squatter?* Who you tink you *fuckin* talkin to? Me bawn yah, me grow yah, an me will bury right yah so.

*A t'ousand acres.* It was a meaningless number.

Turner Buchanan sighed. He lifted his hands, palms facing her, in a gesture of peace. Look, I know this is a shock. I know it's bad news, and I'm not a terrible person, I'll give you some time to relocate. I'm spending about another week here trying to find the other—aah—people who are on my land, hoping you'll all be reasonable. After that, it'll be up to the lawyers. Expensive for everybody. But that—he pointed at the title beside her—says the land you're living on is mine.

She was caught between outrage and despair. How to react? Should she appear reasonable and lull him into complacency? Should she threaten? Unleash her vocabulary of Jamaican badwuds? Turner Buchanan must be aware of Jamaica's crime rate. She could suggest that life was cheap here and few things call forth violence more readily than a claim to land. Not time for that yet. She stored her anger.

Awright, *Mister* Buchanan, she said. You find me, an you sey what you come to sey. Me hear you. Not only you can find lawyer, still. You write down where me can find you. We have more to speak about. This not over.

He stood. There's a letter in the bundle which has my address. Goodbye, Miss Sinclair. Hope you'll be reasonable. Easier for everybody. I'll give you a month to let me know what you're going to do.

You hear from me when you hear from me, she said through clenched teeth. He shook his head and walked down the front steps of the stone house she, Clive and the people of Mason Hall built.

*Backra*, she whispered to herself. Then her father's words: white massa. Slave owner. The words didn't make her feel any better.

# Chapter 20

Nan-an-an, the stone woman moans that night, a muted clanging like a rusty bell. Sounding an alarm. Anansi? she wonders, the trickster spider, his stories told to her by Granenid so long ago? Nan-an-an. A name? She's grateful to leave the familiar dream of darkness thick enough to taste, the unreachable blue light from the sky, the smell of water. Her body feels both heavy and light—and she thinks of soil, how it can clod into thick clumps and resist all tilling, but then dry up and blow away on the wind. She listens for sounds from Lamont but there are none. A rooster crows and she hears the beginnings of the dawn chorus. She'll wake Lamont as soon as it's light, they'll eat together, and go to the library as soon as it opens. She will look at the names of her relatives, the ones who came before.

When she hears Lamont moving around, she gets up and dresses. He's made himself tea and is sitting on the front steps. There's a little tea left in the battered pot she uses for steeping mint leaves, and she pours it into a cup. She stands beside him, looking out.

Dat bed a di bomb, Mummi, he says. She suppresses the urge to stroke his head.

You hear anyting last night? she asks. The morning air smells of smoke and manure. Probably someone was moving their cows past her gate at dawn.

Anyting like what?

Jus' anyting strange.

Like tief, you mean? Shotta?

Me mean anyting.

No, Mummi. Mi sleep like a dead man.

Hard dough bread for breakfast, she says. Today we go library.

He doesn't object, although she knows he must have been hoping for a cooked breakfast.

They sit in front of a computer at the library. The new librarian doesn't come out of her office and Miss Pauline is glad they have the larger room almost to themselves. Lamont shows her new pictures on Kelly Buchanan's Facebook page—one of upturned fishing boats on a beach, the other of a sunset. She probly still in Treasure Beach, he says. People post dem holiday pictures soon as dem tek. Then he shows her what he calls a family tree, a map of sorts made of little boxes and straight lines. She traces the connections with her finger. This one married that one and had all those children, and they married, and had ever more children. The names she's never heard before, the dates and the mysterious abbreviations make her feel foggy. The sheer number of people. Me cyah memba all this, she says to Lamont, who's staring at his phone.

Confusin for true, he agrees, turning to face the screen. He points. Here is you, where Justine did start. She peers at the screen and there's her name, Pauline Evadne Sinclair, b. 29 December 1918–?, Mason Hall, St. Mary parish, Jamaica.

The machine in front of her knows who she is. Somehow it has found her, like a soldier looking for a ganja grower. To suppress her anxiety she asks, What the question mark is for?

Mi tink it mean you don't dead yet. See, how these have di date di person pass? "b" mean born, "d" mean dead.

Dead, she whispers, thinking birthday plus dash and then deathday. A dash seems a poor way to describe a life.

The screen freezes. Lamont curses, moves the small device he has explained is inexplicably called a mouse, strikes some of the keys. What happen? she asks, feeling vindicated by her lack of trust in the machine. She hopes it's dead.

Internet drop out, he says. Soon come back.

She considers asking—drop out to where?—but decides against it. She doesn't really want to know how the computer works. She sees the names of her sister and brother in little boxes next to hers, both with question marks, although her sister died shortly after Clive's funeral. Cancer, the telegram from Lyn's baby father had said. Miss Pauline had not known Lyn was ill. There are the names of her mother and father. And then Granenid, her mother's mother, Enid Cameron. *Now I lay me down to sleep.*

It come back, says Lamont, moving the small device. New names appear, rolling, coming up and then disappearing.

Jus' what in front of you, she whispers out loud. Lef the rest. She turns to Lamont. Show me this Kelly.

Lamont moves the mouse and all the names blur. Here. Lamont points. Dis ah di Buchanan man fam tree.

She sees Kelly's box—b. 28 June 1978.—d.? Turner Buchanan's daughter is about Justine's age. She concentrates on the information on the screen. The whiteman was an only child. Married to one Sandra Buchanan. They had three children, Jeffrey, Nicole and Kelly, all born in America. If the computer is right, Jeffrey is the only one of Turner Buchanan's children who had a child although she wonders how frequently it is updated. Only Sandra Buchanan had a deathday.

The screen freezes again. She tries to move the mouse, but the little arrow on the screen skids crazily around. Lamont has walked over to the window and is tapping on his phone. The computer goes dark and then an image of a blue sky with clouds comes up. She pushes back the chair, close to tears of frustration.

Lamont turns. What happen, Mummi?

She shakes her head, wipes her eyes with her sleeve.

Hush, the boy says, sitting beside her. Move over.

She forces a smile and says, Internet drop out.

R-i-g-h-t, he says, smiling with her. See, is not so bad. Tell you what. Lemme set up a Facebook page for you. Send dis Kelly a message. Maybe she don't block one elder. Tell her you tink you is fambly. People always doing dat, seen? Ask for a phone number. Internet come back.

He takes his place in front of the computer, snaps a picture of her with his phone, which he shows her too quickly, the keyboard rattles and images appear and disappear on the screen. Okay, Lamont says, what you want sey to Miss Kelly Buchanan?

On the way back to the stone house on the yeng-yeng, they pass sound systems being set up in the village center. Christmas comin, dance a keep, Lamont says. He leaves her with a breezy promise to keep checking Facebook for a response from Kelly Buchanan, but the day crawls by and she doesn't hear from him. She dislikes that he's an intermediary—that a message could be sitting somewhere unopened, unread, because he's forgotten to look or the internet dropped out again. She's ashamed of the emotion she showed at the library and doesn't want to call him, but after a glowing evening drains away, she does try, worried she'll forget how the phone works. But Lamont doesn't answer the phone's urgent, tinny sounds.

Deep in the night the stone woman is loud. Nan-an-an. Sea. Wah-tah. Ay-gee. You-ou-u. Fear swells in her groin like arousal. Her skin shrinks. When she gets up in the morning, the floors are gritty with dust and fallen mortar. She forces herself to eat, drink, sweep and dust, to make her slow way to River, down the concrete steps, holding on to the rope, to bring water back in the plastic bottle. She doesn't know any of the young women who beat their clothes on the rocks and laugh together.

Her rock is shaded by a rudimentary shelter with a sagging tarpaulin roof, containing a few bamboo benches. A boy she doesn't recognize is selling sodas from a cooler. She leans on the rock she named Sollah, now far from River's edge, palms spread, taking her weight. She thinks about rocks—perhaps they are the earth's true occupants and will be its only inheritors. You nuh want sit pon a bench, Mummi? says the boy.

Me is good here.

You want a drinks? Pepsi, Bigga, CranWata, Boom?

She shakes her head. The sight and sound of the water might bring comfort, even guidance. She wishes she could pray.

She needs to understand what Lamont has launched—this

Facebook thing. She's called Justine twice on the new phone, but she too hasn't answered. Facebook holds her image somehow, an image she herself doesn't have, and that is worrisome. She remembers her father telling her to use a pet name, so neither government nor duppy could find her, a piece of advice she rejected. Now some edifice of smoke has found her, *here*, in Mason Hall, has captured her name and her image.

The boy selling drinks is looking at her and she wonders if he can tell her about Facebook, but she doesn't ask. She gazes at River until her vision blurs and water, bare earth, plants and air become one. Cyah be hard to find a foreign woman in Treasure Beach. She knows nothing about the place, whether it's coastal or inland, urban or rural, large or small. Another place would be good. Then, for the first time in her life, she thinks: Anyplace but here.

The day clouds over and without warning, she's assailed by a longing for Clive so sharp she groans and bends over; Clive with his knowledge of the island gained in his years as mule cart driver and once the road he helped to build came to Mason Hall, his red mail van; Clive with his love of journeys, his optimism. He would know how to get to Treasure Beach, what they would pass on the way, and he would chat to strangers, leaning on bar counters, eating boiled corn from roadside vendors, buying a pineapple or watermelon, depending on the season, from farmers working in their fields. He would concoct a good story to tell the people in Treasure Beach and he would find Kelly Buchanan.

A journey will take her away from the voices in the stone house. Away from herself.

# Chapter 21

Before sunrise the next day, she leaves for Treasure Beach with Puppy to find a white woman. She hopes she'll fail, and she won't think now about returning, about having nowhere else to rest. Not until she has to. Her full basket is on the back seat, containing hands of green banana and plantain, both green and ripe, grater cake, sweet potato, cerasee, and an uncut pumpkin. She holds the file of papers on her lap, with the copy of the title given to her by Turner Buchanan, his letter to her, and the annual receipts for the property taxes she paid after Lyn suggested that would strengthen her claim to the land. At the time, she had no proof of her own birth as she wasn't born in a hospital, so Miss Glad didn't get the small piece of paper to begin the application for a birth certificate. Until Miss Pauline applied for and received a birth certificate, she had never had a bank account or a passport, and had paid every bill she owed in cash. Sitting in the front passenger seat of Puppy's taxi, she has now understood that it was the birth certificate that allowed her to be part of the family tree. That's how the computer found her.

Justine had called the night before, apologizing for her lack of response in a jumble of words, explaining that Carol's health is poor and there's been some *kass-kass* with the Jamaicans looking after her.

No test results yet, Gran? she asked.

January them sey. You was there. Her daughter's health is failing, yet her own life keeps unfolding.

Miss Pauline told her about the messages to Kelly Buchanan and Justine said she was sitting at her computer right now and would send her a friend request so she could also check the page. She could block you, Miss Pauline said, and feels a sense of unreality that she has spoken these words.

She could. It might be better to wait. I miss you Gran, she said. Miss the sunshine.

House empty wit' out you, Jussy.

Look after yourself, Gran. Eat.

She didn't tell her granddaughter of her plan to visit Treasure Beach.

As the taxi heads down the potholed, treacherous road in the dark, Miss Pauline tries to remember when last she left St. Mary parish but can't. When she was young, she'd wanted to, but by the time the stone house was finished, those impulses had gone. Here was enough, had always been enough. Her thoughts turn to the curly-haired woman she saw in the computer. What has brought her to Jamaica? Has she also come to claim land in Mason Hall, as her father did? No, she thinks. She wouldna be in Treasure Beach if that what she come to do.

What to hope for. What.

Junction Road bad, Mummi, Puppy says. Hillside come down 'bout two month gone. Just has to patient.

Miss Pauline has driven Junction Road to Kingston to

pay the property taxes at least once a year since Turner Buchanan's visit, although during the last ten years or so, she's had a lawyer in Port Maria pay the taxes for her. Still, that must be at least twenty trips. Yet she's surprised at how unfamiliar the drive seems this morning.

Cyah be worse than what we just drive over, she replies. Then she realizes she's forgotten her stick. Well, she doesn't plan to do much walking.

They reach the coast just as the sun comes up. The road hugs a sheer cliff on one side, and on the other, the azure sea stretches away, unruffled. They pass the church where Carol and Evon Marshall got married, its stone tower more imposing than she remembers, past the brick courthouse and then over a bridge into the town of Port Maria, crowded with people and cars. Construction in the town ranges from rusting shipping containers with windows and doors cut into the sides, through dilapidated colonial structures to brightly painted, flat-roofed concrete buildings. They drive by the cemetery where Jiwan and Zepha were buried and she's glad to see the spreading guango tree is still there. She considers asking Puppy to stop but decides against it.

Jiwan. Early January, 1977, the state of emergency still in place, the grass just beginning to show signs of dry time shriveling, she, drinking her tea on the veranda. Payment for a ganja crop had gone without a hitch the day before. Clive was due back that night after his bus route. She thought: This is happiness, a full circle, nuttn missin, nuttn to covet. Then she heard a woman's voice raised in anguish. Zepha, on the path to her house, arms upraised, wailing at the sky. She ran to her, and her old friend fell to her knees as she approached.

What happen Zeph? Hush, hush, talk to me.

Is Jiwan, Zepha cried. Police kill him, shot inna the back. *Inna the back*, Paulie. Him was runnin away from him field.

Miss Pauline held Zepha's shaking body. Where Jiwan is now? she said, swallowing her fury and disbelief. A stupid question, because what did it matter where his dead body was? But Zepha might have been mistaken.

Them took him, she sobbed. T'row him inna the back of the jeep like him a hog for the slaughter man.

How you know him dead then?

Two shot him get. One, inna the back. Him fall. The police walk up to him on the ground, *on the ground*, an shot him inna the head. Man cyah survive head shot, Paulie.

You was there?

No. Wilful see it. Him see them kill the only man him know as fadda. Is him tell me what happen. Zepha wailed without restraint.

Fuckin Babylon, bloodclaat murderer, every last one of them. Hush, Zeph. Me know it hot like fire. Where Wilful is now? Come inside. Mek me tink what to do. She helped her broken-hearted friend up the front steps.

But there was nothing to be done. The entire hillside where Jiwan's ganja plants flourished was burned to rocks and dirt by soldiers. After a month, his body was returned in a pine casket Zepha had to pay for. The police story was that he attacked them with a knife. Zepha met her baby father's extended family for the first time at his funeral and she understood from their whispers that they disapproved of his occupation and of her. The day after his nine-night, Wilful left Mason Hall for Kingston, according to Steady, and Zepha

never saw or heard from her eldest son again. She heard that
he died years later, a bystander victim at an armed robbery
attempt on a bank. Wrong place, wrong time, according to
the police. Mebbe, Miss Pauline thought then, we all in the
wrong place and no time will ever be right. She had always
been sure that Wilful was Pastor Edmond Slowly's biological
son. Woman rain never done, she thought, standing at Zepha's
side at Jiwan's funeral. Woman rain always waitin.

Beyond Port Maria, the road turns inland. Nort' Coast
Highway, says Puppy, explaining the relatively good road.
Foreigner buil' it. Breakaway one place at Albany.

Former cane lands and cattle pastures, now in ruinate, large
guango trees, African tulip trees just coming into their scarlet
blooms, fields and fields of coconuts, signs offering eggs for
sale, a shop front covered with a display of silver Dutch pots,
the Feel Gud Bar, roadside tire repair places, and plywood
sheds, men in oily clothes at work on cars. They pass clusters
of houses, fruit stalls with no one in attendance, small shops,
many with their doors closed.

A line of trucks waits at the side of the road—the sand
mining operation at Agualta Vale where perhaps her brother,
Troy, had worked while still a child. Yellow machines are
already digging and scraping and growling despite the early
hour. She doesn't know if her River connects to the Wag
Water River and eventually, the sea. They drive on a newly
built stretch of road with a modern bridge leading off to the
right. She thinks: Use to be a huge cotton tree right there.
The road goes over a narrow metal bridge and turns toward
the mountain spine of the island.

The road follows the valley, and as it rises, the river on the right recedes far below. Children walk in the road with buckets on their heads, collecting water from streams that trail down the rocky cliffs and are channeled into bamboo gutters or PVC pipes and she thinks of the bamboo irrigation system for her ganja plants.

You waan stop at Oriental Fry Chicken when we reach di top?

Too early for fry chicken. Mek we get wey we going.

A bridge takes them across the Wag Water, and now it's on the lefthand side of the road, the water low and scummy, the riverbed full of gray boulders of many sizes, some enormous. No women wash on the river's banks. They pass piles of smooth gray river stones on the roadside, awaiting a sale, and the burned-out shells of cars. Castleton comin up, says Puppy, referring to the botanic gardens.

Vendors sell green *gungu* peas in plastic bags at the side of the road. Good addition to her basket. Mek us get some *gungus*, she says and Puppy pulls over, but Miss Pauline is appalled by the price of a food item she has never paid for in her life and they drive on.

The winding road has made her feel queasy. She wants to stop, but also to reach her destination. She wishes she had a clear idea where they were heading after Kingston. Cars, busses and trucks begin to jostle for space on the narrow road and their progress slows. Road patching brings them to a halt twice. The vegetation is covered with dust, and billboards are so bleached out by the sun it's impossible to tell what they were once selling.

Stony Hill Square, says Puppy. We comin inna Kingston.

She thinks of Clive's bus route, which started and ended in Stony Hill Square. As with Mason Hall, there is no real square.

You have to drive t'rou Kingston? she asks.

To a point. Wi guh down Constant Spring to di Boulevard an get on di Mandeville highway. Wi stop at one gas station on di Boulevard. Mi nuh like di bahtroom at di toll plaza.

Miss Pauline wishes she could see the whole island from above, like a bird. She knows the shape of Jamaica from long ago school books and murals, but the flat green lines on paper with a few town names meant nothing to her. She understands there are mountains and flat lands, rivers and the coast, but she doesn't know how much of each or where they lie in relation to each other. Yes, they've crossed the island from north to south, and now will head west, but these directional words lack meaning. She supposes once she arrives in Treasure Beach, she'll be able to orient herself by the rising and setting of the sun, if she's there long enough. She's prepared to stay overnight, has brought her nightgown and housecoat, a towel, washcloth, comb and toothbrush. She's sure a room will be available in a tourist town, and she has money with her, but she hopes to find Kelly Buchanan easily and conclude her business in a few hours. That's how she's decided to regard what she's doing—as a business transaction. She'll either want the land or she won't. If she wants it, there will be a price. She thinks of her money, stored and hidden in various places in the stone house, as well as in the bank account she was finally persuaded to open by Lora. Maybe it will be enough. She knows in her heart, though, that she's lying to herself. This is about much more than land.

*

Kingston presents an atmosphere of suppressed rage, a cacophony of vehicle noises, thin men offering to clean windscreens at traffic lights. A naked man sets fire to a pile of trash on a pavement and people step into the road to avoid him. They stop at a gas station, and she's given a key to the bathroom, which she wrestles with until a young woman wearing shorts and a bra top helps her. She splashes her face and hopes her nausea will subside now they're off the Junction Road.

Smaddy still growin cane, she says to Puppy, observing cane fields on either side of the main road out of the city. Cane. The crop that brought the whitemen to these shores, mostly grown on flat, well watered lands. The *backra* house she found was high up, in the forest, and the man himself would have looked down on all that was below him. Was cane his crop? She doubts it. Yet still he found himself to Mason Hall.

They drive up and onto an enormous road, a highway, the biggest she's ever seen. She considers the strength of the pillars underneath and decides it's best not to think about them. Puppy speeds up until they are almost flying.

They get to Treasure Beach just after ten. It's not at all as she expected—dry, scrubby, with a large, shimmering pond and plain concrete buildings, some painted in bright colors. The grass is the color of sand and the land is dotted with *lignum vitae* trees. There's no town square, where perhaps people might gather, but they come upon a grocery store and an L-shaped line of small businesses. Puppy pulls into a parking lot, but Miss Pauline says, No. Mek us drive aroun' a likkl. She wants to imagine Clive showing her around the place he spoke of as if it were a different country.

You di boss.

The road tracks the coast, and they pass a variety of buildings, tourist-type places with gardens landscaped in cactus and bougainvillea, small cafés and cook shops, older concrete nog houses, a hotel whose sign is painted on a derelict car, a driveway to another hotel, swampy areas, dry land covered in the strange blond grass like an animal's hair. Treasure Beach seems to be a string of villages, clustered around small bays, rather than a single place. Calabash Bay, Frenchman's. Billy's Bay.

They arrive at a big yellow NO TRESPASSING sign and see another sign about sand mining. They've seen the extent of Treasure Beach and she asks Puppy to turn around. Yeah, Mummi, mi nuh like di sand miner-dem, he agrees. Dangerous people, you see mi. Had her brother Troy become dangerous?

They return to the small plaza and go into the supermarket. Miss Pauline is thirsty but she dislikes the taste of bottled water. Puppy buys a Red Stripe beer and the last two patties in a display case, very likely from yesterday, pays, and goes outside. The sodas of her childhood, cream soda and kola champagne, are not on the shelves. She buys a grapefruit drink called Ting and a pack of four bulla cakes, knowing she can't eat that many. When she pays the cashier, she says, Mawnin. Me looking for a white woman name Kelly Buchanan. You know her?

The cashier is young, with locs dyed dark red, wearing a tunic over her street clothes. Her fingernails are each painted a different color. Plenty white ooman dey 'bout dis time a year, she says, counting the bills and coins. Me nuh know alla dem name. You is who?

Me is Miss Pauline Sinclair. From St. Mary. She remembers Lamont's advice and goes on, Me tink the woman is fambly so me want find her. She mebbe working here. Some kinda charity work.

The cashier looks over Miss Pauline's shoulder, as if to check if she's being overheard, but there's no one else in the shop. She points with a pursed mouth. Ask at the ooman place 'round di corner. Ooman Peace it name. Them do charity work an plenty white people over suh.

Is far? Me can walk?

The cashier looks her up and down. Better you drive.

Miss Pauline is annoyed with herself for leaving her stick and forgetting to bring her own water. She thanks the young woman and leaves. Puppy sits on a low wall around the trunk of a massive shade tree she doesn't know, eating and drinking. Beside him, she takes small bites of one of the bullas. It makes a ball in her throat. She doesn't want Puppy to accompany her to the charity place. She feels for the phone in her pocket and is pleased that she remembers how to check the signal. Three bars. Good enough. To Puppy she says, Come back for me right here suh in two hour. If anyting, you call or me will call you.

Wha' 'bout di basket?

Leave it inna the taxi. Is for later. She hands him the remaining bullas.

Mi can have one? You is really going walk aroun' Treasure Beach inna di sun hot by youself?

Me is not dead yet, snaps Miss Pauline. Two hour. Eat the rest of the bulla, if you want.

*

The road to the charity place is deeply potholed and deterio-
rates to a marl track in places. She's glad to have the time to
think. Will she find Kelly Buchanan? What has she come to
Jamaica for? Then: What me going tell her? A high white sun
beats down, reflects off the road, and the sea roars off to the
right. Raas, it hot. She begins to feel light-headed.

Mummi, what you a do out inna di sun hot, says a voice
behind her.

She turns to see a teenaged boy on a bicycle, wearing
a peaked cap with a tick mark on the front. He stops
beside her.

Mawnin. You know which part a charity place is? she says.

Ooman Peace? Just roun' di corner. You want mi carry you?

How you going carry me on a bicycle, yout'?

He hits the bar between his legs. Right yah so. Is not far,
but you look like you ah go pop down if you keep walkin.

She thinks of Lamont and the yeng-yeng and the general
and often expressed opinion that young Jamaican males are
vicious and beyond salvation. Irredeemable, a politician had
famously damned them back in the day. All depend who
grow them, she thinks. She thanks him and he helps her to
sit sideways on the bar. He's very close to her and smells of
fish, diesel oil and sweat.

You a fisher? she asks, as he begins to pedal, the bicycle
wobbling too much.

Ma fadda. Mi help ma mumma inna dem cook shop. She
cookin up a *serious* brown stew fish—you come fah lunch.
Mi get you a special price.

They pick up speed and a hot, salt-laced wind dries the
sweat on her face. The boy chatters away and they pass an

area where the bush has been cleared and she can see the rough, shining sea. Her spirits lift in the revealing light.

He stops outside a flat-roofed concrete house, painted white. There's no sign, but the front door is open, and she can hear voices inside. See it dere, the boy says.

Me grateful. What your name?

Yellowtail.

She smiles. Where you mumma cook shop?

Near di fall down casha tree. Evrybaddy know it. Nuh wait too long, else di good fish sell off. He rides off in big, slow loops, and when he picks up enough speed, takes his hands off the handlebars.

She goes up two steps, knocks on the open door, but there's no response. It's dark inside and she needs to get out of the sun. She steps into the room, trips on a bunched-up rag rug and falls hard. Pain shockwaves up her right arm and her vision goes dark.

She's lying down, sick and washed in cold sweat, her eyes seem gummed shut. Her elbow throbs. The last thing she remembers is being in the taxi, but she's not there now. She retches once, twice, and a bony hand eases her onto her side, brings a bucket up to her mouth. She vomits chunks of bulla. The hand wipes her mouth with a wet rag which smells of carbolic soap, and she lies back. Feel for some ginger tea, Mummi? someone says. Sekkle you stomach.

She shifts her body a little and pain slices through her elbow. She bites her lips, forces her eyes open. She's lying on a lounger, the kind she saw on the hotel beach. Two women stand over her; one stooped and gray-haired, the other a teenager.

She nuh look like she hurt bad, says the young woman. Just faint from di sun.

She drop hard, says the old woman. She coulda break sumpn. See, she holdin her elbow.

The young woman takes Miss Pauline's arm and bends and straightens it. She yelps.

See? Not broke. She can move it.

Hmm. Get her some ginger tea.

Water better. You stay wit' her. The young woman leaves, and Miss Pauline senses the continuation of a long argument between them.

The old woman brings over a folding chair and sits beside her. I'm Joan Bentley, she says with a certain emphasis. And you is who?

She's being chastised. She says, Sorry, Miss Joan. Forgettin ma manners. Musta lick ma head too. Me is Miss Pauline Sinclair. From Mason Hall in St. Mary.

Joan Bentley smiles. You a long way from home. You prefer ginger tea? Me get it, if you want.

Miss Pauline feels a sisterhood with her. Ginger tea sound good, she says.

Both women have left the room. She's embarrassed by her fall and her determination to set things right has gone. She did what she did and that's the end of it. If Kelly Buchanan has come for her land, who is left to care? Her granddaughter had not seemed to. She sits up, retching once more, glad she's alone, but nothing comes up. She cradles her elbow. She'll just call Puppy when she feels better and go home.

She looks around. Wooden floor, old-time sash windows with filmy white curtains, a narrow bed, bookshelves and a dressing table. Cool enough, thanks to a turning ceiling fan. Someone's bedroom.

The young woman brings her the ginger tea. The older woman must have won the unspoken argument. The mug is almost too hot to hold; the tea is scalding, much too sweet and very strong. Her nausea eases.

T'anks. Musta been carsick. Sorry for the inconvenience.

Is awright. Anybaddy can sick.

Me can have some water now?

Okay, says the young woman. Me trainin to be a practical nurse; when me come back, me mek a sling for you, keep the elbow quiet.

She returns with a bottle of water and a bandage and deftly fashions a sling.

T'anks. Me is Miss Pauline Sinclair. From Mason Hall in St. Mary parish.

Whoy. You old to travel so far. You ready for the sling?

Yes. What you name? You from Treasure Beach?

Great Bay. Over suh. Me is Coral. She puts the sling around Miss Pauline's neck and eases her arm into it.

Pretty name.

So what you a do in Treasure Beach, Miss Pauline?

She'd rather speak with the old woman but doesn't know how to ask for her. Lookin for smaddy. Seem like she workin in a place like this—charity place.

Only two charity place in Treasure Beach—where you is now, and a boardin school for boy who give trouble. Man or ooman?

Ooman.

What she name?

Kelly Buchanan.

But see here now! Miss Kelly work here!

Kelly Buchanan work here?

Ee-hee. Two, t'ree month now. She from the U.S.

Where she is now?

Dunno. Mussi go eat lunch. She nuh keep regular hours.

Where me can find her?

Just wait. She soon come. You want anyting more?

A bahtroom. Lef the bucket. Mebbe me need it again.

Coral nods. Come wit' me.

She uses the toilet and splashes her face one-handed, looking at herself in the mirror. She's grateful it's been so easy, that she literally fell into the place where Turner Buchanan's daughter works.

Back in the bedroom, she sits in the chair, her nausea easing. She still doesn't know what she will say to Kelly Buchanan. She waits, beginning to feel restless.

Finally, the door opens, and a white woman walks in. I hear you're looking for me? she says in an American voice. She wears red cotton pants and a loose blouse in an African print, the same beads Miss Pauline remembers from the photograph Lamont showed her. Her hair spirals loose around her shoulders, the tips bleached either by sun and salt or a hairdresser. She's sunburned across her nose and cheeks, the skin on her forehead peeling.

Miss Pauline stares into the river eyes of Turner Buchanan.

Well? says the white woman. Say something. Who are you? She wrinkles her nose at the vomit smell from the bucket.

Mawnin. Me is Miss Pauline Sinclair from Mason Hall—

Did you say Mason Hall?

Mason Hall, yes. Me come here to find you. You fadda—
She stops.

The woman grips a glass of water. Her knuckles are whiter
than her skin. Are you the woman he found long ago? How
the hell did you find me here? she says.

Facebook. A youngster help me.

Good Lord. I did get a couple messages from folks claiming
to be family. I was afraid it was a scam and blocked them.
That was you? What do you want?

Miss Pauline feels trapped by this unfamiliar room, by her
fall, by the journey which seemed endless while it was occur-
ring, but now has already become the past. By the words she
must soon utter. Ee-hee. That is me. We can go somewhere
an talk? In the shade? Mebbe by the sea?

Kelly Buchanan considers. Miss Pauline understands she's
reassured by her age, just as Lamont anticipated. She's a
threat to no one now.

I don't know what there is to talk about and I have things
to do but there's an almond tree just down the coast, says
Kelly Buchanan. Good shade. Nice benches underneath it.
You want us to go there? It's a little walk.

Sound good, she says. Then she remembers Puppy—must
be a good two hours since she left him. She tries a call, but
he doesn't answer.

Miss Pauline gets up, cradling her arm. She reaches for the
bottle of water, drinks it all, makes a face, and picks up the
bucket. Which part me can t'row this? she says.

*

They walk together down the same road, the sun overhead. Kelly Buchanan has put on a straw hat with a wide brim, but Miss Pauline sees how the sun dapples her face in tiny dots of light. She should tell her the hat is not good enough for her fair skin, but she says nothing. She'll try Puppy again as soon as they're seated—she needs to pay attention to where she puts her feet on this rutted, unfamiliar road.

They round a slight bend, and she sees a spreading almond tree, the ground underneath thick with its fallen leaves, orange, brown, yellow, green. Two wooden benches, side by side, face the sea. She nods. If there is any good place talk, this is it. She was born in the hills, planted, rooted and grown there but the sea has meaning too. Walking beside her is a white woman who was born and grew elsewhere but has some connection to Mason Hall, according to her father and the title. Maybe this woman can explain what all the boxes on the computer screen meant. And she owes the foreign woman the truth about her father's second visit. *Story come to bump.*

# Chapter 22

You again? she said to Turner Buchanan. Nineteen eighty-seven, the year before Hurricane Gilbert tracked right through the center of Jamaica. She leaned on the veranda railing, a new addition to the stone house, along with gutters and a water tank, which had also allowed the construction of an inside kitchen and bathroom with a flush toilet in the corner rooms. She still preferred River's water for drinking. The whiteman stood at the bottom of the front steps. She had not heard from him in two years or so, despite his promise to follow up a month after his first visit. She was just beginning to believe that his claim to her land would never be made. You nuh give up yet?

May I come in? he said.

You is mannersable, me give you that, she replied. Come out of the sunhot.

He held a brown envelope. More documents. She gestured at the wicker chair, and he sat. This time she offered no refreshment.

You paid the property taxes, he said. Smart move.

Is not no *move*. Is ma land.

Turner Buchanan sighed. Miss Sinclair, I don't want to

cause you unnecessary grief. I've sought legal advice and while your payment of the taxes does strengthen your claim, the fact is you've not been given any permission to be on this land. I know you don't want to hear you're a squatter, but that's what you are. Now I'm prepared to give you decent compensation if you'll leave without a fuss. I've had my property surveyed and in addition, I will offer you and two others small parcels of land for a nominal fee, just to make it legal. That's more than fair, wouldn't you agree?

Fair? she objects. How this can fair? *Your* property? This place is nuttn to you. *Nuttn*. How you can just tek it an call it fair?

Don't you want to know how much I'm offering? Or look at the land I'm willing to settle you on? It's a generous offer but it won't be on the table forever. The next visit will be from a lawyer. Is that what you want?

You nuh interest in what me want. She gestured at the house and land around it. Ma pickney grow here—how much that worth?

He named a sum. Plus another piece of land, he added. You can build another house. And where did you get the stones to build this house? You took them, right? Stole them. His conciliatory manner was gone; his jaw was set, eyes narrowed.

Somebody must have told him about the stones. Probably for cash. She searched for the right words to respond to the accusation of theft but found none. She wanted to rage at the whiteman, just the latest in a long line of oppressors, ready to take what he wanted. Well, she would not be so easily overcome. She spoke softly and he leaned forward to catch her words. Awright, she said. You want see where this house come from? Mek we go. After that, you tek me to this piece of land you want give me.

Now you're being sensible, Turner Buchanan said, and his lips trembled into a brief, triumphant smile.

She went inside, drank some water, used the toilet, put on her hat, and settled her cutlass into the scabbard under her skirt. She touched the stone wall just inside the front door as she went out.

Early October, the summer heat finally releasing its grip. They walked together over old paths and new. Purple clouds massed behind distant hills—there would be only a few hours before the afternoon rains started. She lengthened her stride, and Turner Buchanan kept up without complaint. Beautiful land, he said. She was silent.

She touched the rough, knobbly trunk of the giant cotton tree as they went by. Turner Buchanan stared up at its canopy. How old would this be? he asked. Again, she said nothing. They passed the single remaining gatepost to Mason Hall, and he stopped. Is this the entrance to the site of the old great house? My father called it *backra* house. His voice was breathless, whether in exertion or excitement she couldn't tell.

You don't come here before this? she demanded. You claimin land you never see?

Nobody knew where it was. He was defensive and she marked a small victory.

She pointed to her chest. Me. *Me* know where it is. He looked away.

They gazed at the bush. I don't see anything, he said.

Nuttn much is lef, she agreed. She hung back, as he walked ahead, pushing through the vegetation. He stopped to kick at one of the few remaining stones lying on the ground. She followed. The bush was thin on the site of the dismantled ruin, and Turner Buchanan stepped over foundations, pushing aside vines and small shrubs with his hands, breaking some, stepping on others. An owner, nothing more or less, inspecting his property. He brushed by a cowitch plant, and she did not warn him, thought, Good, you nah sleep for now. She turned her back on him, left him to prowl around in what was left of the sanctuary of her youth. *Her* room. Her place, now all gone, even the walls she had initially left standing, removed stone by stone in the years after the people of Mason Hall built their village of stone. What me must do, Dadda? Clive? she whispered out loud. Help me.

*If you kill him an bury him, problem solve.* The words slid into her brain, as if they were new, thought for the first time. But they were not new. They had been eating away at her since the whiteman's first visit. She felt the outline of the 'lass under her skirt, she kept it sharp, a tool she used every year to clear acres of bush, chop clean through the muscular length of yellow snakes and once even the neck of a wild boar, which rushed her out of the undergrowth. The whiteman would not see it coming. A good death. An me bury him right yah so. Say the right word over him grave.

*Who you is, really? Who?*

She looked around for Turner Buchanan, adrenaline rising, and for the first time, *backra* house was a sinister place, heavy with torment and suffering. She imagined the slice of the cutlass through the back of the whiteman's neck, the pumping blood, bright as it left his body, turning red-black before it seeped into the earth. He would not have time to cry out.

How long would it take to dig a grave with only the 'lass as a tool? At least there were still enough small stones around to mark his resting place. She wanted to howl her distress. Her fury.

Her thoughts spiraled. How did Turner Buchanan get to Mason Hall that day? Did he drive as before, and if so, where did he leave his car? Whose car was it? Who knew he had driven to Mason Hall? If he disappeared and his car was found in the village, there would be a search—white people, visitors, attracted the diligent attention of the police if they disappeared. Any good search would find the disturbed soil of a recent grave and it was much easier to get to the site of *backra* house than it had been in her youth because most of the forest was gone. She was rigid with indecision, rage and fear.

He was near the old kitchen. You people pulled the whole damn thing down? he shouted over his shoulder.

The whole fuckin ting, she yelled back.

He left the kitchen and strode toward what had been the smallest room. She was about to call a warning when it happened: he stepped onto what looked like solid ground covered by the relentless vegetation and, with a cry of shock, disappeared into the sinkhole.

The two women sit in silence under the almond tree. It's the coolest time of year, but the sun pounds the land and reflects off the sea in innumerable points of light. Miss Pauline closes her eyes, swaying a little in the heat. Something rustles in the leaves at their feet and the foreign woman looks down. I love the insects here, she says. Every day I see something different.

Miss Pauline's wavering intention to lay things bare—to confess to Turner Buchanan's daughter—shrivels and dies. She cannot—will not—tell this woman what happened to her father. Not today. Not here. Not yet. Her brain casts about for something to say. She realizes she's trying to rock the bench, as if it's the glider on her veranda and she's suddenly desperate for home—desperate to rewind the journey all the way back to Mason Hall and have Puppy's taxi break down so that she would not be sitting by the sea with Kelly Buchanan. Home, she thinks, is the land. Not the house. The land will never turn against her.

The white woman says, So how did you find out about me? Why do you think we are related?

Ma granpickney find you on the computer. Then a youngster help me an him tell me to say we is fambly.

The white woman nods. The internet. Nothing is hidden anymore.

Miss Pauline thinks: Evryting is hidden. Tell me about youself, Miss Kelly. What you is doing here?

Kelly Buchanan shrugs. Looking for home, I guess. Maybe some roots, Maybe an adventure. I don't know. I never felt at home in America, never.

Wait. Start over. Although she already knows the answer, she asks, Where you bawn?

New York.

Okay.

I knew we had Jamaican roots, we ate the food, listened to the music, thought we spoke the language. Her face is shadowed. My grandmother told us duppy stories and taught us proverbs. A rock at the river bottom never feels the heat of the sun. A donkey says the world is not level. Kelly Buchanan pauses. The English translation of the old proverbs grates on Miss Pauline's ears but she says nothing.

Kelly Buchanan goes on, When I was young, in school, everybody wanted to be Jamaican and I was popular. But once I left school I was not white enough for Americans, too white to be Jamaican. Got rid of any trace of an accent. Then, my father went to Jamaica when I was ten and disappeared. We knew he had inherited some land here from his father, my grandfather, Earl Paisley. I never knew him—he went to England and died there. Anyway, my father, Turner—you must have met him the first time he came, right? He said he met an—aah—old woman who was living on the land. You, right?

Miss Pauline nods but says nothing. Her throat closes up.

The second time he came here he never came back. Kelly Buchanan kicks at a leaf and it rises and falls. He was presumed dead eventually, killed by a taxi driver. It broke my mother. When she died last year, I started imagining what it would be like to start over on an island. This one. I had roots here, right? I hated winter as well—the short days. The gray skies. She makes a sound of irritation. It sounds so stupid now. Like I'm nothing more than a snowbird.

Miss Pauline doesn't know what a snowbird is, but she doesn't want to interrupt, doesn't want to ask why the white woman didn't fear Jamaica, given her father's murder. Searching for common ground and hoping to delay the inevitable questions about their relationship, she says, So both of we fadda dead when we was ten.

Is that right? How did yours die?

Him chop himself by mistake. A accident. Him was a farmer. Go on wit' you story.

Kelly fans her face with her hat. Okay. Then I lost my job at the greenhouse—I always loved plants—my fortieth birthday was coming up, I had time on my hands, so I started going through my mother's papers. Found a family tree, which I guess my father had done and was what led him to the land here. Started to look online myself and found the story I'm sure you already know—how the first man who came to Jamaica, to Mason Hall, our ancestor, Hananel d'Aguilar, was a slaver, had children with a slave woman—

*Sey* what? Miss Pauline says. You know *backra* name?

*Backra?*

Slave massa. Sey that name again, Miss Pauline whispers.

Hananel d'Aguilar. Portuguese man. Jewish.

Whoy. She says, Hananel? Not Nananel? The stone woman's voice comes back to her. *Nan-an-an.*

No, Hananel. He's easy to find on the internet. His father was some kind of aristocrat.

Sey him last name again?

D'Aguilar.

DAG-U-LAR. A-G-U, she thinks. The letters on the broken stone above her front door. Maybe the D was lost. A rogue wave hits rocky shelf in front of them and they flinch from the spray. Miss Pauline shivers.

You seem surprised. If you tried to find me, you must know all this.

Miss Pauline shakes her head, clenching her teeth. Me only know as far back as you fadda. She sees the dozens of names

on the computer screen at the library, scrolling and scrolling.
Han-an-el.

Oh. Well, it's quite a story. As I said, the man d'Aguilar
was a Portuguese slaver, came to your village, Mason Hall,
and had children with an enslaved woman. One of—

Wait. What the name of the woman?

Nancy. Nancy McLean.

Nan-an-an. Sea. Nancy. The stone woman.

Are you all right? You look—

Me good. How much pickney them have?

Maybe seven, but definitely six. Born into slavery. One of
them, David McLean, is my direct ancestor. You're descended
from a brother. Hananel freed him—

What you mean? What you sayin? You an me is related?
*Me is related to you fadda?*

Well, yes. Isn't that why you're here? Because you found
out our relationship? Your message said you thought we were
family! I'm confused.

Jus gimme a minute, Miss Pauline says. She gets up
and walks away. At the edge of the sea, her mind churns.
Everything she knows, everything she believes about herself
is shaken. Maybe shattered. Tink, she says out loud. Use you
brain. The whiteman come to Mason Hall in slavery time.
Mebbe him have a wife, mebbe not. Him rape a slave woman,
she have him have pickney. One boy chile ma ancestor.
Anodda boy chile is Turner Buchanan ancestor. Is possible.

She remembers how Pastor Edmond Slowly used to read
from the Bible at the beginning of lessons, and one of the
most boring was about a man who lived for hundreds of
years and begat a man who in turn begat countless sons and

daughters. She never could remember the name of the man or the names of all the children until Noah came along, but she remembered him and his sons, Shem, Ham and Japheth because then, as now, she thought it strange that a child would be named after the smoked flesh of a pig. Begats are an old preoccupation of humanity

Turner Buchanan's children and grandchildren could be part of her family tree, not just aspiring landowners. Could be blood relatives. All with their own stories, lives, graces and transgressions. She's part of a tangle of ancient knots she doesn't know how to unravel, or even if she should try. She turns to look at the foreign woman under the tree and thinks: Blood is not black or white. One of her parents, she doesn't know which one, sprang from the white people—the *slavers*, she corrects herself—who came and settled at Mason Hall.

Which means, she did too.

What will she say now to Kelly Buchanan, who will ask again why she's here? Will she now have to tell her what happened to her father? She thinks: Why you fuckin couldna lef it all alone?

She returns to stand in front of Kelly Buchanan and tries to buy some time. How you an me is related? Exactly?

We're seventh cousins. Like I said, you're descended from my ancestor David McLean's eldest brother, McLean d'Aguilar.

So you tellin me we is both descended from the *backra* man who come to Mason Hall? This Hananel. Him an a slave woman name Nancy?

Yes, that's right. I can't understand why you don't know this if you did the research. Didn't my father tell you?

You fadda don't sey anyting about that.

But you said you looked online?

Me never look so far back.

The white woman nodded. It's hard to keep it all straight on a screen. I have the whole thing printed out on paper—that's easier.

Kelly Buchanan frowns then. So if you didn't know we're related, why did you come here? What do you want with me?

What will she say now? Land. Inheritance.

You fadda bring a title. Him sey him own the land ma house is on. Him sey him own most of Mason Hall. One t'ousand acres. Me is old-old, Miss Kelly. Me want to mek sure ma fambly don't have a fight on them hand after me is dead.

Kelly Buchanan sighs. Plain old land. Then: You don't want to hear the rest of the story?

Might as cheap, says Miss Pauline and sits.

Where was I? Well, as I said, I don't know anything about your direct ancestor, the brother. But Hananel freed Nancy and her son David McLean—maybe the other siblings too, I'm not sure—before Emancipation. Settled money on her. David was a child.

How you find out those tings?

Old records. Wills. Christenings. Kelly Buchanan is animated, describing her search, her eyes shining, hands waving. Anyway, I got interested in Nancy McLean. That's her European name. Some of her children were named d'Aguilar and some McLean, almost as if Hananel and Nancy negotiated that between them. I got in touch with some people in the UK, doing research on the legacies of slavery. Of course, there's no information on her own history, whether she was born in Africa or here, her own family, how old she was, anything like that, but they found her surname on a list of slaves at another plantation in a different part of the island. Clarendon, near a place called Mocho. Those people were named McLean and you know they used to give the slaves the name of the owner. So I think Hananel bought her from the McLeans and took her to Mason Hall. I guess we'll never know for sure.

Miss Pauline tries to imagine it all. The woman, Nancy, captured from her unknown birthplace. Transported some-how, by ship if she was born in Africa, maybe a mule cart if she was born in Jamaica. Sold at some point, taken from Mocho in Clarendon to the hills of St. Mary, then along the same hidden track she, Pauline, walked to *backra* house in Mason Hall. Nancy McLean, enslaved, raped, birthing her children in a hut near the plantation house where, more than one hundred and forty years later, Pauline would believe herself welcome. She thinks of all the times she imagined the woman of *backra* house, always with a white skin. Was Nancy McLean a house slave? Or was she a wetnurse for David McLean's wife? Is she the stone woman who speaks? She shakes her head. More than likely *backra* massa would have used her and sent her to sleep in a slave hut. Six children. Maybe seven.

I like to think he loved her, says Kelly Buchanan.

Sey what?

That Hananel loved Nancy.

Miss Pauline glowers. He *raped* her. Forced her to have him pickney. Stole her whola life. Took her from her people. From her place.

Yes. Sorry. Raped her. And she was mixed race herself. A mustee, according to the papers. She falls silent and all Miss Pauline hears is the slow drum of the sea. She thinks of her own surname: Sinclair. Sin-clear. A white name. Like Nancy's. Rape upon rape.

She's never been one to obsess about Africa, or the meaning of Blackness, never been preoccupied with going back to a place across an ocean to a people both her own and not her own, but now, standing at the island's edge, she understands she's both Black and white, landowner and squatter, a bawn yah and a woman of nowhere. She feels gutted; severed from herself. All her life she's been content with being *from* Mason Hall. More than content. Proud. Grounded. Planted. *If me plant you, you will grow.* But her blood swirls elsewhere too, in places she has never been, will never see. Nancy McLean's origins will never be known, nor her travails, nor her triumphs, but this woman's blood lives in her. Lives *here*. Nan-an-an. And *backra*'s blood lives in her too.

*Who you is, really?*

Are you still listening? says Kelly Buchanan. David McLean left Mason Hall, must have sold it—I don't know when—and went to a place called Middleton near Morant Bay. He got compensation at Emancipation—you know the British compensated the slave owners but not the slaves themselves. You can look it up online, find out how much and for how many slaves—

Wait. What you a sey? This David, born innna slavery, him grow to own slave? How that coulda happen?

The white woman shrugs. It probably happened a lot.

Miss Pauline meets the woman's gray-green eyes. How much him get pay? she says.

Nine hundred and twenty-seven pounds, nineteen shillings and ninepence.

Miss Pauline feels dazed. The pain in her elbow throbs without cease. Don't sound like much.

It was a lot for those days. His descendants sold their land at Middleton, maybe after the Morant Bay Rebellion—you know about that, right?—and some stayed here and many left. That's it.

How many people the McLean man got pay for?

Slaves, you mean?

I mean fuckin people! snarls Miss Pauline.

Jesus. Take it easy with me. I didn't mean anything. Forty-five.

Nobaddy *ever* mean anyting. So this Ha-hananel, him get pay for him owna slaves? Them in Mason Hall?

That I don't know. He's not on any list I've been able to find. He must have sold Mason Hall before Emancipation.

Land transactions. Lists. Paper. Now the internet. Miss Pauline thinks of the document in her bag in Puppy's taxi.

What happen to him?

Hananel? Kelly Buchanan is composed, her hands folded in her lap, hat back on her head. Her story, thinks Miss Pauline, but also not her story. She is too distant from it, whether measured in time or miles. For her cousin—she stumbles over the word in her mind—it's a story in a textbook. Words on a computer screen.

Yes. Hananel. Him first.

I don't know when he sold Mason Hall or if he left it to one of his children, the foreign ones. He did have a legal wife in the UK. He was buying and selling land up to 1822, here in

Jamaica, but there are no more records after that—no will, no weddings, births or funerals. No one has ever found his grave.

So how you granfadda get the land?

She shrugs. I don't know. After independence, I guess you could seek a new title if you could prove you owned land. Maybe Earl bought it from Hananel's other descendants.

What happen to David?

He was murdered. Something about trying to rig votes for white people. Buried in an Anglican church in Morant Bay.

An the other pickney for Hananel and Nancy?

Kelly Buchanan shrugs. What can I tell you? Some stayed, some left, went all over the world. They married, had children. Lived their lives.

What happen to Nancy?

Kelly lifts her hands. I don't know. The only records of her are her manumission—that means freedom—papers, Hananel's will and her children's christenings. She's gone from the records.

Miss Pauline thinks: Nan-an-an. She doesn't have the energy to correct Kelly Buchanan's assumption that she doesn't know what manumission means.

Kelly turns to face Miss Pauline. We have somewhere in the region of twelve hundred blood relatives in twenty-four countries. I did a DNA test, and every month, I get a notice of more people who might be related to me. To us. Back then, they had huge families. That's another reason I came here. I thought I would look for the ones still here. I didn't think—

Who else you find?

Once I got here, I didn't look. I was afraid.

Because you fadda—aahm—disappear?

Yes, partly. But I knew that before I came. She shrugs. At first we—my mother and me—thought he might have just run off. They were going through a bad patch. Then that taxi driver was found with his things. But it also seemed a long time ago, and I didn't want to stir any of it up. She bends forward, elbow on her knees, chin in her hands, her face hidden.

You mumma never know why you fadda come here?

Yes, she knew. She didn't agree with it, though. Or understand it. She told me after that they had a huge fight about it. She didn't like Jamaica, said it was an evil place. They brought us here as children—I don't remember it—and my mother came down a few times after my father went missing. But once she got the papers saying he was presumed dead, she never came back. She died last year, as I said. My father wasn't Jamaican either. He was born in the U.S.—it was his mother who told us about the island.

You granny, the one who tell you Jamaica story, she was Black?

Kelly doesn't look up. Brown, I guess you would say, she mumbles.

What about you sista and brudda?

What about them?

Them white like you? Them ever come here? She inhales. Them going want ma land?

They're both older than me, and yes, they look like me and came on that one family trip. I don't think they've been back. My sister won't be interested in any land—she married a cardiologist and they're pretty settled in Atlanta. My brother, though. Hmm. If I tell him about the land, he might—

Might what?

I don't know. We don't really speak.

So you come here to look for fambly—

Sort of.

Awright, sort of. But you don't look. Why?

Well, look at me. I did all right in my life. My parents did all right. Suppose I came here and the relatives I found were poor? What would I do?

*Black* an poor, Miss Pauline thinks. That what you mean. Then, a word she's often dismissed when heard from Mason Hall's village lawyer, Legal: reparations. She had scoffed at him every time he mentioned it: You nuh know how the ting set?

She's so thirsty. So why you don't go home? she asks. Come for a visit, leave. Like tourist. Facebook ting sey you been here a while.

Hard to explain. Yeah, I was a tourist at first, did visitor things, but then I came across Ooman Peace and started to help out. She takes a tissue out of her pocket and wipes her face. I like the women there. I like working with my hands—I was always good at crafts, sewing, knitting, that kind of thing. It's simple. Useful. She shrugs. I've felt safe here for now. It's plenty cheaper than New York. It sounds so stupid, so shallow, but I love the warmth. She waves at the scene in front of them. The sea. The sun. The bright colors. The plants—we had one variety of croton in the greenhouse—here you must have twenty. Here, you garden with a machete. *Mash-etty.* Here everything grows. And I love the way strangers greet you in the street. I love that it's small. That's all. I thought this—Jamaica, Treasure Beach, I'm not sure—could become home. That it would be something different. Somewhere different.

Miss Pauline remembers what Coral said about Kelly Buchanan's working hours—they were flexible. She thinks: You is smaddy here. She doesn't say it.

So you don't interest in the Mason Hall land? The question thuds between them and Kelly Buchanan does not answer right away.

I guess—I guess I'd like to see it. How much land is it? My roots too, right?

Miss Pauline wants to shout: No! Not you fuckin roots. But her own roots look different to her now.

The sun goes behind a large cloud, the light turns flat, the sea booms, and Miss Pauline wonders aloud if it will rain, hoping this might bring their meeting to an end. She feels scraped raw by what she's heard, and she's marked Kelly Buchanan's question about the size of the land. She knows what it means. She needs time to think about what she's learned. Time and solitude. It's about five hours' drive back to Mason Hall, and she hasn't spoken to Puppy. He might have become bored and driven away, stranding her here.

It hardly rains in Treasure Beach, says Kelly in response to Miss Pauline's comment about rain. She gets up. Well, I'm glad you found me. Are you going home tonight? Or staying here for a while? We could—

Miss Pauline surprises herself: Me want to tell you about the stones.

Stones. What stones? The white woman sits back down.

Me an ma baby fadda took the stone from *backra* house. The house this Hananel build. We make we owna house from them. Pull the whola ting down. Plenty people in the village do the same ting. She looks at her hands. Me—she breathes in, holds it, and lets it out—start look for you because the stone-them tell me to.

What?

Me know how it sound. But me is not mad, Miss Kelly. The stone of ma house start move an talk an them call the name of *backra* massa an Miss Nancy.

Kelly Buchanan makes a sound of disbelief. Impossible. You probably just had bad dreams. Where's your driver waiting? Let me walk with you.

She's being dismissed. Word only tek a person so far. Word can lead to cliff an swamp instead of sky.

What?

Miss Pauline realizes she's spoken aloud. Nuttn. You come here alone?

You mean, did I travel with anyone? No. I've made friends here, but yes, I suppose I'm alone.

Me come here in a taxi. Pack a few tings an come wit' me. You can see Mason Hall. Jamaica. Some of it, anyway. We can talk more. Get to know—

Apprehension crosses Kelly Buchanan's face and Miss Pauline knows she's thinking of her father. She says: Miss Kelly, we just meet, an you nuh have any reason to trust me, but like me sey, me is one old-old woman. One hundred year end of this month. Me can barely kill a maskitta. You is here, an is right you see where you blood come from. She thinks: Come to.

Let me think about it. Give me your phone number. If I decide to come to Mason Hall, I'll call you.

Nuh wait too long, says Miss Pauline. Me will sit here for a while. Kelly nods, and Miss Pauline watches the white woman walk away, back to the new life she has imagined.

When Puppy finally answers his phone, it's clear he's been drinking. A stranger takes the phone from him and explains to Miss Pauline that the taxi driver can hardly stand and will have to sleep it off before going anywhere. She remembers the bedroom at Ooman Peace and returns to the house, thinking she might be able to rent the room for the night. She makes her slow way there but the only person still present is Kelly Buchanan. She's washed her face and tidied her hair.

Miss Pauline says: Ma driver drunk. Me can rent the bedroom over suh for tonight? Me gawn tomorrow.

No, I'm so sorry. We have a Peace Corps Volunteer in that room. She'll soon be back.

Miss Pauline nods and turns to leave. Then Kelly Buchanan says, Wait. I have an Airbnb with a couch. We could talk more. I could show you the family tree on paper. I don't, I don't know—

Miss Pauline has never heard of Airbnb, but she accepts the offer of a place to stay for a night in Treasure Beach. She can't search for anything else. She's exhausted and every joint hurts. She wants to rest before she faces the long journey over the island's spine, whether alone or with this woman she's found. This member of her family. Much—maybe everything—has been left unsaid between them.

The apartment is simple—two rooms at the side of a flat-roofed concrete house, one furnished with a couch, wooden chair and table, a galley kitchen to one side, and the other is a small bedroom with a double bed. A tiny veranda looks out to a grassy field where goats are tethered. There's a hammock strung under a *lignum vitae* tree and Kelly Buchanan tells her that she spends a lot of time there in the shade. She points her to a tiny bathroom. It takes her a while to figure out how to flush the toilet because it doesn't have a tank high on the wall with a chain as hers does.

She joins Kelly Buchanan on the veranda. The afternoon is ebbing, and Miss Pauline is hungry, her basket still in Puppy's taxi. She doesn't know how to mention food, doesn't want it to seem as if she's asking to be fed, but she's also uncomfortable with offering to buy the other woman supper. Well, it won't be the first night she goes to bed hungry. She wishes again for River's water.

I have some *gungu* pea soup, Kelly says, getting up. My neighbor, Maggie, grows them and she showed me how to shell the peas and make the soup.

Miss Pauline nods and her eyes brim with tears. The offer of a simple homemade meal, made by someone she's wronged, seems enormous. She's ravenous again, the kind of desperate hunger she's not felt since her pregnancies and certainly not in old age.

You relax on the porch, Kelly says, and at first Miss Pauline doesn't understand what she means. The kitchen is too small for two, the white woman explains, and all I'm doing is heating up the soup. Miss Pauline realizes the porch is the veranda.

You have some water? Miss Pauline says.

Of course. Sorry, I should have asked before. Kelly

Buchanan goes inside, takes a bottle of water out of the fridge and hands it to her. Miss Pauline hates cold water, but she accepts it with a murmured thanks.

She considers easing herself into the hammock under the tree but decides she doesn't want to risk another fall. She sits, drinking, wincing at the cold water against her teeth. The house is hot and she's glad to be outside. In an hour, mosquitoes will swarm, and they'll have to be inside with closed doors and windows.

A lane runs in front of the small house and people walk along it, men and women, a woman carrying a basket on her head, another woman holding two small children by the hand, a man pulling two tethered, bleating goats along. These people are going home. Visiting each other. Tending to their lives. Every one of them greets her, a stranger, in their different ways, some with gestures and body language, others with words. The tension and pain of the afternoon begins to leave her body, although her mind still churns.

Fambly. What does it mean? Is it just a blood connection, or something deeper? Kelly Buchanan does not *feel* like fambly. Turner Buchanan, her relative, however distant, had not *felt* like fambly. She has a far greater affinity with the strangers walking down the lane in front of her. Is that just a matter of similar skin color? Experiences? Culture? Or the rootedness that has guided her all her life? But like her own daughter, many Jamaicans don't feel rooted and are desperate to leave— close to a million of them have already left for other shores in waves and waves and waves. For places where it was once cool to be Jamaican.

That elbow still bothering you? Kelly hands her ice cubes

wrapped in a thin towel and a bandage. Let me tie it on for you. Miss Pauline gasps when she tries to straighten her arm.

Take it out of the sling but keep it slightly bent. Kelly wraps the ice around her elbow. There, she says. Should feel better in the morning.

You is a nurse? Why you being so nice?

Damned if I know, Kelly Buchanan says. And the two women laugh together, a little.

Before the greenhouse, I was a grade school teacher, she adds. I've bandaged up my share of elbows and knees. You ready for some soup? You take the table inside, like how you only have one arm. I'll sit out here.

She does not deserve this kindness, not from this woman. When Turner Buchanan walked up to her house, he was an enemy, a foreigner with the weight of the law behind him, a tool of the system, of Babylon, come to take all she'd built away from her. She hears his screams in her mind, his desperate prayers, and she closes her eyes. It's too confusing, too complex, to unravel the double helix of act and consequence, blame and responsibility, of—she hears echoes of her early religious schooling—the sins of the fathers. And the mothers. Unto the generations. She should have paid more attention in Bible study—maybe there were some truths to be excavated from that old book after all.

Come inside and eat, says Kelly Buchanan. We soon have to close the door because of—

The maskitta, says Miss Pauline. Me know. You can tell me about your greenhouse.

You can tell me about *backra.*

*

After they have eaten, the front door barred against the night, Kelly Buchanan unrolls a large piece of paper. Their family tree. It's too big for the table, so she lays it out on the floor with books on the corners. And kneeling, the two women trace the complex, crooked lines of their families together. So many lives. So many names. So little information contained in birth dash death.

# Chapter 23

When Miss Pauline opens her eyes next morning, she knows
it's after nine. She's had her first dreamless and undisturbed
sleep in weeks in Kelly Buchanan's bed—which the younger
woman had insisted on. I wake up very early, she'd said, and
I go for an early swim. The couch is fine for me. It's only for
one night. She didn't say—I'm plenty younger than you.

Miss Pauline lies still, gathering herself, sweat at her temples and under her arms, her elbow aching. She's emptied
the bottle of water during the night, although she doesn't
remember drinking it, nor getting up to use the toilet. Her
mind feels wooly. She wonders if she's dreamed the events
of the day before, if she's wandered away from her house in
Mason Hall, and some stranger has taken her in. There are
the sounds of movement in the other room, and she smells
coffee. She picks up the towel given to her by Kelly the night
before and opens the door.

The living room is empty. Good. The sounds must have
come from the other half of the house, from the woman Kelly
Buchanan called her friend Maggie. Miss Pauline thinks idly
about the nature of that new friendship. She wants to retract
her offer of the visit to Mason Hall, all those hours in a car,

then the time under the same roof, within the same stone walls—what words can possibly fill such dangerous stretches of time? And so much has not been said.

Her stomach growls. She's still hungry. And thirsty. She refills the bottle from the tap over the kitchen sink and drinks it down, making a face at the chemical taste. There's a coffee pot on the stove and a dish, covered with a towel. The pot is still hot. There are two slices of hard dough bread, a chunk of rat cheese and a dollop of jam on the dish. She sniffs the jam—guava.

She washes her face, sets her tie-head, and takes the bread and cheese outside with still more water. It's already hot. Faraway music thumps, cars race their engines and the sea rumbles on. She eats and drinks, then eases her arm out of the sling and flexes her elbow. It hurts, but it's not broken. She reaches into her pocket, takes out the phone which she's forgotten to charge again, and calls Puppy.

Two hours later they're on the road for Mason Hall. Her new relative has packed a small bag, insisted she must share the cost of the taxi, and called her friends at Ooman Peace. Miss Pauline heard her on the phone, telling her friends where to start looking, should she fail to return. Yes, a distant cousin. No, a woman. Elderly. The same one from yesterday. Mason Hall in St. Mary. Pauline Sinclair. I have my phone. Yes, I talked to my family.

Me bring food from country, Miss Pauline says as they drive down the lane from the Airbnb to the main road. Mek us give it to you friend. After they have left the food, Miss Pauline gives the empty basket and the bag containing the papers for her land to Puppy. Put in the trunk. Me sit in the back with Miss Kelly.

The two women speak only a few pleasantries on the journey. Puppy is shame-faced and slit-eyed and groans occasionally. He keeps the radio on, and Miss Pauline is glad because it makes conversation difficult. They buy jerk chicken in Junction and Kelly Buchanan grabs for her water bottle after the first bite. I can't eat this, she says, holding up the tinfoil packet.

Gimme, says Puppy, but he doesn't eat either and the car smells of singed flesh and pepper despite the open windows. Miss Pauline begins to feel sick again.

Kelly remarks on the variety of the landscape—dry and bare, lush and green, flat plains and elevated plateaus, hills and mountains, villages, towns. She asks if they can drive through Mandeville, to see what a bigger town looks like, but Puppy refuses. Too much traffic, Aunty, he says.

We go t'rou piece of Kingston, says Miss Pauline. Then over the mountain.

Well, I did go through a part of Montego Bay when I flew in, Kelly Buchanan says.

They arrive in Mason Hall at four o'clock. Miss Pauline's hundredth birthday is just under ten days away.

Lamont is sitting on her glider. He jumps to his feet as they drive up. She can't remember if she left a key to the house with him. Who is that? says Kelly Buchanan, caution in her voice.

Young friend. Him awright. She counts out the money for Puppy, gives it to him and eases herself out of the taxi.

Kelly Buchanan doesn't get out right away. Her phone is in her hand.

Don't forget you tings, says Puppy, opening the taxi's trunk.

Hi! Come help me, nuh! Miss Pauline calls to Lamont and he comes down the front steps. She lifts her free arm as if to embrace him but lets it fall. He picks up the empty basket, the two bags and her file of papers.

Wha' happen to you? he says, pointing at the sling. Then he peers inside the taxi. Who dat?

Me fall down. Nuttn serious. That is Miss Kelly Buchanan.

Whoy! You not easy, Mummi. She not comin out?

She soon come out.

Hi, Miss! Lamont shouts through the open car window.

Hello, says Kelly Buchanan, staring at his tattoos. She damn lucky she never see the gun in him haircut, Miss Pauline thinks, supressing a smile. Him awright, Miss Kelly, she says again.

Miss Pauline fumbles with the front door key, wondering if the stones spoke to an empty house while she was gone.

Come in, nuh, she says over her shoulder.

Kelly Buchanan stops just outside the front door. So these are the famous stones, she says, looking around. Simple structure. You built a square with a metal zinc roof.

Miss Pauline bristles at the implied criticism. Swallow you spit, she thinks, and remembers how, when the walls of her house were almost finished, talk turned to the roof. There was no wood to be scavenged from the ruin. What kinda roof? Clive had asked, Lizard standing with him.

Flat, she said. The house in her mind was square, a fortress, an unbreachable sanctuary, safe from storm, fire and heat.

Flat roof going leak, Clive said. If it mek of wood, it rotten out quick.

Peak roof better, said Lizard. Mek of zinc sheet.

Hurricane tear off galvanize sheet easy, said Pauline, hating her ignorance about building methods. They settle on a slanted zinc roof, raised at one end on a single plank of cedar wood, the triangular gaps filled with clay and strips of bamboo.

Her stone house was built on land she chose, raised off the earth for coolness and protection from flooding, the floors made from cedar trees felled in the hurricane, the zinc roof supported by wooden rafters cut by the Portland man's small sawmill on the coast. They added no embellishments. There were no carvings, curlicues, cherubs or flourishes, no balconies, balustrades, pediments or columns. Nothing was painted. All Miss Pauline allowed was a single plank of cedar over the front door, carved with the initials of all the people who'd worked on the house, set in a frame of those stones which broke during transfer or construction. This was her public statement of admiration for the work of human hands and backs and eyes, her acceptance of imperfection, her conviction that even broken things had their uses. Right in the center, above the names, the men inset the broken stone with the letters—A-G-U. She hears the stone woman's voice in her mind, like argument.

Kelly Buchanan looks up at the plank of wood over the door carved with the initials of those who built the house. You never gave it a name? The house, I mean? she says to Miss Pauline.

No. Just ma house.

Are all those people dead now?

Miss Pauline sees their faces in her mind. Most were older than she was at the time of the house construction, and although she doesn't know how or when everyone died, they've all exceeded a reasonable human life span.

All dead, she says. Me soon dead too.

A-G-U, says her cousin, staring at the broken stone. Aguilar.

Miss Pauline wonders what the white woman will hear this night; when she will speak of Turner Buchanan's second visit to Mason Hall, and what words will come to her.

# Chapter 24

She shows Kelly Buchanan the spare room, brings her clean sheets. She'll have to prepare something, the white woman—her cousin—hardly touched the jerk chicken. She feels like she's been away a week. She's surprised that the food in her fridge, the fruit in the bowl on the table, is as she left it. She doesn't feel like cooking, or for that matter, slaughtering one of the chickens. Justine taught her how to make an omelet, she has eggs and cheese, and the herbs in her garden. She'll make some fried green plantain to go with the eggs, and the American woman will likely be fine with that. But first, she needs to take in what she's learned.

Afternoon bleeds into evening. Lamont swings on the glider, and Puppy's taxi is parked under the breadfruit tree. He must be sleeping on the back seat. She sits beside Lamont, rubs her swollen elbow. So what you is doing back here? What happen to the job in Kingston?

Aah, Mummi. Pure wrongs over dere, you see mi? Pure badnis.

What kinda badnis?

Gang an gun. He shrugs. How tings run nowaday.

Miss Pauline remembers Zepha's voice so long ago: *So the ting set.*

Lamont says, First ting dem tell you: informa fi *dead*. You unnerstan? No matter what happen, you have to keep you mout' shut. Den dem tell you what dem do to informa.

What?

Dem kill informa wit' a chainsaw. Chop off dem head, sometime it tek to relative inna box. Sometime t'row outta sea. Sometime hand-dem cut off, so nobaddy cyah tell is who when dem find di body. He shakes his head. Man who in charge, him tell mi same so, seen? Tell me sey nobaddy going know what happen to mi anyhow me talk. Mummi, hard-hard man over dey so. Dog-heart man.

Without wondering if he will welcome her touch, she puts her arm around his shoulders and he leans against her, his body humming with tension.

What you sey to him?

Mi tell him nobaddy going look fah mi. Him sey mi awright. But as soon as him tun him back, mi lef. An mi nah go back. *Chainsaw*, Mummi.

What to say to this youngster on her veranda? She remembers Clive's words about the labor riots: Coward man keep sound bone. Lamont won't like being called a coward.

Some tings not good to talk, she says.

True ting, he says, nodding.

Yout'. Me woulda look for you.

He blinks, wipes his eyes. Sits up straight, takes out his phone. They rock together. Her elbow aches. Christmas soon come. She'll sit here, watching the night creatures for a while.

She wonders what the stones will do now that she's home and has brought Kelly Buchanan with her.

The stones rustle, grate and moan for most of the night. Com-um-um, they say. Come now. Nan-an-an. The stone woman's music swells. Miss Pauline smells dank water and rust flaking. Then blood. She's numb now. She waits for the woman or the teenaged boy sleeping on the glider cushions on the floor to rouse her with questions about the sounds, but no one does. It must be her mind. Her guilt. She falls into an uneasy sleep eventually and dreams of thick darkness and one small blue hole to the sky. *Come now.*

At daybreak, she wakes Kelly Buchanan. Come now, she whispers to her, obedient to the stone voice. Better we walk before sun is up. The white woman doesn't argue. I hardly slept in the heat, she says. You should get A/C.

This not hot, says Miss Pauline. Bring you hat.

When they walk through the living room, Lamont does not stir. Puppy's taxi is still under the breadfruit tree. And Kelly Buchanan says nothing about strange noises during the night.

They walk together through dew-drenched countryside, the morning light glinting off droplets of water clinging to leaves and blades of grass and spiderwebs. How utterly beautiful, says Kelly, stopping to look at every plant, sometimes saying long words Miss Pauline has never heard. And the birdsong! Do you know their names?

Some. Not all. That one a nightingale. Never have much time to pay attention to bird, unless them could eat or lay egg. Bird is just bird.

I guess all of this would have been forest back in—

Some forest here when me was a pickney.

Where are we going?

*Backra* house. Where it was. Before. Used to be deep in forest when me see it first time.

Kelly Buchanan stops. I'm not sure—

Me tell you awready. Me too old to hurt anybaddy. You come here to find you roots, nuh suh? You nuh want see the place the whiteman, this Hananel, come to?

I guess but—

But what? You want smaddy else to come? Me wake Lamont if you want. Or Puppy—him still sleep inna him taxi.

N-no. It's okay. Is it far? How did you find it?

A pastor—teacher—touch me an me run away. Just come across it.

Touched you?

Him rape plenty girl in him time. Not me, though. But almost.

Shit. How old were you?

Thirteen. Just got ma monthlies. The Pastor ignored her after her bloody warning to him. She last saw him in death— a blackened, grinning corpse, his own house burned down around him during the 1980 elections. Everybody in Mason Hall said it was some politics business, but she chose to believe he finally got what he deserved at the hands of a girl.

Hmm. Awful. Then Kelly repeats her question, Is the house—ruin—is it far?

Not so far. See that cotton tree over suh? Near to that.

That's not close.

Miss Pauline has not used the walking stick since she left for Treasure Beach. She had wanted it while there, but now it feels unnecessary. The symptoms of illness are gone. Only her elbow aches. It's time to face it's not her body that's failing her.

They walk together through the hills of St. Mary parish, the land rising and falling away into hidden valleys, through a few fields plowed for planting, skirting the abiding Jamaican bush. The sun is up now and where the shape of the land dips, they can see the unruly blue of the sea in the distance.

The cotton tree is closer. A chainsaw screeches in the distance. She thinks of Lamont's account of the construction men and shudders.

Miss Pauline stops at the one remaining gatepost of the entrance to the ruin. This where it did start, she says. Mason Hall. Mason Manor. She points. The house did over there suh.

It's all overgrown, says Kelly Buchanan. Her cheeks are pink with exertion. There's nothing to see now. How much was left when you first saw it?

Wall. Floor. Foundation. Stairway. Bush cover up evryting in it time.

You pulled down the entire structure? How big was it? Was it a mansion?

Call it that, yes. Big. Bigger than any house me ever see.

How far did—does—the land go?

Miss Pauline thinks: *All that parcel of land.* She says, Not so sure. Forest was here when me come but mebbe it grow up after slavery time. Only a few big-big tree was here. Stone house don't rotten away, but wooden shack, mud hut, them don't leave no trace. She doesn't want to say the words: one t'ousand acres.

She had roamed the land around the great house ruin when

she was a teenager. She remembers her find of a blackened hand mirror, the glass long shattered and lost to the earth. She held it, but the broken mirror gave up nothing of the woman who once owned it. She left it in the soil. Later, she found the large rock with the small, rusted iron shackle attached to it, of a size that would be used to restrain a child. She stared at it, imagining its uses, and much later, asked Clive to chisel it free of the rock. It still lies in the cedar chest in her bedroom, attached to a piece of the rock. She never found any other artifacts of enslavement—no branding irons, no coppers for boiling sugar, no chains, and she wondered if someone else had taken what they wanted and if so, when. She found the stone jar she still uses and fragments of other containers—jars, bowls, bottles. But all that was left of the Mason Hall *backra* house then was some of the rotting wood used to build it, the floor tiles, and the immortal stone walls. Until even those were taken away, although still, they lived.

Did my father come to this place?

Here is the moment. Her heart pounds. Walk where me walk an watch out for cowitch, she says.

Miss Pauline doesn't have the cutlass with her, so they fight through shrubs and vines and small trees. She knows the white woman's skin will itch this night and thin red welts will rise. The flagstone paths under the vegetation that used to guide her steps are long gone or buried deep in the earth. She stops. She's not sure of her memory anymore.

Why're you stopping?

Shh. Lemme tink. Lemme memba. Miss Pauline shuts her eyes.

Kelly stands too close, and Miss Pauline senses her growing

fear. She sees the old walls in her mind, the kitchen with the huge sink, hauled away by Maroon Titus and five other men, used as a water trough for his cows. Still there, in an abandoned pasture. When she first discovered the sinkhole, it was enclosed by the walls of the smallest room and she imagined its use as a toilet but perhaps it was a source of fresh water. Maybe it had been both. She opens her eyes. Follow backa me, she says to the other woman.

When she thinks she's near, she gets down on her knees.

What the hell are you doing? says Kelly Buchanan.

Miss Pauline doesn't answer. She takes her arm out of the sling and begins to inch forward on hands and knees, the pain in her elbow awakened. Then she finds a rotting plank of wood, half hidden in the vegetation. It's one of the pieces of wood she put over the sinkhole, she recognizes it for its length, remembers levering it at one end. Afterward. Ants boil out of the wood.

She struggles to lift it, but it's caught in the vines. Let me help you, says Kelly Buchanan.

Listen me. Just 'tan where you fuckin is.

She gets the wood free, pushes it out of the way and continues inching forward. Beneath the weave of plants, she glimpses faded floor tiles. She smells water, finds another piece of brittle wood, thinks: Evryting is food for sumpn. A cloud of mosquitoes settles around her head.

Right here suh, she says. She kneels beside the hole in the stones, feeling for the smoother fire bricks that lined it.

What's right here? says Kelly Buchanan. She slaps at a mosquito and scratches her bare arm. Miss Pauline tries to get up and almost falls over. Mind *an* body dyin, she thinks. Take my hand, says the white woman and Miss Pauline holds her soft, plump fingers and pulls herself up. She eases her arm back into the sling.

They stand side by side, staring at the black hole in the earth, the edges half hidden by vegetation. What *is* that? says Kelly Buchanan. I smell water.

Miss Pauline turns to face the white woman. Is a sinkhole. Mebbe the house build over water so them draw it up, like a well. Mebbe them shit inna it. Her guilt and shame rises. It would be easy to say nothing else. She steels herself, shuts her eyes, and speaks, This is where you fadda did dead. Here suh. Him fall in an him drown.

She hears the panic in Turner Buchanan's voice and the echo of his splashing far below and she smells the water of the whiteman's tomb. Rotten water.

# Chapter 25

Fuck, he had spluttered in disbelief. Then: Jesus, help me! She felt the full depth of his terror. She lay on the ground, feeling for the edge of the sinkhole and found it. Pulling herself to the edge, she peered into an abyss. A man thrashed in water stored underground. Help me, Turner Buchanan screamed, his voice ragged with dread, bouncing off the walls of the underground cavern. I'll double the offer. No, I'll withdraw my claim. Leave Jamaica today. Get a rope and pull me out. Get help. Please. Please, Pauline. I have three children. You're a mother yourself. Don't leave me down here! Dear God. I'm begging you.

She rested her face in her hands, smelled the earth heaving with unseen growth, and the tainted water far beneath the surface. Could Turner Buchanan swim? How far would water flow underground?

There's no rope 'round here, she whispered.

Except. Except for the vines on the banyan tree, her whirling, frantic brain answered. Chop a long one off. T'row one end to him. Tie the odda end to a rock. Get help.

He prayed in earnest, his voice weaker; the splashing dying down, moving away. Perhaps the water beneath the earth was like a river, maybe it would pull him along, he was a whiteman from foreign, he was bound to be able to swim, bound to be able to keep his head above water, and the river would take him and spit him out, frightened but alive, and he would never, *ever* bother her again, never come back to Mason Hall, never come back to Jamaica, forget about his claim. Yes. That's how it would happen. She saw him bobbing in a black ribbon of water curling through a yawning underground cavern, the roof too high to see, and there he was, emerging alive in a shining green river far away. Dark to light. He would scare the women washing clothes on the banks and the men fishing, and they would cross themselves and pray to Jesus. They would tell stories about the whiteman with river eyes, and in the telling, the events would get ever more outlandish. And then she had covered her face, lying at the edge of the sinkhole, until there were no more sounds from the man or the water.

Kelly Buchanan stares. You. *You* killed my father?

Me never kill him. But is true me did hear him die.

There's more she wants to say, more than the bald re-counting of what happened; she wants to tell of the years afterward when she wished—no, finally *prayed* to deities she had always scorned, to grant her sleeplessness, because whenever she closed her eyes, she dreamed she was drowning under the earth in a trackless darkness, except for an uneven, unreachable, blue hole above. For all of her life since that day, that dream returned—of a desperate search for breath, a fight against the current, of being pulled slowly away from the only source of light, seeing it quartered, then halved, then three-quartered, like a waning moon in the night sky. Sometimes her dreams were only of the absence of light—there were no people, no threats, no sense of a crime committed, no events, no demons, no blood, no fear—just an eternal, erasing night. Her first words when she awoke from these dreams were always: It an accident. Me never mean it. But she has always known this to be a lie. It would not have been easy, perhaps he would have been too heavy, impossible to pull him out, but she did not try to save him.

She turns to the woman beside her and sees her cheeks are wet. Sey sumpn, nuh?

Kelly raises her hands, palms up. What am I to say? She brings her face close, too close, and Miss Pauline feels her breath with each word. You're telling me you murdered my father and you've lived out your shitty, useless life without any consequences. That he was left to drown in a well, what you call a sinkhole. Am I supposed to forgive you? Why've you come here to tell me this? Or have you brought me here to kill me? My brother and sister know where I am. You won't get away with it this time.

Miss Pauline thinks about graves of water, the restless sea where uncounted souls were thrown on their way to this island, discarded as rubbish. A water grave can never be truly visited, will not support a headstone or memorial, flesh and bones are lost forever. Should she defend herself, talk about her nameless ancestors, the hundreds the internet would never discover, who gave their lives to work this ruin, that she claimed as shelter? But how can she claim justice, if she too is descended from *backra*? Should she appeal to their family connection, their shared blood? Should she have lied and told the other story she's played out in her mind, over and over again: how she raced to the banyan tree and chopped down the thickest vine, and it fell to the earth in uneven coils, and how heavy it was when she hoisted it onto her shoulder, and how difficult it was to drag the vine over the rough ground, and how, when she let it fall into the sinkhole, she looked around for something to tie the other end to and there was nothing, nothing, and how distant the splash of the water sounded, and how she shouted to Turner Buchanan to feel for the vine because she didn't know how much he could see, and how she pleaded with him to answer her, and how after immeasurable time had passed, he shouted, I got it! And how his prayers became thankful and full of air and light and hope. How she then felt the tug of his weight on the vine, like a wriggling fish near the end of its fight against the hook, and how she held him, arms aching at full length, turning her head this way and that, looking for anything, anything, to secure the vine to, so that she could leave him breathing in the dark while she ran for help. Should she have told how she saw a large enough stone which she looped the vine around, how resistant it was to the molding, how likely to break or uncoil, and how she piled up other stones, and waited to see if they would hold? How she thought of the waste tires she used for her ganja plants, that they would float, and how she raced across the witnessing land to the nearest of her fields, and ran back, falling twice, cracking the same elbow that now throbs from her recent fall, that bears the scar from the fall the first time she went to collect water at River, and how, when she returned to the sinkhole the vine had disappeared, and the stones she had used to hold it in place were scattered, as if the man at the other end of it had flashed it about like a whip, severing his last connection to the world above and how, when she threw the tire into the sinkhole, and shouted to him, called his name, pleaded with him to answer, there was no voice, no whimper, no plea, no prayer, no gurgling last words at all from Turner Buchanan? Should she have told of a rescue attempt that never occurred, a different outcome yearned for on every subsequent day of her life, or should she finish her account of that day with what really happened, how she lay on the undergrowth as the afternoon rain started, her arms outstretched, her face in a deepening, muddy puddle, as if to know for herself what drowning meant, and how eventually, after the deluge had stopped, she pulled herself up, her body caked in the wet earth, and returned home through the sharp, after-rain light of a Jamaican October, through the flooded land and drooping trees, to wait for Turner Buchanan's car to be found?

Kelly repeats herself: Why're you telling me this now? Here? I'm not a priest or a police officer. You're going to kill me, right? Her voice is choked and there are flecks of spittle on her lips.

Miss Pauline thinks: Me want you to know ma life not shitty or useless.

Ma time comin, Miss Kelly, she says, exhaling and stepping back. Me don't believe in judgment, all them ting pastor an priest tell you inna church, but me believe in truth. You is this man daughter an you deserve to know what happen. Me never kill him, exactly, but me cause him to die. Me listen to him die. Me never tell anybaddy what happen to him. And me still live on the land him come here to claim. Me have grandchildren. You have a brudda an sista. Him have a child. Mek me ask you: who the land at Mason Hall belong to?

So that's *really* what this is about? Land? My God, woman, you're nothing more than a money-grubbing bitch. I'm leaving. She turns, tripping over the vegetation, heading straight for cowitch. Miss Pauline grabs her arm.

Let go of me!

This land nuh nuttn. Is home, she says. Is sumpn. She lets go of the woman's arm. Wait. Me show you the way out. The way home. You will lost.

Kelly Buchanan puts her face in her hands and her shoulders shake. Miss Pauline wants to hold the sobbing woman, but she stands where she is, waiting. There's more she wants to say, about the weeks after Turner Buchanan disappeared into the sinkhole, when she searched the lanes and byways of Mason Hall for a strange car, when she read every word of the *Gleaner*, front to back, back to front, looking for stories about a missing whiteman in rural St. Mary but saw nothing. Nuttn at all. Now she knows he had been driven to Mason Hall by Elliot Gardner, so there was no car to find, and that Turner Buchanan left his suitcase in the car when he came to see her. Perhaps he had not paid the full fare to Elliot Gardner, and once he failed to return, the taxi driver simply regarded the contents of the bag as his. Or perhaps he stole it, was caught in a roadblock, and eventually paid much more than was owed for a crime he hadn't committed. Her crime. She wants to tell how, after many months, after the futile efforts of the police and Turner Buchanan's wife, the search was abandoned. Turner Buchanan became just one more whiteman claimed by a tropical island, where he had no doubt sought ideas of a wealth-yielding paradise, as had so many before him.

She stopped reading the *Gleaner*. The island had covered its own tracks.

Kelly Buchanan lifts her face, and their eyes meet.

What you want do, Miss Kelly? Miss Pauline asks. You want me to dead here too? Now? You is a young woman—pull me over to the sinkhole, give me one good shove an argument dun. Me die the same way you fadda die. Circle close up. You want call the police? It no matter to me. All me want sekkle is for you to know what happen, an me to know what going happen to ma house an land after me dead. Me don't want leave your family an ma family to fight for anodda four hundred year. Don't it high time the fightin done? You know how much people killin over land? Still?

Kelly Buchanan looks around. This is where they were when they woke up in the morning, she whispers. Our ancestors. This is the last place my father saw. Her voice contains wonderment and grief in equal measure. Maybe I should organize a memorial of some kind. But what's the point? None of us will ever visit it.

You is a religious person? You could sey some prayer for you fadda soul.

A bit late, don't you think? If he's been judged, it's happened long ago.

Miss Pauline sighs. When me was young, she says, me look evrywhere for a sign showin the slaves was here. Me look for them grave, them house, me look for them field, them whipping post, even where them did hang. Me don't find anyting, 'cept one shackle. Me still have it. Me come here at nighttime an wait for them duppy—if any place should haunt, is this place, don't it? But nuttn come. Nuttn is lef. Nuttn at all.

You—me—we nuh know who will come here nex week, nex year or nex century. Mek us leave sumpn for them to find. You fadda name, if nuttn else.

Kelly Buchanan bursts into tears again. This time she throws her head back and wails. Miss Pauline reaches out awkwardly with one arm, and the woman she's wronged, confessed to, searched for and found leans against her.

I can't stand to think of his last moments, Kelly sobs.

Me know. Hush. Hush now.

When her tears are spent, Kelly Buchanan steps back. She dries her eyes on her sleeve and says, Did you ever find a grave here?

Ee-hee. Three of them. Near the top of the hill over suh.

Whose graves?

Cyah tell. Writin worn off.

Take me there, Kelly says.

They stand over the three rectangular graves, just visible through grass and weeds. One has a brick base with an arched dome. The second is half covered by a white stone slab which has broken away. There are strange symbols on the slab, but nothing that they recognize as a name or a date. The third is smaller, a simple rectangle enclosing dirt and weeds. No headstone, nowhere that a name could have been recorded. There is no shade and the graves look baked. Perhaps *backra* Hananel was buried here with his legal wife, along with Nancy McLean whose grave merited no slab. Nowhere to write words of tribute. She wonders which one of their children buried them—her own direct ancestor, the ancestors of the cousin standing beside her, or any of the other siblings—and she wonders what emotions lived between these people, what bound them together and what tore them apart.

Kelly Buchanan bows her head and Miss Pauline decides it's right that there are no words on the graves. They stand for all who died here, including Turner Buchanan.

That afternoon, the two women sit at the table inside Miss Pauline's stone house. Now what, Kelly Buchanan says. I should leave. Is that taxi driver available?

That up to you, Miss Pauline replies. You want leave, leave. You want stay, but you want Puppy to wait outside, so you can leave any time of day or night, me pay him to stay. You want find somewhere to stay inna the district, me ask a friend. You want sleep in the bush, fine, me give you a *tra-paulin* an one blanket. You want tell the police, you call them. You want a lawyer, plenty in Kingston.

Show me the papers you have. The title my father brought. Then I'll go.

Miss Pauline goes into her bedroom and gets the papers from the bag she took with her to Treasure Beach. She shows Kelly Buchanan the title for all that parcel of land known as Mason Hall or Mason Manor left with her by Turner Buchanan, hands over the crumpled receipts from the years of paying the property taxes. The white woman spreads them out. Miss Pauline asks about other members of the family, half-brothers and half-sisters, cousins, aunts and uncles, and the connections of blood twist in her mind, going backward and forward in time, and spreading outward like the ripples made by a man falling to his death in water held far underground. Until they stopped. She thinks: 'cept blood go on forever.

Kelly Buchanan looks up from the papers. I want to make a list.

A list? What kinda list?

A list of names. Of all the people who have a claim on this house and land. This place. Do you have paper?

Miss Pauline nods and gets up. She wonders if such a list will be short or impossible to complete. She gets the ledger with the entries of her long-ago ganja sales, turns the pages until she finds a clean one and hands the open book to Kelly Buchanan. The white woman searches her handbag for a pen and bends over the book.

Me outside, pickin some lime, Miss Pauline says. Feel for some lemonade.


It's well past the season for limes, but the tree Zepha gave her more than sixty years ago bears year round. When she stands beside the tree, she sees one of the branches has developed the long, thin leaves of a parasitic tree which she knows as *scorn mi grung*, because it does not need soil to take root. She's seen the work of this strange plant—how it sometimes enters a tree and from the inside, begins to take it over until eventually the branches become something else and the original tree is obliterated. Zepha's lime tree is finished now. Tears prick her eyes.

The limes are small and tough, but will still have some juice. The lime tree survived Hurricane Gilbert, whereas her ganja plants did not and were never replanted. Zepha. She remembers the visit from Zepha's second son, Steady by name and nature, a year after the hurricane. He brought the news that his mother, her lifelong friend, was in the St. Ann's Bay hospital with sugar.

Sugar? she said.

Diabetes. You know how she love sweet tings, cane especially. And she never tek di medication dem give her.

Tek me to her. Now-now.

The St. Ann's Bay hospital still bore signs of hurricane damage—the windows boarded up, parts of the roof covered with tarpaulins. The waiting rooms and corridors were full of people with pain and fear on their faces. She shouted at a nurse who told her to wait her turn and then turned to appeal to an orderly, whose face was familiar but she couldn't place. Probably a son of Mason Hall. A man with a chop wound across his face staggered into the room, the edges gaping, like a second mouth. A nurse hurried over to him.

Follow backa me, the orderly whispered. You, he said to Steady, you wait here.

Zepha lay on the same kind of bed she remembered from Carol's birth, in a long room with many other beds and people, some sleeping, others groaning. The sheets were tucked in tightly across her friend's body, and her were eyes closed. One arm lay outside the bedclothes and was hooked up to a plastic bag on a stand. Dem soon run you, said the orderly. Not visitin hour. So mek haste sey what you come to sey.

She pulled a metal chair up to the side of the bed and the scrape of the chair on the floor roused Zepha. Paulie? she said, opening her eyes.

Is me. Wha' happen, Zeph? Why you never tek wha' them give you?

Is you same one tell me nuh trust no doctor man, nuh so? She smiled to take the sting from her words.

But you did always have more sense than me, Zeph. Nuh worry, them will fix you up now.

Zepha met her eyes. You nuh tell lie, Paulie. Nuh start now. Beg you keep you eye on ma pickney. Me can rest easy if me know that.

Zeph. You and me, we batty and bench since we was pickney. You nuh have to ask me that. Them will never want long as me live. Me swear it.

Good fren better than pocket money. Zepha closed her eyes again.

Come now, the orderly said from behind. Ward nurse on them way. You go get me in trouble.

Miss Pauline took Zepha's hand and squeezed. Her friend squeezed back, but her grip was weak. Eyes still closed, she whispered, You was right about that evil man, Slowly. Is him rape me, him is Wilful blood fadda. Me know you do sumn to him an him never touch anodda young gal again. You never believe the ting set. You brave, Paulie. Me always love that about you.

Her cheeks were wet. She would never recover from this loss. The orderly pulled at her arm, and she let go of Zepha's hand.

Me come back tomorrow, she said.

Zepha died that night. Miss Pauline wanted to bury her in the yard of her house, so she could sit at her graveside and remember, but Steady and Lora insisted she rest with their father in Port Maria under the guango tree. After the funeral and nine-night, Lora brought her a basket of Zepha's embroidered cloths. She did want you to have these, she said.

*

She fills a pocket with Zepha's limes and goes back inside.

I need to take a break, Kelly says when she sees her, arching her back. She's sweating, despite the coolness of the time of year.

Help me mek the lemonade.

At the kitchen sink, they seed and squeeze the limes, strain and sweeten the juice with brown sugar.

Where did that boy go? says Kelly Buchanan, when they're back at the table.

Lamont? Dunno. Him come an go as him feel like.

I didn't put his name on the list.

Him not a relative. But then she thinks, why not? Out loud she says, Why evrybaddy in Mason Hall not a relative? Evrybaddy here 'cause of that house, evrybaddy here share some drop of the same blood that bring the white people an the Black people to this place back when. And what 'bout the people who dead here? The ones that did quarry the stone— them pickney an granpickney? What is to mark them life? Them death? She shakes her head. Is too much to unnerstan, she says.

Speaking of relatives, Kelly Buchanan says, I called my sister again. And my brother. I'm amazed I found him. She drains her glass of lemonade.

True? Me tink you sey you nuh in touch.

It was true. But I called my sister before we left Treasure Beach. In case—

In case what?

Well, this affects them too, right? It's not my decision alone.

So what them sey?

My sister says she's not interested.

She don't care how you fadda die?

Didn't seem to. Said Mama told him not to come here. I told her your age and she said you'll soon be dead, so what does it all matter?

That all?

Pretty much. She said I should come home, that I was crazy to go anywhere with you, and it's time I behaved like an adult and stopped thinking life is one big vacation.

An you brudda? Jeffrey, right?

Kelly Buchanan meets her eyes. Her face is swollen and sad. She nods and holds up her phone. My brother says he's coming here. I just got a text. He's at the airport in Miami, standing by for a flight here.

# Chapter 26

Her house feels overfull of clamoring people, present, absent, living and dead. She needs time to process the idea of a new relative, a man, about to visit. Wait, where're you going? Kelly calls after her but she doesn't turn or answer. She's wearing her house slippers. Cyah go far. One time, coulda go anywhere barefoot.

It shouldn't surprise her that Kelly Buchanan contacted her own brother and sister. Whatever she owes to Kelly, she owes to them as well. But it has. It's as if she has turned over a rock in the forest, one that's been long in place, and revealed what's underneath—seething insects, fungi, rottenness, evil. Death, but also life. The Buchanan children. Their descendants. Hers. Their ancestors. And the extended family of Elliot Gardner. Even if she replaces the rock, all that has been revealed, all that scurried out of the darkness, will never return to hiding. What she did has finally come to light. She feels the first glow of relief.

She walks down the faint pathway from her front step to the road. The strength she felt earlier has ebbed. It'll soon be dusk and after that, night will fall quickly. She thinks of the physical markers of her life in Mason Hall, all so familiar, but now she fears there is no meaning left in any of them. Certainly no redemption. Plain an straight, she tells herself, me just live too bloodclaat long.

The square stone at the center of Mason Hall is close. She walks to it, trying not to shuffle. The stone throws a long shadow and no one is about. She leans against it. Her feet are dusty. The mystery of the square stone remains unsolved, but then it comes to her—it was not taken here. It was always here, a rocky outcrop, a sentinel of the land itself. And the craftsmen who quarried and shaped the stones for *backra* house carved this right here. Made it over into a shape men liked, regular, ordered, a shape which showed their skill. Pastor Slowly's Bible words come back to her: *Every mountain and hill shall be made low; and the crooked shall be made straight, and the rough places plain.*

How long will it take for Jeffrey Buchanan to get to Mason Hall? She's sure his willingness to fly to Jamaica forbodes anger and distress. Pure *bangarang*. She's sorry Justine returned to New York but also wants to spare her the wrangling. This is her poisoned cup and hers alone.

Well, she'll have to face it all. Her secret could have died with her, and unknown people of the future would have laid claim to the stone house, and lawyers in Kingston would figure out the legalities, and maybe that would have been the better way. None of the people involved—her relatives, she reminds herself—have any wish to live in Mason Hall. Not even Bernice Gardner, who worries for her son in Kingston.

She wishes she could settle for herself the question of who owns the land on which her house sits. Even if others disagree, and battles of different kinds wage on for years after her death, if she was clear in her own mind what would be a just outcome, that would be enough. But every possible outcome slashes at her soul. And there is no rewinding of history to be had, the slave ships that came from Africa will never turn around, the dungeons on the coast will not crumble to sand before a single human spends a night in filth and misery, the swoop of Jamaican hills will not return to forest, the sugar cane and tobacco will not downgrow, all the *backra* houses will not deconstruct, the quarried stones will not return to the island's bones, and her ancestors cannot be unborn.

*Nor can she.*

At least, she thinks, me did pull one *backra* house down. Me an Clive an the people of Mason Hall, we remake it for we.

Night is falling and she must go home before it gets too dark to see. She lays her palm on the rock of Mason Hall. She wishes it had been the one to speak to her, this rock, with its long and patient horizons.

Tomorrow late, she thinks. That when Jeffrey Buchanan will come. Will he choose to stay in a hotel on the coast? She imagines Bernice Gardner cleaning his room, both in ignorance of each other.

The late evening sky blazes in the west, the orb of the sun already a memory.

It's full dark by the time she stumbles up the front steps of the stone house. Every light in the house is on and Miss Pauline closes her eyes against its harshness.

Where the hell have you been? Kelly Buchanan says walking up to her. Lamont went to look for you. I was—

Worry?

Yes. No. I just didn't know—

Me just have to be alone for a likkl.

She sits heavily on the glider. You cook some food for youself?

No. I don't know my way around your kitchen. There's no microwave. I gave Lamont some money to bring something. He said he would, but he's been gone a while.

Him waitin for the jerk pork to ready. Miss Kelly, me can trouble you for some water? It inna the stone jar beside the sink. Bring it an we talk.

Kelly returns with the water, rubbing her neck. Your pillows are hard, she says.

Miss Pauline drains the glass of water. You free to leave anytime. Plenty hotel on the north coast.

Kelly looks abashed. I didn't mean to criticize. I used to camp, slept on the ground. I guess I'm getting older, right? I'm staying until Jeffrey comes if that's okay. I don't think he can sleep here, though, so I guess we'll have to leave together.

Miss Pauline pats the seat beside her. Tell me about you brudda, she says. You did sey him an you not in touch. How come him decide to come here? What him want?

Kelly Buchanan shakes her head. Jeffrey, she says, as if his name itself is an explanation. She sits. He's the eldest, eight years older than me. Then Nicole three years after him, then me. As you might expect, he was my father's favorite. Miss Pauline doesn't interrupt but she's not sure why favoritism for Jeffrey is expected of Turner Buchanan.

He was sickly as a child, Kelly goes on, got everything that was going around. If he got a cold, it became flu. If he fell down, he broke something. If he cut himself, it got infected. He was always at the doctor. So they—my parents—overprotected him. That's what I think anyway. He wouldn't agree. He got away with murder his whole life—trouble at school, never had to help at home, plenty of back talk. My father turned on him when he was a teenager, and Jeffrey went from being golden child to problem with a capital "P." He scraped through high school and refused college. Said he was an entrepreneur. He left my parents' house at seventeen—I was only nine—but he kept coming back for money, which my mother gave him year after year until my father found out. They had a huge fight over it. That's when my father went—came—to Jamaica the second time. And never came back.

They hear the yeng-yeng and see the beam of headlights coming up the hill. Miss Pauline is relieved. She doesn't think she can put food in her stomach, but Lamont's arrival will bring the conversation to an end for now.

Bring chicken for you, Lamont says to Miss Pauline, running up the front steps. He glances at Kelly and looks away. Pork for mi.

Kelly Buchanan says, I hope it's not as hot as the jerk chicken we ate on the way here.

They eat on the veranda, using their fingers, Lamont on the front step. He has brought cold Red Stripe beer with him, and Miss Pauline accepts one, thinking it might be a good substitute for food, but she takes one swallow and returns it. She picks through the foil packet of jerk chicken until she finds a bony piece with hardly any meat. She sucks on it, enjoying the flavor.

What's this bread-like fried thing? asks Kelly Buchanan.

Festival, says Lamont. You never eat it in Treasure Beach?

No. At least no pepper. It's good. Not diet food, though.

Mek sure you wash you hand good after you eat, Lamont advises, his mouth full. Don't rub you eye.

You still in you room in the village, yout'? Miss Pauline asks, handing the chicken she has not eaten to him.

Ee-hee. Miss Bridget sey me can stay anodda month. After dat, me nuh know.

You have nowhere to live? Kelly says.

Lamont's watchfulness rises on his face. Mi will find somewhere, Miss.

He looks down, avoids her eyes, searches for one more piece of chicken among the discarded bones.

After Lamont leaves, the two women sit together, looking out. The sky is scalloped with moonlit clouds. Thank God it's cooled down a bit, says Kelly Buchanan.

You believe in God?

Yes. Sort of. Don't you? She fidgets on the glider, perhaps feeling they sit too close.

Not me. Go on wit' you brudda story.

I don't know how much more I can tell you. He left Miami—you know that's where he was born, right?—went to the west coast for a while, LA, I think, tried to get work as an actor, but that didn't work out. Too much competition, he said. Took up photography at a community college— Dad paid for his camera equipment. Gave that up. Bought a motorcycle and went touring with a girl. We used to get postcards and then even those stopped. Then we heard she was pregnant—turned out she was from somewhere in eastern Europe, wanting U.S. citizenship. We think she paid him. They married. We weren't invited to the wedding. He was most in touch with Nicole, they were closer in age, but one year she just said she was done. He was always in some drama, landlords, police, banks, credit card companies. She sighs. I dunno.

Him have a child, right? What happen to the wife an son? You never meet them?

Me? No. I never did. Nicole did; in fact, once Jeffrey dumped the child on her because he'd been evicted. Sweet little boy, she said. I think—not sure—he divorced after that. I don't know who raised the child.

What him name?

The boy?

Ee-hee.

Um. Simon? Stephen? Something like that, anyway.

When last you speak to you brudda? Before now. How come you just call him sudden like that? How you even has him number?

Kelly Buchanan shifts on the glider and doesn't answer right away. Miss Pauline waits. Another child—Stephen or Simon— to think about. She wonders if she's hearing the truth. She has a lost brother too and she hates it that she will die without knowing what happened to Troy. His name should be added to Kelly Buchanan's list. Just in case he's still alive.

Kelly Buchanan says: I called Nicole first, obviously. We're in touch, not every day or anything, but we talk about once a month. I think I told you, she did well for herself. She advised me not to tell Jeffrey about all this, that he would just cause problems, but I thought I should. He's still our brother. We argued. In the end she said probably he wouldn't be able to buy a plane ticket, so why not.

You sista don't want the land but you brudda coulda.

I don't know. I mean, it's not beach land or anything.

Miss Pauline frowns. Nobaddy want land inna the useless Jamaica bush, don't it? But you fadda did want it. Land is land.

You know, I'm tired. I'm going to bed now. You've got the Jeffrey story. How quickly do you think he'll be here?

Dunno. Even if him get to Jamaica tonight, probly have to wait 'til mawnin for a taxi. Mebbe tomorrow evenin him will reach.

Kelly Buchanan stands. Maybe at the end of all this we'll wish my father's death stayed a mystery.

Never come to an end, Miss Pauline says, although she thinks Miss Kelly might be right.


They are woken by a ferocious banging. At first, Miss Pauline thinks it's the stones, but it's too loud, too human. The two women meet in the living room, Miss Pauline carrying her 'lass. Kelly Buchanan looks at the blade and takes a step back.

Someone is pounding on the front door and then they hear an American voice: KELLY! It's me! C'mon, man, I'm tired, you know how hard this place was to find? Open the fucking door.

Jeffrey, whispers Kelly. What time is it? She goes around the living room, flipping all the electric light switches.

Near dawn, says Miss Pauline. She opens the front door, holding the cutlass at her side. The dogs of Mason Hall howl at the disturbance.

The light on the veranda falls on the man on the doorstep. Jesus, he says, staring at the cutlass. You people are fucking something else.

Miss Pauline bristles. If this man thinks he can win a swearing contest, he's mistaken. He's not young but she's unprepared for his good looks—floppy hair graying in a dramatic streak over his left ear, high cheekbones, fleshy lips, too white teeth. Unshaven. He wears a tight black T-shirt tucked into jeans. Tall, with a body softened by a layer of good living. His skin is the tan of outdoor play and there is nothing about him that looks Jamaican. You best come inside, she says to him, noticing that the door of the car parked in the yard is open. You drive youself?

Of course. Rented a car at the airport. Easy drive from Montego Bay, but Jesus, the road up here! You're this Pauline Sinclair person? This is the house in question?

She's impressed with his navigational skills and annoyed at his rudeness in equal measure. Me is *Miss* Pauline Sinclair, eh-hee. How you find Mason Hall?

Google Maps, of course. He waves a phone at her. Sis, he greets Kelly Buchanan, and she grunts in reply.

Lemme get my stuff, Jeffrey Buchanan says and returns to the car. He pulls out a duffle bag.

Park under the breadfruit tree over suh, Miss Pauline says.

Inside the house, Kelly Buchanan seems nervous. Shall I make us some tea?

Ee-hee. Me going into ma bedroom. Give you an you brudda some privacy. Mek we talk after the sun come up.

In her bedroom, she hears the murmur of foreign voices. She needs the bathroom, but she'll have to wait. She makes her bed and pulls back the curtains to let the dawn light in. She's never abandoned the practice of always having a pitcher of water and a basin in her bedroom, and now she's grateful she can wash her face. She settles into the chair in the corner, where she reads when the weather is bad, listening for the noises of morning coming to Mason Hall.

They all sit at the table in the living room. The man—her cousin, Jeffrey—seems to take up all the air in the room. He looks around and pushes himself back on the chair. She hopes he'll fall over. If he's eight years older than his sister, he must be late forties. His gaze contains possessiveness and judgment. Kelly Buchanan sits up straight with her arms wrapped around her middle, her hair tightly tied back, revealing the contours of her face.

Jeffrey's going to find a hotel today, she says to Miss Pauline. I told him there's not enough room here.

There's not even coffee, the man sneers.

Lamont must have finished the coffee Justine brought with her. Miss Pauline glares at Jeffrey Buchanan. You in a strange place, she says. Mebbe you tek time wit' what you sey.

He leans forward. Well, fuck you, old woman. From what I hear, you killed our father, and my next stop could be the police. *You* watch yourself.

Miss Pauline smiles. Whiteman, me no 'fraid of anyting you can do to me. *Nuttn*, you hear me? So talk up now, what you come here for? You have question, me will answer them. Me have some question too. But you not going disrespect me in ma owna house. Seen? she says in the voice of Lamont.

Let's all calm down, says Kelly Buchanan. Her voice

trembles. Is she suppressing fear or anger? Miss Pauline understands the history between the two siblings contains much more than she knows.

I told him what happened with our father on the phone, Kelly says to Miss Pauline, nodding at her brother. I told him it was an accident.

Convenient story, that's all, Jeffrey Buchanan says. Kelly says you have a copy of the title? How much land are we talking about?

How much land you *want*? What you going do wit' it?

Not your business what I do with it. You don't own it anyway. If you pack up and go, I'll forget about how my father died and you won't rot in prison. He sits back in his chair, pushing out his chest.

You don't want see this land you claimin? You just want it?

Land is money. Wealth. I'm sure I don't have to explain that. You killed for it.

Wealth. Miss Pauline thinks: Him right, but not for the reason him tink.

So you plan to come live here? she says. Migrate?

Of course not, he scoffs. I'll sell it, or maybe develop it. I'll have to walk around, see what it looks like before I decide. It's no good for tourism, for sure; that road is just impossible. He glances at his sister. Don't worry, sis, I'll see you and Nicole get your share.

Kelly looks down and says nothing.

Tell me how you fadda come to own this land, Miss Pauline says.

I haven't a clue. You met him. You're the one he gave the title to. You know more than we do.

The title is in Grandpa's name, Kelly says to her brother.

Probably he just left it to Dad in his will, Jeffrey says, shrugging. No big mystery. Maybe the will wasn't probated. Or maybe he died without a will and that whole process took time. A lawyer will sort it out.

Miss Pauline says to Kelly Buchanan: You never tell him about the *backra* ancestor? How it all start?

No. He's not going to care about any of that.

Miss Pauline nods. She turns to Jeffrey Buchanan. Who clear this land? Who cut the tree, plow the earth, plant the crop, reap them, feed the animal, put up fence, carry water, cook food, build road an house? Who do that, Mr. Jeffrey? You? Miss Kelly here? You fadda? You granfadda?

Of course not. What's your point? Working land doesn't mean it's yours. Do I have to explain the laws of private property?

His disrespect enrages her. In her mind, she lists the strikes against her he'd have enumerated, probably unconsciously: Black, female, old, rural, foreign, poor, powerless, friendless, uneducated. He's like a bulldozer revving its engine, poised to flatten the side of a mountain, push its trees over, turn its living terrain sweep into a wasteland of churned-up dirt and rock, down to the earthworms and galliwasps crushed. A bulldozer nah tink, she says out loud.

What? the man in her house asks. Speak English. Are you going to show me the title or not?

You sista here tell me you have a son. Wey him is? How old? You close to him?

Stephen? What does he have to do with anything?

Stephen, Kelly Buchanan says.

You answer ma question an mebbe we talk about the title.

Kelly Buchanan looks at her brother. Yes, Jeffrey. Where's your *son*? My nephew. You abandon him too? She leans forward, half out of the chair.

Jeffrey kisses his teeth and for the first time, Miss Pauline sees the ghost of a Jamaican heritage. Stephen is just fine, he says. He's what, must be close to thirty now. Last I heard he was working one of the Seattle ferries. But thanks for your *concern*.

And when was that? demands Kelly, her chin jutting out.

What the fuck is your point? I speak to him. He's a man now. Miss Pauline sees Jeffrey's defensiveness. He's not immune to guilt.

You left him. Just like you left us. Left Mom and Dad. They never got over it.

*They* left me, Jeffrey Buchanan shouts, jumping to his feet. One of the chair's legs cracks like a gunshot and it falls to one side. They were happy to see me starve! And you, you were just a hippie, grubbing around with plants and dirt.

Starve? They gave you *everything* and you threw it all away.

Miss Pauline hates these people and wishes them gone. *Stay away from* backra. She's sorry she told them the truth. She wants her granddaughter. Then she hears the sound of the yeng-yeng. Lamont. Almost as good, she thinks. She gets up, still in her nightgown, housedress and slippers, and rushes outside to meet him. Tek me for a ride, she says, and without speaking, he turns the motorcycle around. Someplace this ting can fly, she says.

The sun is fully up but the coast road air is cool, and she shivers in her thin night clothes. She curls her toes so her slippers won't fall off. The speed makes her eyes water. She closes her eyes and lays her check on Lamont's back, holding on to his waist, her elbow throbbing at the new position. She's glad the noise of the motorcycle makes conversation impossible.

She thinks about the family argument she's just witnessed, an over-privileged young man feeling hard done by, leaving home, heading into the world to inflict damage. She wonders again about the impetus that brought her ancestor to these shores; greed, of course. But maybe also a sense of grievance. Her father used to say: When Black man tief, him tief penny farthing. When whiteman tief, him tek evryting.

After a time, Lamont slows and steers the yeng-yeng to the side of the road. There's a small rocky cove with a sliver of beach and a single fishing canoe tied to a dead coconut tree. How far you waan go, Mummi? Lamont says. Soon need gas.

Gimme a minute, she says. She struggles off the back of the yeng-yeng, her slippers still on her feet. She stumbles down to the shore, and stands, blinking to focus her vision. The scene sharpens; an uneven line of white surf sheltering the cove, lumpy blue sea and the dead straight horizon so far away. She sighs, thinks: Cyah escape you owna life. Cyah lef it until it lef you.

What would a young Jamaican man with no prospects say about the ownership of the land at Mason Hall? She glances behind her. Lamont is still astride the yeng-yeng, looking at his phone. She feels the tributaries of inheritance converging on a delta of the young—Justine. Jacob and a baby soon to be born. Bernice. Bernice's son and her sister's unknown child or children. A new name today: Stephen.

Yet none of these people are rooted in Mason Hall. They

have not lived their lives here, were never fed and watered by the land, never hungered, never withstood heat, hurricane or drought, did not build a house of stone, did not pay for their presence in blood or toil or hard-won cash. They have no connection, no experience, no memories here. No losses. No *love*. It's not a word she uses lightly, knowing how much it masks. For them, this place is a commodity. Like the weed she grew and sold.

But, she thinks, them have ancestor who was here.

A memory: She was big and pregnant with Carol. Clive was home as gas rationing was still in place due to the war in Europe and his stores had run out. He pushed the first glider seat back and forth with his foot on the railing, which soothed two-year-old Alvin, finally sleeping, his head on his father's lap, feet on hers. Clive touched her rounded belly; the baby kicked her full bladder and she groaned.

Better worl' for the new pickney when war finish, he said.

She kissed her teeth. Not our bloodclaat worl'.

Lina, you too damn miserable, Clive said, but she remembers the warmth of his voice and the way his hand slipped down to hold hers, his thumb stroking the back of her wrist. She softened, but then thought of the labor of childbirth ahead of her. To Clive she said: Miserable? You try shit a pumpkin.

He threw his head back and laughed. You shit the pumpkin, me try mek a better worl' for the two pickney. Right here suh. He touched her forehead with his.

Standing where small waves break, traffic building up on the road behind her, she wonders: How much blood connection matter? Perhaps her responsibility is not to her relatives—distant relatives, she corrects herself—but to the young man waiting on the yeng-yeng—a true child of Mason Hall. A Jamaican. If the looping circuitries of blood could ever be untangled, ever laid in a straight line with all the junctions and connections evident, who's to say she might not be related to Lamont?

Yet the man-child behind her is desperate to leave Mason Hall. She cannot fool herself he feels love for the place in which she was born and grew. *The girls breed an the boys leave.*

A man—a blood relative—died in front of her at the site of a historical crime. She made no attempt at rescue and said nothing afterward. That cannot be undone. The laws of man say his descendants own the land. She already knows the only one of his children who wants it is unworthy. Her own children and their children have moved on in every way. Me cyah save it, she cries to the sky.

Mummi? says Lamont. You awright? He's beside her and she turns into his wiry young arms.

# Chapter 27

It's mid-morning and four people sit in silence on the veranda of the stone house—Miss Pauline, Kelly and Jeffrey Buchanan and Lamont. No one has eaten and Miss Pauline doesn't care. The yeng-yeng is parked under the breadfruit tree beside the rental car. She wishes again for Justine. Will she tell her granddaughter about Turner Buchanan's death now? By what means? She cannot imagine making her confession into a computer screen or on her phone.

Jeffrey Buchanan knits his eyebrows, Kelly's eyes are puffy. Miss Pauline believes that while she was with Lamont, the siblings exchanged long-avoided words. Lamont is bent over his phone, but his body looks sprung, as if held in readiness for an attack, and Miss Pauline senses his protectiveness of her. The veranda, usually so pleasant at this time of year, feels oppressive. Maybe her house has already begun its descent into ruination. She imagines the stones spread across the landscape and some future set of heritage people from Kingston wondering about their origins.

She's at the end of things. Stones do not move or speak, they do not rustle or wail, make music or beat drums. Spirits do not live inside them. They bear no witness, do not yearn.

All her life, she's tried to face whatever came without fear, trusting her own guiding hand. Yes, storms of various kinds had torn through her life, but she responded as she saw fit, and she believed that those who tried to hurt her came to regret it. She broke the laws of men but also committed a crime according to her own set of rules. She has lived with lacerating regret, but she is glad she had been *able*. Now she cannot solve the issue before her. She must leave it to those who live after.

And yet. If the stones had not spoken, had not moved, whether they were the invention of a failing mind or not, she would never have met the people on her veranda, not even Lamont. She looks at the closed faces of the two Buchanan relatives and thinks: Me did bring them together *here*. And mebbe them can talk now.

A whiteman crossed an ocean to find himself on a hillside forest. A Black woman was his victim. Fuck, no. Nancy McLean was no kinda victim. Them give her *backra* name, work her, rape her, but she mek her owna life. She do what she had to, Miss Pauline thinks, she fight, she survive an she get what was her own, what shoulda never been taken from her—her freedom. The freedom of her children. Miss Pauline is sorry she will never know her real name or her story.

All the children these people begat. The families in England, those who stayed in Jamaica, the ones who left the island and spread out across the world. Her own children. The various skin colors emerging from the crimes of history. How many of her relatives have her eyes? Puss eyes, as her father called them? How many do not? How many are brave and resolute? How many kind? Cruel? Two brothers with the same father and mother, the same blood, headwaters for them all. The lives of those on her veranda took their haphazard journeys across cliff and slope and plain as any river does, meeting obstacles, disappearing underground, emerging into the light, always seeking the sea. One brother enslaved others, received money for his evil acts, and his descendants prospered. The other brother's course is her particular tributary. Had she and her children prospered?

Jeffrey clears his throat. Are you going to show me around then? he says, but his voice is tentative.

She has avoided his direct gaze up to now. She looks at him. His eyes are the rich brown color of a Red Stripe bottle. Not the eyes of Turner Buchanan or her own. Nuh-uh, she says. You find youself here, you want this land, you walk it. Like you ancestor do. Like me. Chop you way t'rou it.

You showed the ruin to Kelly, he whines, as if he's in the middle of a playground argument with a parent. He doesn't say it, but she knows what he thinks: It's not fair.

If she want tek you, she can.

I could never find it again, Kelly says. And I don't want to. I'm ready to go home.

Bring that book we write the list on. An the pen. Me want to write down how to find ma granpickney, Justine she name. Mebbe she know how to find ma odda grands. For you all to decide what to happen on this land.

At least give us the volume and folio number on the title so we can find it easily, says Jeffrey.

She scowls at him. This land not 'bout that piece of paper. You find youself here, good. Mebbe you roots is here, mebbe not. But you mek you search wit' you feet an you eyes an ears wide open. Tek you sista wit' you. All me ask is that you tell Justine what you a go do with ma house.

And then she hears a roaring sound, something wicked coming fast, the breadfruit tree bends and shakes as if fighting a gale, she feels a sharp jerk underfoot, rising up and up, as if the house itself is trying to rid itself of its inhabitants. As if it strains to throw them skyward and then swallow them whole. Terror floods her limbs, coming from way back, her genes understanding what has come to Mason Hall long before she does. Then another jerk and dishes fall off shelves inside the house, a piece of furniture crashes to the floor. The stones move and scrape and shudder and moan and the stone woman's voice says: Run-un-un. Miss Pauline grabs the arm of the swaying glider.

Kelly jumps to her feet. Is that an earthquake? We should duck and cover!

This fucking place, says Jeffrey. He stands too but doesn't move toward the front steps. His chair falls over. The floor heaves again and he stumbles, almost losing his footing. Lamont slides off the veranda railing, grabs Miss Pauline's hand and tries to pull her to her feet. She resists and lifts her head. Is not an earthquake. Is just the stone-them. She says to Kelly, Me told you before an you did not believe. You nuh hear what she sey?

Ridiculous, Kelly hisses, holding on to the railing. Shit, this is terrifying.

Lamont pulls again at Miss Pauline's hand and the floor rolls like the sea. She lets him lead her down the front steps, her legs as weak as rope.

They stagger together outside, and Lamont swears and

swears. She sees her own fear mirrored on his face and she quells it. He drops her hand. The earth rises and falls, no longer a solid, everlasting presence underfoot and she's suddenly drowning in a tsunami of grief. She should have stayed under her owna roof and her grave should have been the fallen stones of her owna house, excavated from the island's bones centuries ago. Trees still shake their leaves as if in response to a driving wind coming from all directions at once, but there is no wind. She hears the familiar scraping noises from the stones and the crash of more things falling inside her house; then, the raised voices from the people of Mason Hall. The stone woman does not speak again.

It's an earthquake. Just an earthquake and she has survived them before.

They stand in an open area of the yard and the tremors subside. The trees cease their thrashing. The air is still. The birds are silent. Voices call out: You feel that? Dat was a bad one! Merciful Jesus. It last long, eeh?

I've n-never b-been in an earthquake before, stammers Kelly. Shit. What do we do now? How long do we stay outside? I guess a stone house is not a good place to be.

I left my phone on charge inside, says Jeffrey Buchanan.

Power probly gone, says Miss Pauline, calm settling over her. A sense of arrival.

Lamont walks over to the breadfruit tree and pushes the yeng-yeng out from under its branches. A few breadfruit, too high for anyone to pick, have fallen to the ground.

Is this to be the final explanation? Tremors before a big earthquake, the one the scientists have been predicting as overdue, a natural event, like a hurricane, like lightning, like an October rainstorm; this is what kept her awake and caused her to begin the search for the family of Turner Buchanan? That the use of cement was wrong all those years ago or the stones just grew softer and softer with time? That stones do not speak, will never speak, that it was all just a new nightmare, evidence of her brain cells sputtering out. And then finally, today, the warnings of the earth coming to pass.

You awright Mummi? says Lamont, returning with the motorcycle. You look sick. Eart'quake dun. Dat a bad one, don't?

Miss Pauline nods. How to accept that whatever comes next is not up to her? Her back is to the house and she's reluctant to turn around, to assess what damage the earthquake has done. She remembers the university people and their talk about a fault.

She sees Lora approaching, fully dressed, with a bag in her hand. Miss Pauline lifts her chin. How the district fare? Anybaddy dead? Anyting fall down? she says to her old friend's daughter.

Miss Pauline. Glad to see you awright, Lora says. She bends over, breathless, but goes on, The old part of Mason Hall—di stone buildin—them shake up bad. Some fall down. New part look okay. But me hear sey di road break away again. One *massive* landslide.

What you mean, buildin shake up?

Them not straight anymore. Them chaka-chaka like—Lora looks a question at the strangers but doesn't ask who they are.

Miss Pauline opens her arms. Ma fambly, she says, and the word is like the call of an owl, full of meaning and mystery and threat. She speaks the names of Kelly and Jeffrey Buchanan. To them she says, This is Lora, ma old friend daughter.

Good t-to meet you, says Kelly.

Miss Pauline turns around to face the stone house and sees what Lora means—the stones have moved out of plumb, and her house looks like something a child might have drawn.

They stand in the yard, wordless, waiting for more tremors, hearing voices from the village, until Jeffrey Buchanan says, What d'you mean, the road is blocked?

The two males leave on the yeng-yeng to assess the damage to the road and the three women peer into the house, ready to run if there is more shaking. The floors inside are covered with fallen mortar, chips of limestone and dust. The stones are askew, a few smaller ones on the ground. The wooden floors sag in places but the zinc roof is intact. Dishes and cooking pots are on the floor, everything breakable is shattered. The stone jar which held River's water is in pieces. Miss Pauline is sure another earthquake, even a small aftershock, will cast the stones of her house wide, like chicken feed thrown by a giant hand. Lora touches one of the walls. Alla the stone buildin in Mason Hall look same way, she says, shaking her head. Mm-umm-mm.

Pauline takes a step inside, but Lora stops her. Nuh safe in here, Miss Pauline.

She stops. You house okay? she says to Lora. She's ashamed not to have asked before.

Some crack inna di wall. Is a nog house, memba? Not stone. You want come over?

Miss Pauline glances at Kelly Buchanan. Her cousin's eyes brim, but she makes no sound. Tek it easy, Miss Pauline says to her and puts her good arm around the younger woman's shoulders.

Come, nuh, Lora says again.

Is a lot of us.

An nuh nuttn. Mason Hall people used to crowd up. Plus Selvin is on the north coast—him cyah reach back for now.

Selvin is Lora's baby father, but her children are grown and have long gone. Miss Pauline smiles at her friend's daughter. Want to wait until Lamont and Jeffrey come back. Hear what them have to sey. Then mebbe we come over.

Me wait wit' you then.

The three women sit on the veranda steps. Miss Pauline is ready to run if there is more shaking, but as the afternoon wanes, her hyper alertness eases. There's nothing more to say and Miss Pauline suddenly finds her desire for the stone house ridiculous. Despite her efforts, her shameful act, it has been taken from her anyway. The structure that cradled her life has been shaken apart. A John Crow soars in the blue sky, far above concerns of the land. It was a mistake to think she was planted. Now, at the end of things, she's a creature of the air, untethered, unburdened, and she laughs.

Why are you laughing? says Kelly Buchanan. Her voice shakes.

Miss Pauline pats her hand but doesn't respond.

Lamont and Jeffrey return, carrying pan chicken and hard dough bread. Jeffrey's face is serious, and he goes to his sister. The road is blocked at both ends. The entire hillside came down. We're cut off. There's no cell signal and the power is gone in the village.

Jesus, says Kelly Buchanan. We can't sleep here. What're we gonna do?

Lora says, Aahm—but doesn't complete the sentence.

Who makin pan chicken in a eart'quake? Miss Pauline asks Lamont.

You memba Soupbone son, Mummi? Him operate behind Miss Bridget bar. Spinner, dem call him. Him have to t'row away some, 'cause it fall on the ground, but some ready an pack up before di eart'quake. Him jus' pick up the coal an start cook again. Him soon run out, still. 'Nuff smaddy waan chicken.

A whola new generation, Miss Pauline thinks. She barely remembers Soupbone and is sure she has never met his son. She thinks of the aftermath of the two hurricanes of her life and the genesis of her desire for a stone house to withstand the storms of the tropics. Clive had disliked her fascination for *backra* house. Chuh man, Lina, it just one wicked old place, he often said. Fulla duppy. You figet what them do to we? You makin excuse for them? Givin them forgiveness? Them don't deserve it.

Is we who build it, she had responded. Our people. It nuh matter who live in it, is we who mek it. It belong to we. If duppy is here, them is our own. Me nuh business wit' the white people. Now she wishes she had known then that she herself would one day need to seek forgiveness.

Me glad it mash up, Clive said, more than once. Them shoulda burn it raas down, back inna the day.

Earthquake. Not fire, she thinks. Not gale force wind. The ground itself. Stone has finally sundered.

\*

They share and eat the chicken, crowded together on the front steps of the stone house, and Miss Pauline thinks of the gnaw of hunger and what it can lead to. Jeffrey Buchanan's boasyness is gone, and his sister leans against him. This time she eats without complaint; she, who has never been stalked by hunger. At the first taste of the food, Miss Pauline's symptoms of illness return as suddenly and unexpectedly as the shaking of the earth.

You not comin wit' me? says Lora. Me nah leave you here, Miss Paulie. Zepha's nickname spoken by her daughter loosens the tight knot in Pauline's chest.

Me have a story to tell you, she says to the group. Is a duppy story, in a way. History, but not book history. Stone history. A story of wickedness, done by plenty people, including me.

I don't want to hear it again, says Kelly.

Too bad, cousin. She groans and holds her stomach.

You're sick. We need to get you to a hospital. But how?

No hospital. Me haunt you for fuckin *ever* if you mek me die inna hospital. This is what me want—listen good. Me want alla we eat Christmas dinner together. Right here suh. You cyah leave here for now, anyway.

That's just nonsense, says Jeffrey Buchanan. How will we get food? Christmas is four nights away—where will we sleep?

Miss Pauline laughs. Food right here in Mason Hall. Chicken an groun' provisions an *gungu* peas an sorrel for drinkin. Me have plenty rice. Might even have some rum from back when. Lora can bring her pudding. We go drink an eat an tell story. We going talk the truth to one anodda.

There's no power! You can't cook anything. We can't stay

inside this house, says Jeffrey and she sees the panic in his face. He's cut off from all he regards as essential.

Ma stove is gas. We can cook. We can sleep here on the veranda, or outside. Not gonna rain between now and Christmas Day.

Aahm—Lora says again.

No one else responds and Miss Pauline senses their concern about her mind, listening to her speak of Christmas dinner. Hear me now, she says. Me want this place to stay, just like it is, mash up, but still standin. Me want it to be a place where people can come see how new tings can born from old. Me was happy here. Me want people to feel that. Me want you to find Bernice Gardner's fadda an bring him here. Mebbe him old, sick, me nuh know, but find him. If him still alive. Bernice too, an her fambly. Puppy know where she work. And then you fill this house with the name of evrybaddy who live here an die here, like the sign over the door. Start with you fadda, Miss Kelly. Call up the heritage people an mek them protect it like the stone inna the middle of Mason Hall. Mek them cut a path to where *backra* house did build an the grave-them on the hill. Clear the bush. She looks at Jeffrey. Invite you sista to come. Stephen too; you son. And you, she says to Lamont, you stay here. You nuh have to be part of Kingston badnis. You mek people all over the world know them can come here an pay them respeck, cry, laugh, pray, memba, howsoever the feelin tek them.

Mummi, you go live forever, says Lamont, sucking at a drumstick. 'Tap chat foolishnis. Wha di heritage people ever do? Them is pure promise an speechifyin. You tink dem going let tourist go inside a mash up house? No, suh. And mi done tell you awready—mi waan lef Mason Hall. Mi *nah* stay yah so. There's a pulse of silence and then he says, Christmas dinner sound good, doh.

Nobaddy want live forever, yout'. You will come to find that out. She pauses, Me have money, she says. Plenty-plenty.

They all stare at her.

Making it a heritage site is not a bad idea, says Kelly. I could do that. If my father's claim is good. We could set up a trust to run it. Make repairs and a beautiful garden. Native trees. A memorial. I saw a TV special about a house like that. Somewhere in Virginia. How much money?

Miss Pauline laughs. Come down to that, eeh, Miss Kelly? Evry time. Enough never you mind. She's not sure what a trust is, but it seems like a good place to start.

Is the road really impassable? Kelly says. How long will it take for the government to clear it?

Long, says Lamont. Mason Hall nuh important to nobaddy. Dere's anodda way out but is one endless drive an di road is terrible. Mi not sure dat car can mek it, he says, nodding at the rental car. Better we find a donkey.

Better you jus' come to ma house, says Lora.

No. Alla you, go now an see what is what. Buy whatever food you see. Candles. Kerosene oil. Coal. Plastic bokkle to store water. Lef me for now—me need to tink. Tek the car. But mek sure you come back.

Car cyah go where di bike go, objects Lamont. Road fulla rockstone.

Bike cyah tek three of you.

Don't waan leave you, Miss Pauline, says Lora. Just come wit' me, nuh? No sense sittin here by youself—for wha'?

Me is good, *putus*. Me soon come. You hear what me sey about ma house?

Me hear. But you stubborn bad. You head tough like a coconut, Miss Pauline, honestly. Zepha's daughter smiles and pulls her into an embrace. Nuh stay long, you hear?

Some pan chicken leave. Tek it wit' you, she says to Lora.

She sits alone on the glider. The people of Mason Hall are out in the streets, still exclaiming about the earthquake, even laughing, and it makes her smile. We tek serious ting an mek joke, she says out loud. Then she lets the lifelong comfort of solitude flow over her. She's home. Always has been. She thinks of the shadowy whiteman who came, back in the day. She can't see his face, doesn't know his age, will never know how he came to be in Mason Hall. She pictures him standing atop a pyramid of Black bodies who labored under the lash to build the house in the forest. And she tries to imagine the face of Nancy McLean, her ancestor too, a woman of Africa, who birthed her children in a slave hut, raised them, survived to live an unremembered, uncelebrated life, but her features shimmer like steam. Babies, born in slavery, joining the same brutal pyramid. Those that came after, more than a thousand of them in just this one family, diverging in myriad ways—skin color, language, country, occupation, wealth, bawn yahs, migrants, landowners, workers, dog-hearted criminals and people of courage and kindness. She is one tiny drop of water in this torrent of humanity, now here, in this moment, on the veranda of a house assembled with the stones of enslavement, taken from the bedrock of an island, where she hovers now, waiting for nightfall.

*

Three days after the earthquake, a bulldozer clears a single lane of the road to Mason Hall and people begin to come and go, the taxi drivers charging three times the regular fare, some people sitting in open trunks, legs danging. Cars return with sheets of plywood tied to their roofs to carry out repairs. Miss Pauline and her relatives are with Lora, Jeffrey and Kelly sleeping on blankets on her living room floor, their faces creased with discomfort. Lamont left for his room in the village the day after the earthquake and Miss Pauline has not heard from him. Lora and Miss Pauline share a bed. She lies awake, listening to Lora's breathing, and pain begins to stitch circles in her belly.

Christmas Day. Outside, in Lora's yard, two trestle tables from the church hall have been set up, and villagers bring their chairs, tablecloths, packs of plastic plates, forks and cups, and paper napkins; Soupbone's son, Spinner, fans the coals in his drum pan, getting ready for seasoned chicken to be brought by the women. A dutch pot of rice and peas is already bubbling on rocks around an open coal fire and children's voices ring out. Throughout the morning, the churchgoers arrive in their best clothes, the men lament the lack of ice due to the extended power cut, but line up warm Red Stripe beers on the edge of Lora's veranda. The sun is gentle, the breeze soft, and the December light is luminous. The people of Mason Hall cook, share and eat Christmas dinner under the generous shade of a guango tree. Miss Pauline sits with Jeffrey and Kelly, sensing how out of place they feel, knowing they will leave in their rented car early the next day. Lamont has still not shown up.

The afternoon ebbs. Leftover food is shared into containers for those who weren't able to come, or for tomorrow. Miss Pauline is inside, helping Lora to cut up Christmas cake, so that everyone can get a bite before they leave, when she hears the sound of the yeng-yeng. Fear and hope collide in her chest. She drops the knife and walks down outside. Sorry mi late, Mummi, Lamont says, astride. Mi was packin up di room. Food dun?

She sees a bag strapped to the back of the motorcycle then. She meets his eyes and they are full of tears. He's trying to make light of their meeting, as if he's just late for an ordinary meal, but she knows he's come to say goodbye. Plenty food leave, yout', she says, following his lead. Spinner will set you up. But her voice trembles.

The sounds of Mason Hall fall away. Me will member to charge ma phone when light come back, Miss Pauline says to him. You call me an tell me how you settlin. Lamont nods, rubbing his eyes on the back of his sleeve.

She opens her arms to him. Don't mek anybaddy tek you into badnis, yout'. You hear me? Mason Hall always here for you. And me? Anyhow me don't answer the phone, me will always be wit' you inna the mawnin breeze.

Mi know, Mummi. He hiccups, catches himself. St. Mary biggest ganja farmer go live forever, nuh true?

She laughs, but winces at the pain in her core. Me have sumpn for you, she says. Go get you food an come back when you dun. Man can't eat an ride at the same time.

She goes inside Lora's bedroom and pulls out the bag she brought with her from the stone house. She takes out Justine's address and phone number, torn from where it was written in the ganja ledger, and leaves it on Lora's dresser under a vase. She riffles through her cash, selects bills, and folds them. She finds the photograph of herself and the child's manacle she discovered at the plantation ruin. The money will smooth Lamont's way. She can't think of anyone still living she'd prefer to have her picture. And she hopes the manacle will bring him back to Mason Hall, to restore it to its place in the ruin reborn as record and memorial.

She stops in the kitchen, where Lora is putting the shared cake on a tray, and without saying anything to her, takes a piece folded into a napkin. She puts everything in an old bread bag and goes out. Lamont stands next to the drum pan, holding his plate, talking to Spinner. She eases herself down onto the steps, waves at the villagers as they collect their cake and say their goodbyes. Her foreign relatives still sit at the table, alone, amidst the leavings of Christmas dinner. She feels a pang of sympathy for them, but not enough to call them over. She knows there is a strong chance that once they leave Mason Hall, they'll never return and her hopes for the stone house and the site of the ruin will never be realized. So it go, she thinks.

The stones *did* speak to her in Nancy McLean's voice. And in her language. She's sure now. And she, Pauline Sinclair, ooman, elder, Jamaican born, received her meaning. What people build holds their stories, buried, it's true, but sometimes a new fissure lets them escape to find all who might listen. And there are many different witnesses to a life. She thinks: Me is owl, *peenie-wallie* an John Crow, panganat an tree root, me is limestone rock, livin dirt an roaring river, me is bamboo an lime tree, board an stone house, all at the same time. Miss Nancy, she says out loud, me will mek sure you name is remember.

She will not know how her own story ends. She reaches for Clive's ring on the ribbon around her neck and feels its warmth in the middle of her palm and she hears him whistle. Sees Zepha sucking on a stick of sugar cane, her children playing in the yard after the hungry time was over. Her mother, Gladys Cameron, born at the turn of another century, Winston Sinclair, her farmer father who she loved, Granenid and her duppy stories, her sister and brother, birthed in the same house, all sharing beginnings, but not here with her at the end. She will not comfort herself with fantasies of seeing them after she dies.

Not long now, she whispers out loud. Lora will see the paper and call Justine after. Miss Pauline wraps her arms around her body, the bread bag beside her on the steps, waiting to say goodbye to Lamont. She holds herself ready, buttons up the pain. Not long at all.

# Author's Note and Acknowledgments

In 2014, I was contacted out of the blue by a New Zealand television company doing genealogical research for a program called *DNA Detectives*. They claimed I was related to a celebrity chef from New Zealand named Ray McVinnie and asked if I would be prepared to meet with him and be filmed as part of the show. Along with one of my sisters and a cousin, we met with Ray and the program producers gave me a sheet of paper with a history I had not known—that on my mother's side, I was descended from a Portuguese Sephardic Jew called Hananel d'Aguilar, and an enslaved "mustee" woman named Nancy McLean, who lived on a plantation in a place I, as a bawn yah Jamaican, had never heard of: Mason Hall.

This sparked both fascination and a painful discomfort, and over the next several years, I contacted distant relatives all over the world, using the tools now available—online genealogical tools, DNA analysis, Facebook, email—and eventually built a family tree of over twelve hundred names, more being added all the time, of people living in over two dozen countries. Special appreciation to my newly discovered cousin, Robin Turner, in Auckland, New Zealand, who sent me family stories and answered my endless questions about who these people really were.

Then I learned of the Legacies of British Slave Ownership Project and I searched for the name of my direct ancestor, David McLean, the son of Hananel d'Aguilar and Nancy McLean, and sitting in my bedroom at my laptop, I found his name—and that he was paid £927.19.09 for the forty-five people he thought he owned at another place I'd never heard of—Middleton in St. David (now St. Thomas). A man born in slavery went on to own slaves himself.

I have included these actual names of my ancestors in *A House for Miss Pauline*, which is an otherwise entirely fictional account of a rural woman of the twentieth and twenty-first centuries who tries to grapple with what this history has meant and still means for modern Jamaicans, as I myself have done, am still doing.

Mason Hall, too, is a real place, and I thank Danny and Lucille for their generous welcome and introductions, especially to Miss Norma, but all I have described about the physical village is fiction. To the best of my knowledge, there is no village of stone in Jamaica, although perhaps there should be. Thanks to Bruce and Fiona for providing some St. Mary magic and to Sharie for sharing her vivid rural childhood memories. To my Cockpit Country friends, Mike Schwartz and Susan Koenig, my everlasting gratitude for revealing that landscape to me, scattered as it is with stones and stories. They probably don't want to be named but thanks to my informants on ganja growing—they know who they are. I'm grateful to Ann Hodges who told me about old building methods. Thanks also to Ann Lyons for describing Jamaica as a new arrival—I have never had those eyes—and to Isis Semaj-Hall, who talked to me about being a Jamaican in New York, and fielded frequent questions about rendering Jamaican patwa on the page. Anything I got wrong is my mistake alone.

My paternal grandfather (and my father, in his time) ran a mail and country bus service so that reference is a small acknowledgment to my father's side of our family. Older Jamaicans still remember the red mail vans and busses that plied Jamaica's rural roads.

The two hurricanes mentioned, Charlie in 1951 and Gilbert in 1988, are actual storms that devastated Jamaica. I was not yet born in 1951 but will never forget the hours of Hurricane Gilbert, when weather became war.

I've also taken liberties with the likelihood of there being a sinkhole in St. Mary—this is a common feature in other parts of the island, but rare in St. Mary parish. I was taken to the Fontabelle Rising in Cockpit Country by Mike, which did seem to be within the crumbling walls of the Fontabelle Great House and that place lodged in my mind, and inspired this story, many years later. And then more recently, I heard that the stones of Fontabelle had been taken to construct a new house and I thought: What if the houses of enslavement could speak? What would they say and to whom?

I have no answer to what should be done with the remnants of the plantation houses here or elsewhere, although I believe architecture has value as a repository for human stories. The houses constructed by enslaved peoples are often located in some of the most beautiful places in the world, and those that have not already fallen down remain examples of extraordinary workmanship and skill. But you can feel the duppies there too—and the pain and trauma clinging to the stones. I have friends who operate great houses as tourist attractions, and they point to the livelihoods provided to rural Jamaicans who have few other options for employment. I have stayed myself in such places and have had my own nighttime encounters with Jamaica's atrocious past. But I do come down on the side of wanting them to be places of remembrance and regret, as opposed to occasions for a mento band and rum punches. And I know my friends would say: But who would visit those places? You certainly can't envisage them being on the list of cruise ship attractions.

On the day I visited Mason Hall, I did wish I could find the gateposts of the *backra* house where Hananel and Nancy lived and see even just the foundations of the house that lives in my mind, perhaps a flight of steps to nowhere, and the graves without names that I imagined. I've since heard that yes, there is such a place, deep in the bush of Mason Hall, and maybe one day I will go back wearing my own puss boots to find it.

My sincere gratitude to Don Robotham and Jamil Toyo who guided me to the words in the Efik language that could have been spoken by Nancy McLean. They might have been said at an Efik-Ibibio graveside in Eastern Nigeria to acknowledge the unbroken connection between the living and the dead and to celebrate that every apparent ending holds the roots of new beginnings.

Thanks to my husband, Fred, who shouldered all domestic duties while I was writing this book, putting up with milk-curdling glares coming his way when he interrupted me, and read the manuscript at least three times, pointing out all the times I had killed and resurrected people fifty pages later. I'm grateful to my lifelong friend and first reader, Celia, for her always thoughtful input, and to my son, Jonathan, who also read early versions and did not shy away from the tricky task of critiquing his mother's writing. Thanks to my incredible agent, Laetitia Rutherford—who made this novel a better book in every respect, received many despairing wails, kept me going and found a home for Miss Pauline with Dialogue Books in the UK and Algonquin Books in the U.S., dream publishers both. Finally, my gratitude and appreciation to Hannah Chukwu, Betsy Gleick and Jovanna Brinck for their enthusiastic support for and faith in *A House for Miss Pauline*.